Maiden Rites

Also by Sonia Pilcer

TEEN ANGEL
LITTLE DARLINGS

Maiden Rites

A ROMANCE

SONIA PILCER

THE VIKING PRESS NEW YORK

Copyright © 1982 by Sonia Pilcer
All rights reserved
First published in 1982 by The Viking Press
625 Madison Avenue, New York, N.Y. 10022
Published simultaneously in Canada by
Penguin Books Canada Limited

Library of Congress Cataloging in Publication Data
Pilcer, Sonia.
Maiden rites.
I. Title
PS3566.I48M34   813'.54   81-51888
ISBN 0-670-45096-0   AACR2

Grateful acknowledgment is made to the following for permission to reprint copyrighted material:

ABKCO MUSIC, INC.: Selections from the song "You Can't Always Get What You Want," by Mick Jagger/Keith Richards. Copyright © 1969 by ABKCO MUSIC, INC. All rights reserved.

ALMO Publications: A selection from the song "Somebody to Love," lyrics and music by Darby Slick. Copyright © 1967 by Irving Music, Inc. (BMI) All rights reserved. International copyright secured.

Chappell Music Company: A selection from the song "People," by Bob Merrill and Jule Styne. Copyright © 1963, 1964 by Bob Merrill and Jule Styne. Chappell-Styne, Inc., and Wonderful Music Corp., owners of publication and allied rights throughout the world. International copyright secured. All rights reserved. A selection from the song "Exodus," by Ernest Gold and Pat Boone. Copyright © 1960, 1961 by Carlyle-Alpina, S.A. Chappell & Co., Inc., Publisher. International copyright secured. All rights reserved. Used by permission.

Joan Daves Literary Agency: A selection from the *Selected Letters of Gustave Flaubert*, translated by Francis Steegmuller. Copyright 1953 by Francis Steegmuller.

Intersong Music Publisher: A selection from the song "Tears on My Pillow," by Sylvestor Bradford and Al Lewis. Copyright © 1958 by Gladys Music and Sovereign Music Corp. Controlled in the U.S.A. by Chappell & Co., Inc. (Intersong Music, Publisher) and Sovereign Music Corp. International copyright secured. All rights reserved.

Page 282 constitutes an extension of the copyright page.

To les femmes; *friends of the bosom, chorus and family. You all know who you are.*

And to Carl Brandt, agent provocateur.

I would also like to thank Yaddo for the time, space and attention that helped this writer summon her book.

"This tape is not for you," Moshe's voice began, "but for me. To have the solace of others' tears, fears of loneliness, eternal lovelessness.

"You don't have to listen to this. Our bond is severed. You did it. But this is my final statement, a kind of memorial to what we had, the dying ashes of our relationship. I put it together one cold night last week and stayed up till the light came through my broken venetian blind.

"I had been talking to time, Hannah. Screaming that love was transient. It runs out like a magazine subscription! I'm crying right now as I think of you. You've probably forgotten, moved on. . . .

"I loved you. You were such a sweet girl when I met you. Hopefully, you can return to that innocent state. Forget drugs, meaningless sex.

"Our love was a beautiful thing, untarnished by all that zeitgeist crap. But now it's lost. I'll let Little Anthony say it for me." Several moments passed. "Just a minute. Here goes. 'You don't remember me but I remember you. 'Twas not so long ago, you broke my heart in two. Tears on my pillow, pain in my heart 'cause of you—o-o-o. If we could start anew, I wouldn't hesitate. I'd gladly take you back and tempt the hand of fate. Tears on my pillow, pain in my—' "

1967 Part 1

*Only you can prevent
refrigerator entrapment.*

I saw him standing there, this young man with hair the color of Wise potato chips. That light. He was from Oklahoma, Alabama, Indiana, Kalamazoo, somewhere in America where they ate small portions, contentedly, that was as exotic to me as Mahatma Gandhi. I thought how much he looked like people you saw on television but rarely encountered in real life.

An anchorman. A baseball player. Even a Republican. He wore a green knit shirt with an alligator insignia, and I knew what that meant, pressed jeans, Weejun loafers without coins because they need never be ostentatious with money, and as I built up my nerve to meet his eyes, ah, the epiphany which jingle-jangled in my ears like a pocketful of change: class, refinement, yes, goddamn couth. Slung over his right shoulder in a careless manner, which is their style, was a white cotton jacket with blue piping and letters that spelled C-O-L-U-M-B-I-A.

So with swift and shameless enterprise, something we've been working on since Egypt, I parked myself several feet from where he stood reading Plato's *Phaedo*. (No dummy was this—which I could never abide, no matter how lovely.) I took out my copy of *The Great Gatsby* and began reading too. After all, it wasn't for naught that I had taken one bus and three subways to the City.

Now you have to come from one of the boroughs or New Jersey, starved for culture, meaningful encounters, revelatory conversations where you discuss your childhood and philosophy of life—pâté of the psyche—to appreciate what someone from there means when they say the City.

For eighteen years, my entire life thus far, almost one fourth over, Manhattan was forty minutes away by car. So near. Just across the Queensborough Bridge. I could almost see it as I stalked in the shadow of the Grand Central Parkway with the knowledge that the City was where all those cars were headed. Yet, achingly, I knew it would still be years before I could escape.

Was Manhattan a dream, I sometimes wondered, created out of the heat of my dissatisfaction? Did people really live there? Or was the skyline a frieze erected by some tormenting god, a glittering bas-relief of Time and Life, General Motors, Empire State? And were those *real* women who stepped out of taxis, one sleek leg, then the other, in leather pumps with a band of gold that flashed in the sunlight on the heel of their shoes, who lunched on spinach salad, quiche, and white wine, shopped, clicking plastic charge plates on glass counters, saleswomen kowtowing to them who, out of the corner of their eyes, eyed me with suspicion? Then back into yellow chariots, arms teeming with Bonwit's, Bergdorf's, and a tiny satchel, ice blue with white letters, not to be seen again until dinner and a curtain at eight?

They were right to suspect me, all of them. I was determined—Madame Defarge, eyebrows knitted, memorizing their moneyed ways, their carelessness, their leisure, "Oh darling, let's!"—not for any other reason than I wanted it. *To kiss the bluebird of happiness on the lips!* It took persistence, I knew, work, luck, and talent which I believed I possessed an abundance of, though I had no idea at what. I would have it, I vowed, whatever it was. By hook, angling one: yes, he as authentic as a stiff-back Shaker chair, a scrimshaw comb, with white almost opalescent skin so you could see his azure Mayflower blood with some English and Celt would do just fine. Or crook. I was not above stealing into their ivied enclaves, their oak-paneled sitting rooms, shaking hallowed family trees, trying on a coat of arms for size. And a pilfered white silk scarf which I paid for in nightmares of incarceration—oh, *Les Miserables!*—to give one girl from Queens a fighting fleck of a chance.

I have always thought of Flushing as a most descriptive name for a jiggly toilet unclogger, advertised along with polka favorites on the *Joe Franklin Show:* "Try Flushing. Guaranteed to make those toilets burble like a mountain spring, burble, or your money back. The one and only Flushing. . . ." Now I'm blushing. But as the birthplace of a young hoyden who aspired to a life of the mind, *affaires du coeur,* intensity, cappuccino, sweaters from Bendel's in eleven colors, existential crises, who read *Atlas Shrugged* to the end at the precocious age of thirteen, me, you can't imagine the burden.

It was like some of the girls I went to school with. Perfectly intelligent Marilyn Shmuckler. Denise Plotkin, a sensitive girl, who wrote poems about the moon and how it pulled the sea to its arms like a wet nurse. Poor Eleanor Fink developed hysterical deafness so she wouldn't have to respond to the onomatopoetic repulsiveness of her name called during assembly.

Them:	Where do you come from?
Me:	(gulp) Kew Garden Hills.
Them:	Where's that?
Me:	Near the old World's Fair, you know, Jewel Avenue. . . .
Them:	Oh, Flushing.

Never to be heard from again. How could anyone who hoped to make a shattering impact on the consciousness of the twentieth century appear in *Who's Who in American Colleges,* even burn out like a meteorite if I had to—come from Flushing? I cried out to the heavens of the unfairness, the wretched lack of free will of where one was hatched. Is college really destiny? Sure, Henry Kissinger graduated from City College. But it would have been so much easier to have been dropped in Mr. and Mrs. Bouvier's lap. He, I looked over my shoulder subtly, could help and probably give me tennis lessons too.

To be just, some famous people hailed from Flushing. Paul Simon grew up in one of the attached houses on our very street and went to Queens College too. Whenever "The Sounds of Silence" aired in the college cafeteria, you could have heard a salted French fry fall. Paul Simon gave us all hope. He too sprang from a house like ours, except my family's was ritzier, semi-attached, as my mother called it, which meant it was only connected to its duplicate on one side, Siamese-style.

"We have land," she exulted, arm sweeping across the L-shaped patch of grass, 12 feet by 15, with a Grecian birdbath in which my sister, Stevie, had stuck a bust of Alfred E. Neuman. We were semi-attached, not semi-detached, donut versus hole phenomenon, as I sometimes confused it to her horror, and in case you don't know, this is very important. It's what we have instead of a class structure. Of course, I've read Marx and Weber. In Contemporary Civilization II, Section K. Across the street were the garden apartments where families who bought pastel Lincoln Continentals and didn't know how to defer pleasure—so they could put a down payment—rented. But there was more to life than socioeconomic factors, wasn't there?

That I survived at all is a testimony to the power of imagination. Nothing ever happened. I know because I was a vigilante for all of 138th Street and 71st Road, peering out of my second-floor bedroom window with the blue-tasseled shade in case there was a crime of passion, a suicide, or at the very least, a nasty frying-pan fight. But I saw *nada* (and how's an impressionable *bambina* supposed to learn about life's vicissitudes besides reading library books?) but tricycles that grew into two-wheelers with training wheels which were soon removed, and Corvettes and Hondas followed. There were electric menorahs on our side of the street and lit-up aluminum trees with angels on theirs. Regardless of race, religion, or greed, everyone washed their cars on Sunday except for the *shmootzniks* across the street. They barbecued and gambled. Nothing ever happened, I repeat, except for that woman who was murdered while twenty-three people watched and that other one who stuffed her son in the garbage. And I only saw it on Walter Cronkite.

I was born in Queens General (7 pounds, 3 ounces), went to Queens College, and feared that when I died someone would nail me into a coffin whose mailing address was the cemetery on Queens Boulevard, where they have standing room only. From dust to dust, how unjust. Accursed fate, that I should have been thrust into such an utterly mediocre, unpoetic milieu.

But I was not one to take whatever slop life pooped on my plate, eat it, and say thanks. No thanks. My destiny called. Yale was in New Haven; Oxford, England; Brown—oh, Providence. Columbia twinkled, jewel of the Hudson, in Morningside Heights, a mere double fare away.

Saturday, September 9, 1967, 1:30 P.M. I ventured forth in my lucky pin-striped shirt, inherited from my father, tight camel corduroys which accentuated my upside-down question-mark arse, dotted by a daisy appliqué, yellow suspenders, and desert boots. Indifferent to fashion I was, a touch beat but not without a certain intellectual allure. Underneath these rags, as any perceptive person could see if they just opened their eyes, lurked a hotbed of as yet untapped sensuality. I even wore a gold locket in the shape of my desire. God, I had a mother lode.

The campus effervesced with the rush to register, buy books, move turntables and crates of records into dorms. I strutted my sweet stuff like it was God's chosen: around the great lawn, up and down the steps of Low Library, and across to Butler Library and Ferris Booth Hall. I had little success except for a maintenance man who made kissing sounds as I passed. But I had patience. Years of waiting had taught me that. And I knew what I was looking for: a mild-mannered Columbia sophomore or junior, preferably not Jewish, who would blaze through my mind and body so I would be left a burning pyre after the experience.

I had read enough novels about it, seen films with subtitles. How could I call myself a fascinating woman if I lived the bourgeois life forever? My real self had hidden in my family and school self—six years at P.S. 164, not to mention Hebrew school, three at Campbell Junior High, another three at insufferable John Bowne, and I still had three and a half more years ahead at Queens—poised like a potential assassin to be sprung on the world.

As I was seeming to study notices on the campus bookstore bulletin board of Russian tutors, but ever watchful, a studio to share on 120th Street, the Quicksilver Messenger Service at the Fillmore, he revealed himself to me in a flash of white light. Like Moses' burning bush, I was aflame.

Why him? Why does the earth twirl around the sun like a drum majorette's baton? Such things are mysterious, Zen-ish. Was it the hair straight and fine, sundipped, another species from mine and somehow closer to the gods and movie stars? The eyes blue enough to bellyflop into: Nag's Head, Nantucket, and Rockefeller's Caneel Bay, and tall, athletic? How come? I drank four glasses of milk, took One-a-Day, ate liver even if I did pitch my mother's Wonder Bread herring sandwiches behind the kitchen cabinet. Was it their pork chops, country link sausages (strictly verboten in the house, but we did eat bacon, and spare ribs from Chow Mein, the Chinese restaurant on Main Street)? Was it turkey club sandwiches with mayonnaise and toothpicks? Peas?

Was it the good family where people said, "Please pass the cream. Thank you, dear," and there were cloth napkins, gravy boats, real classical music and not fifty of the best-loved symphonies on a two-record set, hardcover books?

Was it the generations of American living on top of the hill, in Scarsdale, Greenwich, high in Manhattan buildings with views of private schools, colleges, business contacts when you got out, duplexes, triplexes, superiority complexes, and not the suffocation of two-floor brick houses stacked like Post Toasties at Pathmark?

They tucked in their shirttails, bed sheets, did not talk about bleeding ulcers, fallen arches, prostates, Gelusil, Mylanta, Senokot while eating, and monogrammed everything. Sometimes I wondered whether their privates were embossed with their initials in gold, H.D.S., Esq., like attaché cases, so they'd recognize each other in the shower at their club—"You wouldn't by any chance be Princeton '47"—the way Jewish babies bit the bullet while the moyel snip-snipped.

He didn't have a single blemish on his whole body, smooth as Formica. And he probably had to shave less than me. Anyway, it wouldn't show—not like ours that curled thick and dark as the blackboard jungle. *Hirsute.* And he had a last name you could pronounce that sounded important, maybe a few: White. Lloyd. Smith. Edwards. You saw them in the *Wall Street Journal,* on cornerstones, mastheads, bank checks, embossed legal stationery. His first name was Tip, Skip, Biff, Chip for short and actually devastatingly dignified like royalty: Grafton, Quentin, Courtland, Ellsworth, often followed by Roman numerals. I lowered my lids so I would look sensitive. Oh, to be arrogant so I wouldn't be obsessed by such petty conceits and could debut besides.

I actually used to be so naive that I thought they were anyone who wasn't Jewish or Italian. What did I know of Anglicans, Seventh-Day Adventists, Presbyterians, Congregationalists, Lutherans, Baptists, who were all smallnosed, Gentile, and celebrated Christmas and Easter? Then everyone made such a big deal about Kennedy be-

14

ing Catholic. All I knew was he could become President. Wasn't Christ Jewish? We couldn't, no matter what. My father broke the news to me after I expressed interest. Now that I was older and sadder, I understood that it meant other things too: First National City Bank; Merrill, Lynch; Paine, Webber & Smith; New Haven Railroad (as opposed to the L.I.R.R.); Metropolitan, Whitney Museum trustees; Washington, D.C.—so even if they weren't brilliant or talented or trustworthy, they still ended up running the world. Oh, to be allied with them. With their looks, connections, social graces, and annuities and my personality, no paltry thing, think of the possibilities.

If they would have me. Surely I could win them over with my sincerity, high spirits, enthusiasm. It was just a matter of time, exposure. No? In truth, I had noticed in my few attempts that they laughed at my jokes, even danced with me (I should mention here that I have had extensive dance training, poolside lessons in the bossa nova, cha cha, tango at Catskill bungalow colonies), and tried to feel me up during slow dances—at churches, no less!—but when it came to asking me out, it hadn't happened yet. "Anti-Semitism!" I charged. They always dated one of their own, the blond leading the blond, a freckle-studded Muffy, Pooch, an Alex, Cordy, Bunny, who was nearsighted, snub-nosed, with large-calved piano legs, wore green knit shirts with alligator insignias too, headbands, pompom socks, graduated from Miss Porter's and Finch, did editorial work on women's magazines until she married, well, and took to tennis, interior design, and fund-raising. Didn't we have a prayer? If we were a scream like Mort Sahl. Intelligent as Einstein. And changed our names.

Dark-haired, dark-eyed me, could I pass? Sure, *se habla español*, Italian, and Armenian. We were the melting pot. For Halloween, my mother hung oversized golden hoops from my lobes, alternating each year between my being a gypsy and a señorita. Like members of other sensuous, rhythmic New York ethnic groups, I am average size and voluptuous from the rear. But, on the positive side, we tan darker, try harder, and have thick hair. Mine percolated, catching glints of light in its dark firmament. And I have 20/20 vision.

Oh, blond one so miraculously fair (I gazed longingly at him sideways), won't you cast a glance hither? Many say I'm not bad-looking. B+ with makeup and my hair washed, C without. Was it the personality I projected? Too insecure? I turned my head so that the three-quarter profile of my best side came into view. I tried to smolder in a dark, demonic way, look deep, thinking serious thoughts about how everyone has to die eventually, that life is transient and a person can be just walking down the street and a car can hit him. So it was sometimes necessary to take a risk. I tried to pump up my nerve to say something and not just stand there like a lumpenproletariat.

He looked down at his watch. I knew he was waiting for me to make the first move. He didn't have all day. Poof, he would disappear. But what to say? "Excuse me, has anyone ever told you that you bear a remarkable resemblance to the Botticelli Venus? *Faye Dunaway?* Don Drysdale?"

It all began in third grade with Cathy Sullivan, the prettiest girl in my class. By sheer tenacity and bringing her red licorice string every day, she became my best friend. But there was a price. I learned that early. We whipped each other with chiffon scarves and played beautiful princess, who always looked like her, and monstrous stepmother, who resembled yours Jew-ly. Her hair was spun Rapunzel gold, her eyes a cloudless morning on a Roy Rogers prairie. Cathy wore gold crucifixes in her pierced ears and taught me how to cross myself.

Some years later, I saw Troy Donahue's red windbreaker against his hair blazing white in the sun and those eyes so obscenely, unadulteratedly blue. I was astonished by such beauty. Even if my mother said that

16

they resemble farmers with pig's eyes and noses, that dark hair is more interesting, Elizabeth Taylor striking, Debbie Reynolds insipid, girl-next-door, and they have no character to their faces. Character is character so who needs it like a traffic sign on your kisser, especially if you want to be kissed one of these days? When Troy came to New York on a publicity tour, I waited on line for several hours on the fourth floor of Macy's just to see if he really looked like that, because I knew they could do all sorts of sneaky effects in the movies. And even though he did have some acne scars (I saw them), he was still mythological and gave me a signed photograph. Richard Chamberlain as Dr. Kildare followed James Franciscus, Peter O'Toole, and Steve McQueen, right up to and including Jay Gatsby. I was smitten, but they didn't seem like they'd give me directions if I was lost in a hailstorm. Never say die; I kept on trying but it was hell on my equilibrium.

Was it that I looked too Jewish? Tell me. My nose was straight out of the New Testament. I chose it from a catalog that the plastic surgeon kept on a coffee table in his Rego Park office with Chagall prints in the waiting room. After he assured me that Natalie Wood's nose in *Splendor in the Grass* (I clutched a clipping in my cold hands) would not suit my face, we perused the sections on chins, eyelids, skin grafts, and breasts. The model I liked best was a tiny sproutling of a nose that turned up like a leaf which had just been watered, that made you want to tweak it, but the doctor convinced me to settle for the next size, medium. He took off several inches plus a sizable bump received when I walked into the living-room chandelier while the dining-room table was being repaired. It cost one thousand dollars, my nose, a present for my Sweet Sixteen. No, I didn't have a catered affair at the African Tom Tom Room like my other friends, nor an electric typewriter did I receive; I chose vision unimpeded by the gray shadow, my nose. Afterwards, I told everyone the pair of bloodshot shiners and the cast on my nose was the result of an almost fatal car accident (well, it was an accident, of cruel genetic fate) and collected autographs. Sometimes I feel like an amputee searching for the ghost of my old hook, fearing the phantom will angrily erupt—"I am the nose you tried to bury alive. This sin against nature cannot go unpunished"—and not quite believing that my pert non-Semitic model is here to stay. I'm always touching it, I can't help it, to check that it hasn't fallen off like a lump of Silly Putty or turned back into a Durante.

Well, I had to do something to improve my chances in this life. The mountain wouldn't come to Muhammad if he just stood there. I was desperate, a mad Serb, Marjorie Morningstar, Charlotte Corday. Which is why we invented chutzpa: someone who will not only walk right up and introduce themselves to you but come for dinner and borrow your clothes besides. Was it just that he was whiter than me, sultry Jewess?—a lovely word, used only in books, like *aquiline.*

Okay, I chided myself. If you could choreograph an interpretive dance to the "Theme from Exodus" for talent assembly, getting down on your knees and touching the floor: *"This land is mine,"* jumping up and pointing to the ceiling, *"God gave this land to me. This brave and ancient land to me. Though I am just a man"*—I played both roles—*"When you are by my side ..."*—leaping through the air—you can approach him. He's probably lonely, insulated, repressed and is just dying for someone to start a conversation with him, particularly an intensely intelligent and attractive woman. A pyromaniac of the soul. Yes, you. *Me?*

They're not allowed to do it. It's too vulgar and has been bred out of them along with body odors. But he's wishing someone with an overwhelming *joie de vivre* like you could bring him out. A natural woman. They do love ethnic types! Don't be selfish. He needs you. Do you understand? Later he'll thank you and see how indispensable such a woman is when he's running for political office. You'll get him elected. Inauguration dinners at the White House. Stop stalling. Goodwill tours of underprivileged nations.

I summoned my nerve as I swiveled on my heel to face him. No turning back. I could hear the roll of dice. It was my teeth. *Banzai!*

2

"Hi." I smiled warmly but with restraint so he wouldn't think I had a platypus sense of style, plunging in feet first, was crazy or lecherous, which I most certainly wasn't, or pushy. On the other hand, I wanted him to know I wasn't *sangfroid*. A divine balance struck, I thought.

He looked up, smiling faintly, or rather, the corners of his mouth curved like the bottom of a saucer. *Noblesse oblige*. We gave at the office. Then he turned back to the pages of the *Phaedo* without even noticing my soulful expression.

God, didn't he know what stuff I had in me? Couldn't he tell that I had written my own torch song, to be sung in a smoky room, legs beguilingly crossed as I sat atop a piano crooning in a gravel-pits contralto: *I've got the blues. I've got the blues. The blues have got me by the soul, the blues have got me by the s-o-u-l-l-l-l. I never felt so sad. Oh, baby, I've been bad. I'm mad! Until the day I met you. . . . What can I do? I never felt so b-l-u-e-e-e-e. . . .*

"That's a terrific book, don't you think? Although I felt sad when Socrates died. He seemed like a nice old man. Somehow I thought one of those Greek guys would save him, but they gave him the hemlock and—*la mort*."

He stared at me curiously. My French accent did that. "I have to read it for class—" he began.

"So did I!" I exclaimed. "I even did a paper on it for Humanities."

"Really," he remarked, growing interested.

Right from the start, we had so much in common. You see, barriers of religion and class could be traversed in the communion of literature. Education was universal tender. Mentally, I shook my own hand for having had the foresight to take advance placement and start Queens that summer. So I actually knew what I was talking about.

"Do you still have the paper?" he inquired.

"No, the professor kept it."

"Oh." He turned to his book again.

What else could I ask him, so refined, so Gatsby and Daisy and Nick Carraway-like? Were they really like Fitzgerald said they were, careless people who "smashed up things and creatures and then retreated back into their money or their vast carelessness"? Were they really protected, tucked safe in their bulletproof birthrights which kept out pain, disease, rejection? Nothing could ever hurt them. No one. Was it true? Did his parents ever fight? Did anyone ever raise their voice, or was that politeness the way it really was, even when they closed their doors? Do you believe opposites can be attracted to each other and somehow compensate for one another's shortcomings, no matter how severe?

"Do you have to read the *Republic* too?" I asked eagerly.

"Not yet, but it's on the syllabus."

"We did. God, I love the myth of the cave with all those people looking at shadows and thinking they're the real thing. It's a metaphor, you know. Everyone does that. We can never know whether it is reality or its shadow that—"

He looked bored.

"What else do you have to read for your class?" I asked hastily.

"A lot, and it really pisses me off. I don't see why they have to make us take all these lib courses."

"You don't like them?"

"It's not that. I'm in Engineering," he said, "and I just don't have time to sit around and read books."

Tiny pinprick of disappointment, but I didn't show it. Frankly, I had hoped his major would be more artistic, Comparative Lit or Art History, even Poli Sci. So what do you want, perfection? "What year are you?" I asked.

"Soph."

"I'm an upper freshman, English major."

"Do you go to Barnard?" he asked.

Yes, of course, that was it. So easy. He thought I looked smart enough and like my parents would send me to a private college where people had to pay tuition. "What, you want orgies?" my mother cried. "I've seen pictures of girls throwing their underpants out the window. Not my daughter!" Nevertheless I nodded demurely.

"What dorm are you?"

Dorm? I drew a blank. Oh, to be found out because of such a trifling. Why hadn't I researched it, dummkopf! It was simple enough. Just walk around the campus and jot down the names on the buildings. It didn't cost anything. Damn. Should I admit my ignorance? Would it bring us closer, laughing at my peccadillo? 'Ah, remember how we met and you told a little white lie. I was utterly charmed. . . .' Never. I had pride. "McCormick," I said, winging it.

"I never heard of it," he said. "That's strange. Where is it?"

"116th Street," I muttered.

Why hadn't I learned that it didn't matter how hard you flapped your arms, the only way to fly was the American way? Wing it, as I always did, and you ended up in someone's field, recently manured, singing to the scarecrow.

"Funny, I don't remember seeing it," he said, eyeballing me curiously. "It's not that gray building with the broken window on the second floor?"

"Yes, that's the one! You do know it!" Ha, I applauded myself for brinksmanship brilliance. One must take the plunge and dare to be great.

"I thought that was Reid—"

"No," I said abruptly. "The one next to it."

"Oh, I didn't think there was another building. Maybe it's one of the new dorms," he said. "Anyway, I don't know all of Barnard's buildings."

Yes, he did. I would have to choose an engineering student who memorized mealymouthed facts like that for breakfast. He probably knew all the capitals of the United States and what time it was in Tokyo, too. Ego fizzling, I realized he knew that I couldn't possibly go to Barnard. It was just that he had too good manners to embarrass me. Besides, I did it so well myself. Maybe he even thought it was amusing. Ha-ha. My teeth started to hurt because I was grinding down so hard, smiling. They had such fine manners. Finesse. They could tell you to drop dead and you wouldn't know *bubkes.*

Mournfully, I looked away. I was ready to turn in all my hopes, dreams, and aspirations for a better life, lunch on Central Park South, social mobility, to return to Flushing and have a wedding at the Kew Garden Hills temple, where burgundy carpeting climbed the walls— despite the expenditure of a double fare in both directions.

Then he asked, "You want something to drink?"

Even though I was amazed, I didn't shriek, 'Me!' like I'd just won *Queen for a Day.* "Sure," I said most casually.

As we crossed Broadway, I was in a profound state of grace. Kasha varnishkes could have showered me, and I wouldn't know it, my mind filled with visions of flowering meadows, honeysuckle, and blackbirds tweeting.

We sat down at the counter of the College Inn. I glanced around. Columbia and Barnard students sat in pairs, by themselves, biting into grilled cheese sandwiches, spreading half-dollar-shaped tins of grape jelly on English muffins as they read the *Spectator,* studied anatomy and Latin textbooks, or chattered, giggles surfacing like bubbles. I ordered a Coke so he wouldn't think I was after his money.

"And a chocolate milkshake," he told the waiter.

"So." I turned my stool to face him. "You're not from New York, right?"

"Nope." As he shook his head, blond bangs fell into his eyes. "How did you know?"

"People in New York look like their cars. A little battered, if you know what I mean." I thought that sounded provocative.

"I would have given anything to grow up here. The swiftest kids I've met so far are from the city." He brushed the hair away with the back of his hand.

"It's a highly challenging environment," I agreed.

"Did you grow up here?" he asked.

"Queens," I said. "But Paul Simon lived on my block."

"Did you ever meet him?"

"No." I paused. "But I know his brother, who looks exactly like him. You can't tell them apart."

"I really like his music."

"I bet he even doubles for Paul sometimes."

Silence. As I sipped my Coke, I examined him from under half-closed lids. His was a smile unperturbed by tooth decay, his nose came to a gentle crest—some people had to pay for that. Totally unlike our rocky cliffs and treacherous hypote*nuses*. "Where'd you grow up?" I asked finally.

He frowned. "Buffalo."

Hefty buffaloes stampeded across my brain. I thought of Gary Cooper.

"The sticks," he continued. "Upper state. It has a lot of factories and air pollution. That's about it."

"Oh." They turned into White Castle burgers as I nodded sympathetically.

"Have you lived in the city your whole life?" he asked.

"Queens isn't the City. You might as well be living in Hoboken."

"But at least you could come in whenever you—"

"I went to the Statue of Liberty, the Museum of Natural History, and Radio City as a kid. And that was it."

"What's your name?" he asked.

I smiled mysteriously like it might be Mona, Eustacia, or Lara, not Hannah, Jewish version of a poetic name that, spelled backwards, said the same thing—nothing to learn, no secret message—and only rhymed with banana and Copacabana; who my father called Hanka; and when was a song ever written except my mother's: "Hanileh, *maydileh*, oh, my *shayneh* Hanileh."

"Hannah Wolf." And there wasn't a single movie actress or heroine of a book.

"Wayne McMillan."

We shook hands for a moment.

"Well," I said animatedly. "How do you like the City?"

"Oh, it's terrific. I can't believe it. There's so much energy here."

I nodded, sipping. "I know what you mean."

"I was accepted at Northwestern and U. of Penn. But I wanted to come to New York. And, yeah, I was accepted at Chicago State too. That's where my parents wanted me to go."

"Did you have a hard time convincing them?"

"Not really. Columbia has a good engineering program, so they didn't get too upset. I'll see them Christmas, I guess."

"Do you have any brothers or sisters?" I asked.

"Three. Al went to Chicago State, so did Margie. And my younger brother, Bill, is applying to Amherst this spring."

"That's a good school," I commented.

"Was Barnard your first choice?" he asked.

He actually believed me. That my parents would shell out several thousand dollars for my education when we could get it not only wholesale but free? He obviously didn't know much about Jews. I continued blithely, "No, but I didn't really want to leave the City. I was accepted at Vassar, though."

He nodded, impressed.

"And Radcliffe, too."

He smiled, taking my hand in his. Oh, toothy bliss.

"One of the things I'm really into about the city is all the ethnic stuff," he said, staring into my eyes.

"Really?"

"Yeah. You just never see that in Buffalo. Everybody's the same there. Like there's this guy in my math class, Izzy Goldberg. Isn't that a great name? He's such a pisser. From Brooklyn," he added.

"Well," I bragged, "I'm ethnic as all hell. My mother used to keep fish in the bathtub until she made her gefilte fish."

"What kind of fish is that?"

"You never heard of gefilte fish? Where *do* you come from?" I grinned at him. "It's—I don't know—a patty or something that's made out of ground pike and whitefish. I'm not sure, exactly."

His smile grew in girth as he squeezed my hand. "You seem really intelligent."

"You think so?"

"Sure. I've always been attracted to Jewish and Italian girls." He ran his middle finger down my palm. "They really turn me on."

"Have you ever been down to Little Italy?" The question popped out of my mouth suddenly.

He nodded, knitting his eyebrows for a moment, then continued. "I like the dark hair and eyes. How exotic they look."

"Well, it's just the opposite for me. Isn't that weird?" I stared into my soda. "People always want to be someone else."

He dropped his voice. "They're a lot more sensuous."

Chastely, I turned away but still tried for a smoldering eroticism. We'd have blond cherubs.

"Do you like Columbia?" I asked brightly.

"Yeah. It's a terrific school." He squeezed my hand again. "I'll probably be going out for track next term if my grades are good enough."

Normal. Like he ate cornflakes every morning of his life. So what do you want, a pogrom? "Really? That's something," I said, sipping the last of my Coke but leaving several drops so there'd be no unseemly zupping noises.

"Right now I'm running a six-minute mile, but I'm sure I could train."

And sincere. Guileless. I nodded, beginning to chew on my straw.

"How do you like Barnard?" he asked.

One prayed for something, and it finally happened. God had been kind. Wayne seemed interested. But I had to tell him the truth. Otherwise my duplicity could only be the beginning of a cycle of deceit which would ultimately end in despair and disenchantment. I stared into my glass as I said meekly, "I have to tell you something, Wayne. . . ."

"Sure."

"What would you think if I told you I didn't actually go to Barnard?"

"You've never gone to Barnard?"

I shook my head shamefacedly.

For a moment he stared uncomprehendingly at me. "How come you said you did?"

Would he be inexplicably drawn to the *terra incognita* that separated genius from madness, truth from fantasy? I would if I were him.

"I figured you'd find me more interesting if you thought I went to Barnard. Like we had more in common. . . ."

He shrugged. "It doesn't matter."

"But," I rushed in. "I don't believe it's any way to start a relationship—with lies. I want you to know the truth about me. I go to Queens College, and even though I had good grades, I never applied anywhere else but the city colleges. Queens was my first choice, then Hunter, City. . . . I guess it was stupid."

"Forget it." He brushed another stray golden hair from his forehead with the back of his hand, the hand that had just held mine seconds before, covered in an ecstasy of golden down. I felt as if the sun had slunk behind clouds, my heart heavy.

He stood up. "I've got to meet some people pretty soon, so I should probably . . ." He laid a dollar and a quarter on the counter.

"So do I!" I leaped to my feet. "I'll probably be late. . . ." I paused. "I just wanted to be honest with you, that's all."

"Whatever." He slipped his jacket on. C-O-L-U-M-B-I-A. Would he have let me wear it sometime? I added fifty cents for my Coke.

"Well, I guess I'll see you around," I said casually, like a dirge.

"Look," he said, squeezing my shoulder. "Let's get together some other time."

I thought, faster than the speed of impending defeat. "I do have to be here next—uh, next Saturday—to buy this book for a class. So I'll be at the bookstore. . . ."

"Great. I'll look for you."

"Around four!" I called.

He winked at me as he walked out.

3

Winked. Is that what *they* do? Or did he have something in his eye? Wayne. That night, I held the first dress rehearsal for my date. I pulled out everything I had ever purchased, received as a present, hand-me-down, or borrowed and never returned. Nothing, I discovered, expressed the side of me I wanted him to know or, at least, for him to think I had. They were all shadows of former selves: my tartan skirt with the fringe, worn with knee socks when I thought I might like to appear collegiate; the painter's overalls on which I had splattered white shoe polish so they would look authentic and I artistic. The A-line hot-pink dress which I had once imagined sexy was like something Liberace might wear. My newest incarnation, classy yet ethnic, but not too, hungered for the clothes that would articulate its contours like a manifesto.

If I was a Columbia engineering student from Buffalo, what kind of woman would I be attracted to? He said he liked Jewish women. I heard him. I took off my tie-dyed caftan: too flower child. How I ached as I studied my reflection in the full-length mirror on the inside of my closet, attempting to transform myself into Wayne's physical ideal, whatever that was. Claudia Cardinale? Why couldn't he have given me a hint?

As I stood there, trying on turquoise bikini panties with *samedi* written in red letters, my mother walked in.

"What do you want?" I demanded. "You could knock, you know." I tried to cover myself with my hands.

"Have you found something to wear?" She glanced

down at my bed, which was covered with discarded outfits like casualties.

"I don't have anything," I complained, dropping my arms in a gesture of futility. "I can't stand any of my clothes."

"Did you look in Stevie's closet?"

"Are you kidding? All she has is jeans and work shirts."

"I wish you'd talk to her sometime," she said. "She seems so distant, the way she just locks herself down there in the basement and doesn't talk to anybody."

"Well, she doesn't want to talk to me."

"You two used to be so close. She'd follow you around. When I try to talk to her, she looks through me like I'm glass."

"What am I going to wear?" I interrupted. "I'm going to kill myself!"

"Maybe you could wear something of mine," she suggested. "Would you like my leopard shirt?"

I stared at her. "I wouldn't be caught dead in that thing."

"When I wore it to Lucia's last weekend, everyone said how wonderful I looked in it, and thin. . . ."

"It's not my style," I said, opening the bottom drawer of my dresser despondently. "I hate my clothes." I slammed it shut.

"Would you like to wear my mocha silk shirt that ties in front—you know, with the little pearl buttons?"

"You'd let me wear that?" I asked, knowing it was her most expensive shirt.

"I want you to be careful, of course. If you eat a cheeseburger or some other *chozzerai,* make a bib for yourself out of the napkin. I always do that and stick it into my collar. But if you take care of it, why not? I didn't buy it to sit in the closet."

Before she finished, I'd run into her bedroom and pulled the shirt off its hanger. I tried it on.

"Understated elegance," Edith Head announced. "And terribly feminine." I recognized her, the young woman I wanted Wayne to know, admire, and maybe even fall in love with. A refined me that was graceful and sleek. The silk felt cool against my skin. A little loose but perfect. "Fetching."

I returned to my own closet, slipped a pair of black slacks over my long legs, my very svelte behind, stepped into high heels. How could Wayne help but find me sexually attractive? Besides, it was a distinctly *goyishe* blouse.

My mother, who sometimes came through when you needed her, sat on the bed smoking a Newport. "Let's see."

I walked toward her, then turned slowly. "Well?"

"Nice," she remarked tentatively, squinting her eyes.

"What?" I panicked, checking myself in the mirror again. "You don't like it?"

"No, it's not that. Yes, Hanka, I think it looks okay. . . ."

"Why don't you like it?" I demanded.

"Well, I don't want you to get angry, but I have to be honest. Mocha's a difficult shade. It's a little bit more flattering to my coloring, but it'll do, I think. You look pretty. . . ."

"Thanks," I said sarcastically. All of a sudden, I despised both the shirt and her. "Keep it. I don't want to wear your shirt." I began to unbutton it. "Here."

"You see? I was afraid you'd react that way. First you ask me, then when I tell you—what, should I keep my mouth shut? Hannah, why are you always so sensitive? You have to develop a thicker skin or I don't know what. I told you it looked nice."

"It's too big on me anyhow," I muttered, pulling it off. I returned to her bedroom and hung it up in her closet. Then, after slamming the door behind me, I pulled out my jeans from the drawer.

"If that's the way you want it," she remarked, still sitting on my bed. "But remember, what you wear on the first date is crucial. I wore a black dress with jade beads when I went out with your father. He took me to Lundy's at Sheepshead Bay. Much later he told me that I looked stunning that night. That was his exact word. My hair was long then, down to my waist. I wore it up in a twist with little pearl drop earrings." She lifted her hair up and ran her fingers through it. "You should never have cut your hair," she said, inspecting me. "Men like long hair. They think it's sexier. You should at least have yours shaped."

"Some men like short hair better. Wayne said he liked my hair because it was simple, like a French actress," I lied. "And that it reminded him of Lady Brett."

I had cut my own hair that summer, under the influence of *The Sun Also Rises*. "Brett was damned good-looking. Her hair was brushed back like a boy's. She started all that." My hair, which I used to brush until it was electric—every night, one hundred lashes—had been long enough so I could curl it around the nipple of my right breast like that priestess in *The King Must Die* by Mary Renault. A forest of cathedral pines where mortals plummeted, knee-deep in ferns, toes wiggling. My hair had fallen in thickets on the bathroom floor. I cried as I collected them, fastening a green elastic around the lost strands. But it had been a symbolic gesture of my commitment to becoming a serious individual. I never knew my ears screwed into my head like doorknobs. Wasn't despair, after all, part of any true commitment?

"Wayne what?" she asked.

"I don't know his last name."

"It isn't a Jewish name—"

"Yes, it is."

"So who is this *Wayne*?" she drawled.

"For your information," I declared, turning to face her, "he goes to Columbia University, which is one of the finest schools in the country. David Eisenhower goes there. It's Ivy League. And he's a very dynamic person."

"Dynamic!" She laughed affectionately. "What a big shot you've become, college girl. Just don't forget who wiped your dynamic *tuchis* and powdered it when you had a rash. ..."

"*Get out of here!* Do you hear me? Out!" I began to push her out the door. "If you ever say a single word to him, I'll murder you."

"Nice," she said. "So you want to wear an old bathrobe and curlers when he comes and watch television?"

"He's not coming here because I don't want him to meet you. *And I don't care what you do!*" I shouted, grabbing a mascara wand and shaking it at her.

"Why must you wear so much makeup? A young girl doesn't need all that *shmootz* on her face. Look at me. I never wear that stuff. That's why I don't have wrinkles."

"*Leave me alone!* I can't take it, do you hear me? Get out of here! Moloch! Moloch!" I howled like Allen Ginsberg.

"What?" she sputtered. "What did you call me?"

My father ran up the stairs and bolted into my room. "What's going on here? I'm trying to read and all I hear upstairs is screaming. Why can't you two get along?"

I turned away from him.

"I came in here to help Hannah find something to wear for her date and she begins insulting me. I even offered to lend her my silk blouse—"

"Dad," I turned to him. "I was just trying to get dressed and then she starts bugging me—"

"Your mother is not 'she' to you. Do you understand that? We must have some respect in this house."

"You always defend her anyway," I said, walking out. They just stood there.

"And where are you going, fancy lady?" my mother called.

I slammed the bathroom door as the two of them began to discuss me in Yiddish.

"You see how rude she is. No manners. She just slams doors in our faces."

"Can't you leave her be?" my father pleaded gently. "Bella, she's going through a difficult period. And now with this date—"

"Big deal. I had plenty of dates when I was her age and younger, even. The boys were dying to take me out. You weren't the only one, you know. But I didn't behave badly to my mother."

"I'm sure she didn't mean anything by it."

"Did you hear how she cursed at me? Such ugly, filthy words. I don't even know where she heard them. Certainly not from us. What's a Moloch, anyway?"

"That's just the way people talk nowadays. It's in all the books and magazines. Even *Commentary*. She's just nervous because of the date."

He called into the bathroom, where I sat on the edge of the bathtub, staring out the window. "Hanny! Why don't you come out and make up with your mother." He waited a minute. I didn't answer. "Please don't hurt your mother and me. Hanny!"

"Other daughters would be proud of their mother's accomplishments," she said. "Not her. And that her mother is attractive and looks younger. My daugher acts like she's ashamed. Stevie too."

"She'll come out soon," he said. I heard him go downstairs.

My sweet father, chicken that he is, has suffered such disillusionment in his life. And each plucking has seemed only to add nobility to his dark, sensitive face. He was brilliant, graduated with honors from Brooklyn College, and worked on the newspaper there. My father was a starling shot down in the midst of flight. How did he know a family was upon him and he would have to teach high-school English in Crown Heights? When he finally decided to take a risk, give up the excellent pension and medical plan for greater artistic satisfaction, it was a disaster. First of all, my mother was furious. "You have a good job, a respected profession with paid summer vacations—what more could you want? I just don't understand your thinking, Stashek."

Of course, it was beyond her to fathom the heartbreaking frustration of trying to teach *The Scarlet Letter*

34

to illiterate tenth-graders. He showed me some of their papers. One began: "The scalet letter is what she have to wear because she made it with the preacher and gets into trouble. In my option, they shouldn't have done that to her. She didn't kill anybody like that. . . ." How to explain the complex themes of puritanism, guilt, and evil. So he went out on his own and it was probably the only time he defied my mother to try to pursue his literary career seriously.

I remember the little study he made for himself. Stevie had already moved into the finished basement, so he moved into her abandoned bedroom with his old Royal, a package of typing paper with attached carbons—he was that confident—and his books. Must I speak about the humiliation that followed? The odd writing jobs like composing marital announcements: "The eternal geyser of hope springs forth to celebrate the nuptials of Irving Allen Geinser and Myra Jill Rabinowitz. . . ." He proofread until he was forced to wear glasses. He ghostwrote the autobiography of a Wall Street broker who made a killing with Kodak: "Some say that greenbacks are the root of all evil. I disagree. . . ." And all the while, he banged the typewriter keys into the night, trying to write a best-selling novel so he wouldn't have to work at such drivel. But finally, when no advances or movie deals were on the way for *Forgive Us Our Passions,* he was forced to accept a full-time job. Stashek Wolf, creator of a monograph of poems called "Speak to Me in Words of Fire," became the editor of a trade journal, *The Baking Times.* Oh, the embarrassment! But it is a cross all of us bear because poetry does not a semi-attached house in Kew Garden Hills buy—nor a new nose, for that matter.

"Hanny!" my mother screamed. "Some people around here have to use the toilet, if you'll be so kind. Do you hear me?" She rapped on the door. "Stashek, she refuses to come out!"

4

Imagine dyed red hair, not of the tasteful auburn or strawberry-blond school but candied carrot, Bugs Bunny style, which made it possible for me to spot Bella, bane of my nativity, my mother, among thousands at the New York Pavilion of the World's Fair. She is a very large woman, handsome, one might say, statuesque like a Henry Moore, and is never without her long-line Lady Marlene except when she is sleeping. Once an actress in the Yiddish theater on Second Avenue (always a ham), she is fond of dropping names: "*Ach!* I remember when I played with Leppy Feinstein. Now that was an actor. And so handsome, it took your breath away. When you saw him once, you never forgot his face. Like Montgomery Cliff." During the impressionable years of my childhood, she often performed for Stevie and me, while waiting for a cake to rise (which never did), basting a turkey (which she forgot), the Yiddish version of Ophelia's mad scene, which consisted of a lot of hair pulling so you could swear she was screaming, "Hymie, where have you been! And without rubbers! Tell your mother this minute. What do you mean, a ghost? Are you meshugge? What garbage did you eat last night?" Then she rolled her eyes to the back of her head so there wasn't a trace of eyeball.

My father adores her, eats out of her hands, will climb mountains, swim oceans, plummet the depths, for Bella the Gorilla. According to her, Stashek Wolf first saw her act in *The Rotten Apple,* which was adapted from *The Bad Seed,* except in this version there was an evil daughter who abandoned her elderly dying parents in Brooklyn to take an apartment in Manhattan with her *goyishe* boyfriend. My mother played the daughter's confidante, who advised her against such cruelty. Afterwards, my father sought Bella Weingarten backstage in her dressing room, which she shared with three other actresses: Gita, Ella, and Fafie. It was the tresses *paprikash* (then apparently her own, before L'Oréal) and the spunk of bleating Bella that appealed to him.

How could he? I have been contemplating this question since I was old enough to cross the street by myself. And Stashek Wolf, author of countless scholarly essays on the Labor Movement, Jews in the Diaspora, the Rosenbergs' *Death House Letters,* dotes on her, holds her hand while they're watching television, brings her breakfast in bed on Sundays. Do you have any idea what it has felt like to live with a pair of lovebirds coo-cooing through the night who happen to be your parents and should set a good example? He buys her charms: golden sailboats, an August calendar with a ruby on the twelfth, their anniversary, a miniature blackboard made out of platinum with *I Love You* engraved on it, all for her bracelet, which has become so heavy she has to carry it in her pocketbook and wear it only minutes at a time. Just last week, he bought her a 14K gold abacus in which one of the tiny disks was a quarter-carat diamond. Am I jealous? Yes, a thousand times, yes! I'll admit it. Does *she* cherish his essays and poems, saving them in the top drawer of her desk? No. *She* tells him to stop writing nonsense—I've heard her—and if he's such a genius, how come he doesn't make as much money as the *shvartzer* garbageman?

It has always been perfectly obvious to me that she has no idea about the life of the mind. And I have tried to tell him countless times that she isn't the woman for him, she isn't intellectual enough, and it is not too late to find a spiritual as well as corporeal companion. Does he listen? "Your mother's a remarkable woman," says he. "She can even read French." If it's on a menu, I sneer. He shakes his head sadly, putting his arm around me. "Why can't you two get along? It makes me so unhappy."

I would do it for him because Stashek Wolf, befuddled, indiscriminate, blinded by his passion as he is, is a scholarly prince of a man. Quoth: "If I am not true to myself, how can others be true to me?" He scribbles these pithy aphorisms by the bushel. "Integrity is an indelible mark—as is deceit." "Finally, there is only beauty, laughter, and the imagination."

That's why I have never been able to comprehend why he got hooked up with a lightweight, feather-brained floozy—an actress, of all things who keeps old photographs of herself stuck in corners of her mirror, a feather boa on top of her closet, whose reading matter consists of Hollywood books like Hedy Lamarr's *Ecstasy and Me*, who sings, "I'm forever blowing bubbles," as she prepares frozen dinners and instant coffee. They're the only safe things in the refrigerator; everything else has beards.

Clearly, such energy, such talent, such flaming carnelian nails were not meant for being a wife and mother, merely. When I was in fifth grade and came home with Unsatisfactories on my report card in self-control, cooperation, initiative, and good citizenship, she began to cry. "Oh, I've ruined her. She has problems, I can see that now. You want to go to a chiropractor, Hanny?" For several weeks afterwards, she packed real lunches: peanut butter and jelly sandwiches, Twinkies, and fruit. So I would feel like I had a normal home life.

"I've always wanted more out of life," she declared as she left Stevie and me to prepare meals for my father. "You're grown girls. You don't need me to baby you. Now it's time for me to grow." Which at first meant adult education courses offered at Flushing High: gourmet cooking, which she didn't like because the teacher failed her potatoes julienne, which were octagonal: "I don't see why he made such a big deal about it. Julienne, Romeo—he should get his sweetbreads julienned!" Then she signed up for a travel agent's course because she was tempted by color photographs of Dubrovnik. She took a buyer's course at Saks, figuring, "I know how to dress," and that her natural aptitude for color coordination would fare her well. Instead, after laying down my father's one hundred and fifty dollars, she refused to return after the first class. "The teacher's a *faygeleh*. I couldn't even understand what that *boychik* was saying. And he's going to tell me about clothes?" But all that was before American Overeaters.

At first, she attended like other rotund ladies in the Forest Hills branch at Austin Avenue, trimming her meals, counting calories, and learning "the most important exercise": moving her head back and forth to refuse seconds. And Bella the *baleboosteh* shed forty pounds—credit given where due. But then she became an American Overeaters recruiter. Wherever wretched *chozzers* waddled, there was Bella. She began her career by addressing community groups in Queens, giving pep talks, a missionary trying to convert cannibals: "You must never even enter a bakery. Nor a delicatessen. As for Entenmann's, forget it. . . ."

But bellowing Bella was so successful, her impassioned spiel so much from the heart and stomach, like her Esalen-inspired rap sessions—"Let's talk about why you ate that bagel. You didn't have to, right?"—that soon she was part of a lecture circuit that took her, my mother, jetting to Chicago, Sioux Falls, Toronto, where she always began in the same way: "I was a fat slob too. No, let's be honest here. Only the truth will free us. I too thought I was destined to wear half sizes for the rest of my life. I almost got used to the way people would look at me on the bus, in movie theaters where they had to stand up so I could get by. You all know the look. A phony smile that barely masks their disgust and pity." She grimaced. "I can tell that you all know what I'm talking about. But one day, I had what you might call a revelation. When I found that I couldn't fit into a toilet stall and nature's necessity was upon me, I knew something had to be done."

Yes, she was graphic. And earthy. She waxed particularly lyrical the night she went on closed-circuit television. "I was drowning in a sea of flesh. I could hardly breathe anymore. My cheeks were so full they were beginning to cover my eyes. But still I couldn't stop myself from my mortal enemies: blintzes, *galuskas,* mashed potatoes, bananas and sour cream. American Overeaters saved my life—and my marriage, I might add. . . ." She wore a floor-length woolen empire dress matched exactly to the color of her hair. *Oh, the redheaded monster of my life.*

After giving them fifteen minutes to eat their hearts out, I hoped, I left the bathroom and entered my bedroom. A white angora turtleneck lay on my bed like a kitten. As I was examining it, my mother trotted in. "I was thinking," she said, ignoring my expression of rage and snub, "that maybe this sweater would look nice on you. It shrank when I threw it in the machine. I should have washed it in Woolite. Anyway, Hanny—"

I ignored her.

"Please, Han—you'll look like a living doll in it. Sexy, too," she added. "Try it on. It won't cost you anything."

I pulled the sweater over my head. The soft angora felt like fur. And it was so tight, my normal concavity puckered vaguely convex.

"Nice, huh?" she said, coming over to me. "And very *très* sexy. Your Wayne will think so, don't worry."

I shrugged my shoulders indifferently.

She put her arms around me. "We have our misunderstandings, everyone who loves another person does, but you love your mother, don't you? I only wanted you should wear something that would look the best on you. Not just so and so."

"Okay, already," I mumbled impatiently, wriggling out of her arms.

"Maybe this will make you smile, Hanileh." She poked me in the ribs where I was usually ticklish.

"Don't call me that, I told you!"

"Shhh," she said. "Did you hear about how this woman's divorced husband meets her new one? The first one says, 'Well, Hilda's still an attractive woman. Almost like brand-new, huh? Except, of course, she's a little bit stretched out, if you know what I mean.' He makes an obscene gesture with his hand. 'Actually,' the new husband, bless his heart, says, 'When I get past the part where you were, it's really terrific!' Ha-ha! In other words, you can kiss my behind. It's funny, no? Don't tell your father I told you. He's so square. 'When I get past the part where you were, it's terrific!' In other words, he's well-built. A good joke, huh?"

I nodded. She kissed me, leaving an orange lipstick mark on my cheek like the carrot-top vampire she is.

5

Saturday, 4:20 P.M. I darted out of the bookstore, peering down Broadway in both directions, to the College Inn and looked inside, my nose pressed against the window, making clouds. Back to the bookstore. The College Inn. Then around the campus. He had to be somewhere. We were just missing each other, starcrossed lovers that we were.

I returned to the bookstore again. That's the first place he'd look for me. I positioned myself near the bulletin board where I had stood that first time. It was a fatal attraction, yes, as was the insatiable need for each other. Or was it merely a passion of the moment?

He will come, I told myself. In five minutes. Patience is a virtue. I won't get emotionally upset. Breathe deeply. Let the air flow inside of you. It is the energy and the source. Four minutes. I was slipping. I won't cry, dammit. What would Lady Brett do if the date of her life didn't show? But that never happened to her. Men desired her. I walked across to the literature section and pulled out *The Sun Also Rises*. Why couldn't life be like this? "Hello there. I say, give a chap a brandy and soda. Oh darling, I've been so miserable." Imagine having the panache, the style of Lady Brett Ashley. To which Wayne, like Jake Barnes, would answer, "You got the most class of anybody I ever seen. You got it. That's all." I was crushed.

In the midst of my musings, I felt someone looking over my shoulder. I tried to ignore him.

"Excuse me," he said. "Do you screw?"

"Huh?" I spun around to find a young man staring at me. The only thing he had in common with Wayne was a soiled Columbia jacket. Hair thinning, he had it combed to the side, so that when the fan blew in his direction a slice of his head beamed like a hard-boiled egg while the other side looked like it had Daniel Boone's beaver tail hanging from it. With a sweep of his hand, he tried to reknit it. "What'd you say?"

"How are you?" he asked.

"Oh." I turned back to my book. "I'm waiting for someone."

"Hemingway is full of shit." He pointed to my book. "A fraud, that's what he is. But you must know that already."

"What do you mean?" I demanded.

"He's so stylish with his ennui. Oh, and the despair of the Lost Generation. What a crock!" His expression was pensive. "But he does have a following among college girls. . . ."

Not to be outdone, I arched my eyebrows so I too would appear serious, deeply committed to the written word. "What about college girls?" I retorted.

So just because he was an intellectual, the inkstains on his shirt pocket and the manila envelope he carried were sure signs of nights spent penning stream of consciousness, why couldn't he dress? Not that Bertrand Russell was a beauty, but did Jewish guys have to wear white socks and puddle jumpers? Was it one of the laws? Gemara? My mother would love him.

"Come on," he carped. "I suppose you think Hemingway is an important writer and his suicide such a tragedy to American letters, tsk-tsk. Papa shot himself when he couldn't get it up, that's all. What neurotic, sniveling, infantile shit!" He grabbed the book from my hands and started flipping through the pages like he was looking for a phone number. "Crap, that's what this is." He gestured wildly, shaking the book.

"Can I have my book back?"

"What the critics haven't realized is that Hemingway

creates caricatures, not characters. I wrote an essay about that. Jake Barnes with his thinly veiled disease. He's impotent, from the war, of course. And his hopeless love for that whore Brett—"

"Don't you think you're being judgmental?" I interrupted, keeping my face a *tabula rasa* re: Brett and why I looked like that Disney elephant who had such big ears he could fly.

"Listen, you got to take a stand on what you believe. All his characters do is drink and fuck each other. There's no responsibility or sense of conviction. It's trash, existential trash but you know that, don't you?" He examined me critically.

Should I reveal myself as in my poem that appeared in *Therefore I am,* John Bowne's literary magazine: "I am now fighting my greatest battle/ And the odds are all against me / I am scared / I will be swallowed by society / and I have neither the strength nor courage to fight / Should I conform, even against my ideals / And be accepted? / If not, it will be a long, lonely battle / And I may lose everything / even my integrity." Dedicated to Howard Roark.

I nodded thoughtfully so I'd look like I had deep thoughts that were unutterable, and I struggled inwardly.

"Look," I said finally, figuring that I had to say something or he'd think I was Suzy Creamcheese wrapped in lox, "he was writing after the war about disillusioned, damaged people"—verily quoting Mr. Blum, English 42, an elective I audited.

"What do you know about the war?" he demanded. "Have you had any personal contact?"

I dropped my eyes so he'd know that nevertheless it still had an overwhelming effect on me. "I've met people who have, and—"

"Have you read Bettelheim? Victor Frankl?"

I shook my head.

"Then you don't know. Hemingway's expatriates are self-centered hedonists. He writes without a heart."

"And who do you consider an important writer?" I challenged. "Malraux? Nabokov? Norman Mailer?" Yes, I had studied *The New York Times Book Review* since high school, in search of a world of ideas that still hovered in the distance, like financial independence.

Suddenly he grabbed my hand, led me through the aisles of the bookstore, and stopped, running his finger over a shelf of books until he pulled out *Nausea*. "If you want to read something important, with substance, that attempts to grapple with the issues, read this." He paused for a moment, then the words seemed to rip out of him. "Don't you understand?" he demanded. "Life is serious. Deeply serious. Hemingway is merely a dilettante."

I must admit I was *engagé*. There was something romantic, almost Dostoevskian about him. How his eyes burned, his fingers gesticulating across the black-and-white cover.

"Sartre understands this!" he cried.

Even if there were shiny spots on the knees of his pants—he could save on mirrors. His manic speech. Or was I desperate? Furnishing a hovel with a mahogany breakfront? Hastily I glanced around, but Wayne wasn't there. Had I been stood up? Or was I being unfaithful?

"Roquentin attempts to define his despair, and so Sartre performs a service for all of us. 'The only way to come to terms with life on this planet plummeting to its doom is to face reality as it is,' " he recited, " 'as one meets it in all authentic moments of agony and joy. . . .' That's from a paper I wrote for an independent study in Despair." He wiped his brow with the back of his hand, rearranging his hair. "I'm getting overexcited. This always happens to me. I can't just talk about ideas like it's all a cocktail party. And I tell myself I won't. Am I acting overbearing and obnoxious? Manipulative? You can tell me. I sometimes have the tendency. My name is Moshe Wozinsky."

As I was about to tell him my name, he interrupted. "No, I don't want to know your name yet. When there is a reason, if we know each other several months from now, then tell me your name. In Greece, names are never exchanged before there is a relationship."

"Have you been to Greece?"

"No, I read it in Kazantzakis. But I'll go there soon. It's a country where the spirit of art still lives." He looked directly into my eyes. "Is that important to you?"

"Yes," I answered, nodding vehemently.

"Good. Would you like to join me for breakfast?"

This was an existential moment. A fork in my path. True, I had wanted apple pie, but stuffed derma was sent. Wayne was not coming. I understood that now. Should I send it back to the kitchen? Then, what of the road not taken?

His body looked okay, I supposed, like other males'—what did I know?—an utter stranger, different in its logic, not delicate or graceful, rather hulking, thin arms that were too long for the sleeves of his Columbia jacket. Not too hairy, I was relieved to note. His beard was nattily cut, a goatee, freshly mowed by the next-door neighbor's son, shadowing the bottom of his face, pale, olive-hued. He had an oversized nose, portly *nuncle* of mine before going under the knife, a beer-bellied protuberance which mooned from the center of his face. But his eyes stopped me.

How had I failed to notice them? They were green as a lagoon—by the shore of Gitche Gumee, conjuring dragons and bullfrogs, the land of Oz, I was Dorothy—not just plates of glass like everybody else's: brown or blue, a flat lampshade. No, his were kaleidoscopic, shifting greens, blues, Central Park, *Sea Hunt,* Van Gogh's night sky. They glistened in a half-moon grin one moment, taking mine by the hand—come hither, they twinkled—and I wanted to linger awhile. Then without warning, rain clouds formed as they turned taciturn. "Do you or don't you? I have to get something into my stomach."

"Sure," I said, noting the clock above the register.

46

Breakfast at five o'clock? Hannah Golightly!

Outside the store, Moshe handed me the copy of *Nausea*.

"Did you pay for it?" I asked.

"Of course not," he answered. "They shouldn't be allowed to charge for them. Books are written for all of us. It's a present."

As we walked down Broadway, he continued talking. "This is the time I always have breakfast. I never get up before three in the afternoon. Then, without washing or anything, I always go to Duke's and have my eggs over easy. Do you like your eggs that way?"

"I like scrambled better—"

"It's the only way eggs should be prepared, and it has to be done right. The yolk has to be hot without being overcooked, so you can break it and dip your toast into it. You know what I mean?"

"Very Freudian," I replied wittily. "But don't you ever have to go to classes?"

He turned toward me. "You really didn't seem that middle class."

"What I mean is—"

"As a matter of fact, I've dropped out of Columbia. I didn't find the work meaningful."

My heart fell like a set of keys. So how come he had on the jacket? False advertising.

"Actually what happened is that I freaked out during finals last semester," he began as we continued walking. "I just couldn't study. All I did was play pool at Guys and Dolls." He poked an invisible cue in the air. "According to my analyst, David, it's this fucked-up perfectionism where I have to get all A's. Still trying for my parents' love or some stupid thing like that. Standard Jewboy neurosis."

An analyst. I was repelled and fascinated at the same time. He was the first person I ever met who was psychoanalyzed. Of course, I had seen *David and Lisa,* which inspired my cutting bangs and talking in rhymes, but this was the human drama occurring right before my eyes, live, not on the *David Susskind Show*. How much he must know about unconscious drives, the id and sexual perversions. Did I have any?

"You see, I went to this yeshiva where everyone was going after grades like it was a war. All anyone ever did was study. Study! Did they look at girls? No. It's a miracle I'm not a queer too. All morning, Talmud and the laws which we had to memorize, one thousand of them or more. In the afternoon, we had all the other subjects—"

"Sounds like a lot of work," I said idiotically as I ransacked my brain for some glimmer of a penetrating insight. Nothing came.

"It was goddamn hell! And I try to reason with myself that I don't have to get all A's. My mother won't die, even if she says she will. My father won't have a heart attack. Goddamn them! And, of course, I had to go to Columbia for them."

"Will you go back?" I asked hopefully.

"There are hundreds of rapes and muggings. God is too busy to look down and say, 'Moshe Wozinsky, I see you didn't get an A in Statistics 15. You know what that means!' I didn't murder anyone. So I totally freaked out during finals." He looked up at me. "What did you ask?"

"If you'll go back."

"I don't want to unless I think I can stay. Do you understand?" He peered into my eyes plaintively. "No, you don't, do you? You probably think I'm demented going on like this, but I'm just trying to tell you who I am, not the bullshit people tell each other when they first meet. You've got to be honest. Why else bother? God, I wish I had tapes so I wouldn't have to tell you the same thing I told Ellen, and Claire before her. Anyway, this is Duke's."

We entered a coffee shop on 111th Street and Broadway. Moshe took a corner booth; I sat opposite him. I thought of Wayne, the innocence of the College Inn as contrasted with this joint, which was empty except for an old woman who talked to herself in a nearby booth. "Fuckin' preverts," she muttered into her empty coffee cup.

"You don't know about my parents, my brother who's in the Peace Corps in Africa—that's how far he had to go to get away from my parents—and Schwarzbarth, who used to be my best friend but we're not speaking since he started seeing Claire's roommate. Can you imagine that? I've known him since kindergarten. Oh, tapes would make it bearable. To tell you everything. I'd just play tape number 58244 and you'd know how I visited Claire at Camp Mohawk where she was a music counselor. I convinced Eliot Feinberg from my Psych class to drive up there by telling him all the girls were from Mt. Holyoke. So was she happy to see me? Remember, we were supposed to be in love and I had driven six hours. She hardly greeted me." He paused. "You'd never do anything like that, would you?"

"Did you tell her you were coming up?" I asked.

"Of course not! It was a surprise. Our fifth-month anniversary since the first time we fucked. Later I found out she was getting it on with the swimming instructor. But she was a beauty. Honey blond hair, freckles, a real shiksa." He studied me for a moment. "You're really easy to talk to. I like that. Unfortunately you're not my physical type."

I swallowed hard. Why was there a potential minefield wherever you stepped, especially when you thought it was a grassy nook—and didn't look? I tried to stretch several strands of hair to cover my ears.

"I want you to know that I like you so far. But sexual attraction—I just don't think so." He shook his head, after appraising me like a sports jacket at Barney's.

"Thanks a lot," I said. "You're not my type either." Baldy, I wanted to call him, but I didn't. Lousy dresser. *Shlepper.* He had about as much sexual appeal as a jar of

Mother's dill pickles. A shnerk—which was what you got when you crossed a shnook with a jerk. Bigmouth. Instead, I looked down at myself. Who was I trying to fool? I regretted my clothes, wished my hair was longer, my nails unbitten.

I hated him for not thinking that I was a beauty. Not like *Glamour, Mademoiselle, Seventeen,* which I studied for hair and makeup tips (a flicker of brown shadow just under the cheeks emphasized the bones), but I believed I had a secret beauty (dark, dank like a wine cellar, Irene Papas, Susan Sontag, smoked eel) that had not yet been fully appreciated by the world. But one day, when my photo would be found under the debris of civilization like the Rosetta Stone, I would be vindicated. Toward that end, I had even sent a picture to the *Daily News'* Most Beautiful Girl Contest, grinning, in my camel loden coat. Elizabeth Taylor was voted first, then Grace Kelly. Jackie was third.

"I didn't mean to insult you. It's just that I like girls who don't look like they read books. Blondes. Redheads with fair skin and long legs. I've never been attracted to a Jew."

I looked at Moshe, thinking of the two old women sitting in the sand, each wishing the other was a man.

A middle-aged waitress with a painted beauty mark near her mouth greeted Moshe. "The regular?" she asked, her dark eyes flirting.

"Right, Loretta. And what do you want?" He turned to me. "You can have anything on the menu under two dollars."

"I'm not hungry," I snapped.

"There's a minimum of seventy-five cents at tables," she added, holding a pencil poised over her pad.

"How about a toasted corn muffin?" Moshe suggested.

"Do you want that, honey?"

"I don't know."

"I'll be back," she said. "Don't rush."

"Okay," I cried hastily. "A cup of tea and a chicken salad sandwich on toasted whole wheat with a pickle."

Moshe made a face. "I thought you weren't hungry. Where was I? Yes, Ellen. Tape number 24731."

"What are you talking about?"

"We met at a Barnard mixer. Last year. And I believed her when she told me I was the first one. We spent every weekend together, staying at my place. Then I found out she had this old boyfriend up at Cornell. She didn't tell me, naturally. She lied. If she had just told me, I could have forgiven her. But she went up there to see him behind my back. Told me she was seeing her friend Meryl. What a laugh. But there was something funny about the way she was acting when she came back. I let it go for a while but I sensed something. I even dreamed about her being unfaithful. Then I found this letter—"

"You read her mail?" I asked, outraged. Damn, there I was again, waist-deep in another of his cockamamy *bobbemyseh.*

"Look, it was right on her desk. David says that she probably unconsciously wanted me to find out because of her own guilt. And the letter was from him, Phil Taylor, and he said how terrific the weekend was and how great she was in bed. And Ellen didn't say a single word. How can women be so dishonest? A man wouldn't—"

"I don't know about that."

"When I confronted her, she actually tried to convince me it was all over between them, how she just had to see him one more time to say goodbye. A goodbye fuck! I knew she was lying. I almost lost my mind. That's when I started fucking up and dropped out."

I nodded impassively.

"I didn't mean to hurt your feelings," he said. "I think you're good-looking, in a way. What I really meant is that every time I'm with a Jewish woman, I start thinking of my mother. I just don't know if I could respond."

"Who's asking you to?"

The waitress returned with our food. I reached for

the salt at the same time Moshe did. Our eyes locked in combat. Mine narrowed. While I salted my chicken salad, Moshe looked restlessly around. Then he grabbed the salt shaker and doused his eggs. As he started to mop the yolks with his toast, he looked back at me. "What did you say your name was again?"

6

Okay. He didn't meet any of my specifications. Zilch. Except Columbia, and he had dropped out. So why did I sit vigil on my high-rise cot which converted into two beds for sleep-overs, nervously nibbling Dipsy Doodles, and wait for the phone to ring, *Nausea* near my palpitating heart? I even memorized passages, particularly Anny's. I too wanted to make my life a work of art. "I know that I shall never again meet anything or anybody who will inspire me with passion. You know it's quite a job starting to love somebody. You have to have energy, generosity, blindness. There is even a moment, in the very beginning, when you have to jump across a precipice: if you think about it, you don't do it. I know I'll never jump again."

I would, of course, as I always did, three, four, five steps, bruising elbows and knees, requiring stitches, a crazy-legged jumping bean I was, or, as my mother was fond of saying in front of my boy cousins, "In this behind lives a pincushion." But if you sat still, life could just pass you by like an overcrowded bus. So you had to leap up and down, yell, make like Road Runner, but scoot on. Much later, when gray and wizened, you could drink tea in a glass and menopause. Besides, so far nothing had ever happened to me, and I don't just mean sex. Who in the galaxy noted: one cherry saved in Kew Garden Hills? People were flying out of skyscrapers in the luminous haze of acid. Hitching to California, Katmandu, *somewhere;* freaking out, heads rolling, flashing like pinballs. I was riper than ripe, afraid I'd go rotten and turn soft and black like a banana. Without ever tasting or being tasted by real life and *l'amour.*

I looked around. God, my room seemed like a cocoon and I, the butterfly, strangling to fly. My desk of blond wood matched my dresser and vanity, for which my mother had sewn a skirt to coordinate with the bedspread and curtains. Yellow fetid daisies that I loved not.

It was a college girl's room full of college-girl artifacts. My school books were lined up: psychology, anthropology texts, *The Norton Anthology of English Literature,* volume 1, *Les Fleurs du Mal* and Gide's *L'Immoraliste* for French, *Earth Science Review, Growing Up Absurd;* subscriptions to the *New Yorker* and *New Republic* were stacked on my desk along with spiral school notebooks, QUEENS emblazoned on them. But I had other notebooks, a lone-wolf nymphomaniac's entries—*I must meet somebody or I'll die*—hidden behind my *New World Encyclopedia.*

Moshe. It rhymed with *gauche.* Not the Yiddish like the kosher butcher on Main Street or Moishe Katz, who my mother used to act with. Moshe. What a marvelous name for a green-eyed lover, and aren't you getting wanton? Oh, I wanted to so much.

My room seemd to mock me with its yellow walls, my mother's efforts one summer while I was away at camp, and the new fluorescent light fixture on the ceiling. "I thought it might cheer you up, improve your disposition," she scolded. "Such a beautiful sunny room. I only wish I had such a room when I was a young girl."

Didn't she understand her daughter at all? A sunny disposition was the last thing I wanted, the opposite of my desired temperament—which was, to my horror and shame, cheerful like hers. I wanted to teeter on the edge, a tightrope dancer spinning to the trill of a lunatic flutist.

Like Stephen Dedalus, I prepared. "Words which he did not understand he said over and over to himself till he had learned them by heart: and through them he had glimpses of the real world about him." That's exactly what I did, copying words like "anomie" and "existential crisis" into my notebooks. "The hour when he too would take part in the life of that world seemed drawing near and in secret he began to make ready for the great part which he felt awaited him the nature of which he only dimly apprehended." Maybe Moshe was the messenger from that world, sent to help me confront my inner life, which until now had been nil, unexplored like Mars.

How I longed to meet Moshe at his garret, where I was sure there was a mattress on the floor and *c'est tout.* Where we could sip espresso and Kahlua and talk about ideas. I'd had enough of the Songs of Innocence. Where were the dark ones, my Songs of Experience? To shatter me, So I would be reborn. Different.

It was Bella's Lucille Ball influence, I thought, that I hadn't developed *internally.* I was flighty, nary a serious thought in this foggy noggin. But how could anyone possibly kamikaze into life when you were stuck inside a square lemon, an anachronism, and every morning your mother said, even if it was raining, a respite from all that glaring, hopeful sunlight, "It looks like it's going to be a good day." In my blackest moments, I feared that I was like her, a superficial person like everybody else, nothing special about me; that I wouldn't recognize a profound thought or concept if it smacked me between the eyes like a wad of soaked toilet tissue; that I was a Hollywood set where the building looked real from the outside until you walked through the door and discovered it was fake and there was an impenetrable wall. Instinctively, I drew the shades and tried to think about important issues as befitted the potential mistress of Moshe Wozinsky. Angst. Ennui. Metapsychosis.

Moshe, I now understood, could save me from the unexamined life which Socrates said wasn't worth living. And he probably had no idea of the impact he could have on my existence, undistinguished so far. "Weakness and timidity and inexperience would fall from him in that magic moment." Maybe that would happen to me too. Oh, I could hardly wait to awake from my three-square-meal bourgeois slumber. Moshe, my dark prince, would brush his lips against mine. I would stir slightly. And before I knew it, I'd be reading R. D. Laing and understanding it too.

In an all-encompassing vision, aided by five of my mother's Newports, I now saw that the other one, Wayne, was fool's gold. But what a looker! And he had seemed nice. Nevertheless, a gilded reflection of the real thing, like the golden calf. Besides—and this is the truth, no sour grapes—hadn't I always responded to Ben Casey more than Dr. Kildare? And to make a further confession, Wayne's hair was closer to the hue of grapefruit juice. Colorless. Yet it was necessary to err so that I could find out the truth: that *they* were shallow, a glacial lake. Moshe was as deep as the Bay of Bengal. And earthy, sexual in a subterranean, bearded, but definitely nonrabbinical way. If only he would call.

Monday night had passed in silence. Tuesday too. Today was Wednesday. It was the last chance for our love. If he called tomorrow, I would be forced to refuse, foolish pride. Only the desperate accept dates without at least three days' notice. You don't want to seem to be waiting around. I lit a candle, converted, reciting the Hebrew blessing over wine, the only one I knew by heart, figuring that perhaps a Jewish god could catch a Jewish guy and if He was truly omnipotent, omniscient and ubiquitous, He'd make Moshe call. "I enjoy being a Jew," I sang aloud. Soon the candle extinguished itself. "Sunrise, sunset . . ." Was that some sort of sign?

Moshe would call. Of that, I was confident. He had to. He wasn't the sort who took your number, told you about all the wonderful things you'd do together, and then never called—like Johnny de Noto. I could hardly believe it. How could Johnny have said all those nice things about my eyes and hair, how I had a good figure, and not call? When I ran into him several months later,

I had asked him. Once he remembered who I was, he said he took lots of girls' numbers, and it didn't mean he'd call. It was just in case.

Moshe was not that kind of person. He had too much integrity to lead a woman on, especially a passionate one like me. Besides, he too had been burned in the crucible of love. "There are no adventures—there are no perfect moments. . . . We have lost the same illusions, we followed the same paths. I can guess the rest." I sighed as I studied *Nausea*.

Besides, there had been others. Yes, I had been loved and admired. The drink stirrer from Hawaii Kai and the Mamma Leone menu tacked to the back of my closet proved it. But with the wisdom of hindsight I could see that Michael Weinstein had been a mere boy. Sweet but immature. He attended Milford Academy in Connecticut. We exchanged letters. His were matter-of-fact—"Everything's okay here. I have a lot of work. Hope I can see you Thanksgiving. I'll be in on Wednesday evening . . ."—while mine, heated, strained to be a memorable correspondence that perhaps would be collected posthumously. "It was a melancholy day. A kind of gray fog covered everything like a smudge. The raindrops resembled rhinestones. It reminded me of London. . . ." Michael was from one of Long Island's Five Towns, new Jew money, and we spent hours messing around. The death knell of our relationship sounded when I wouldn't spend the weekend with him in his parents' house while they were in Florida. He called me frigid. Sometimes I thought I could have been happy, or at least comfortable with him. It would all be his one day: a ranch-style mansion in Lawrence, membership at the country club, a turquoise outboard motor yacht named *Golden Breed*.

Then there had been Eddie Jackson of Gun Hill Road, the Bronx, who belonged to a house plan, Think Pink, at Hunter College. He had a blond pompadour, brown eyes, sounded terrific as he described himself over the phone. A perfect blind date—for the blind. He had potholes on his face filled with capfuls of Clearasil, sported a black leather jacket (indoors too), and shiny gray pants upon which a spot would appear during the grinding sessions to the Duprees' "You Belong to Me."

But neither Michael nor Eddie constituted mature, important relationships where you are transformed by the synthesis of love and desire and talk about personal things. And that's what I wanted, had held out for in the private hell of my solitude: a truly passionate love affair in which mind, body, and spirit collided in a three-part harmony of the spheres.

Finally I had met someone who could understand my deepest *innards* and share my thoughts about life, death, the nature of the universe. A tight pair of jeans would improve his appearance immeasurably.

When the Princess sang out with a thunderous, glorious ring, I screamed downstairs, "It's for me! Don't anyone pick it up!" I almost tripped over the cord from joy.

"Did you read it?" Moshe asked while I bumbled hello-how's-it-going, beaming like a smile button, trembling too.

"Huh?" I asked stupidly.

"*Nausea.* Did you read the book?"

"Of course I did! Every word of it."

"Then maybe you can understand me," he said. "What did you think about the relationship between history and everyday life?"

"Well." I paused. "I think Sartre's saying something like that history, while making order of things, isn't true to the chaotic nature of life."

"Good, good," he muttered. "Have you ever felt that kind of nausea?"

Sure, at the moment, having eaten half a bag of Dipsy Doodles. But I said in an intense voice, the way I imagined Anny might speak, "I often feel it. Especially when I see people around me leading superficial lives and never questioning it. They just drive their cars, go to work, then come home, watch TV, and go to sleep. It's a kind of death. I want to find the privileged situations and perfect moments! But it is impossible in this world where every experience is transient."

"Yes!" Moshe cried. "You do understand. That's exactly the way I feel, every moment of my life."

Moved by my own rhetoric, I continued, dropping my voice as I imagined Ingrid Bergman in *Notorious,* "I've felt this way since I was little. Of course, I never had words for it then. But I always wondered why I felt such an outsider, so horribly alienated in the sandbox. Why I sat by myself, building mudpies which I would later destroy, stamping them out with my feet as if they were symbols of a world which was already too painful for me to live in."

"I must see you," Moshe said. "Love is the only thing that transcends the arbitrary violence of everyday life, the assault to the psyche and heart, how time destroys everything."

"Yes!" I squealed.

"Where do you live?" he asked.

I told him. "Just take the #1 I.R.T. subway to 59th Street, change for the D train to Seventh Avenue, and go downstairs and get in the last car of the E train to Continental Avenue. Then, right outside in front of the exit, wait for the Q65A bus, they come every fifteen minutes, and take it to 137th Street and Jewel Avenue. Walk two short blocks. It's the first house to your right with the—"

"How can you live so far away!" Moshe exploded. "Scott Fitzgerald called Queens the valley of ashes. They don't have anything there except the Chiclet factory. I can't understand why you can't live in Manhattan or at least Riverdale, like a normal person. It's impossible this way!"

Before he could change his mind, I offered, "I'll come in to meet you."

"It's inhuman," he ranted, "for any woman to expect a guy to spend all that time, pay a double fare in each direction, so we can just come back here and I can blow twenty bucks for food and a movie. It's unfair."

"But I don't mind meeting—"

"No, no," he interrupted nobly. "I'll come all the way out there. Spend an hour and a half, at the very least, on public transportation, when I could be finishing my Anthro paper so I could get a grade and complete the course. If I don't, I'll never hear the end of it. Like if I don't pick up my mother's shoes from the shoemaker even if she says, 'No, do it only if you can. If you happen to pass the shoemaker. Don't go out of your way.' So when I see her, she demands, 'Where's my shoes? You can't even do that for your mother? It's not enough that you live by yourself, who knows how you eat, who you see, in Manhattan. . . .' I'll do it, Hannah. This one time. Besides, your mother probably wants to check me out and all."

"You will?" I sighed. A guy who wasn't interested wouldn't do that.

"Can I just ask you some things before the date?"

My left ear was beginning to sprout buds. I moved the receiver to the other ear, reaching for a handful of Dipsy Doodles. "Yeah?"

"Just some basics. You go to Queens?"

"Yes," I said bravely. "But I'm in the Honors Program. And they have an excellent English department."

"Year?"

"Upper freshman. I went to summer school so I could get started." I bit down softly on the chip.

"What are you eating?" he demanded.

"Melba toast," I lied, thinking it more dignified.

"Didn't you get a Regent's Scholarship?" he asked.

"Sure, but they wouldn't let me go away."

"Hmmm, overprotective," Moshe mumbled. "How would you describe your relationship with your father?"

"Why are you asking these questions?"

"Listen, it's important to know certain things about a person you're going out with. That way we can know each other's neurotic patterns and try to deal with them in a constructive way."

"Oh," I conceded. "I guess we're pretty close."

"Do you ever sit on his lap?"

"I used to, but—"

"You used to." Moshe repeated the words like they had an awful significance. "Electra Complex," he pronounced.

"We didn't do it all the time or anything like that." I swallowed the chip.

"Don't be defensive. What about your mother?"

I paused, then said with some control, "We don't get along that well."

"Why?"

"She treats me like a child."

"Probably threatened," he said. "Any sibs? Brothers or sisters?"

"Moshe, I feel like you've got a questionnaire in front of you and you're writing all this down!" I protested.

"What if I am?" he answered. "This is just preliminary stuff I've got to know. Once I know it, then we can forget it."

"Okay. I've got a younger sister named Stevie."

"Stevie? That's a strange name for a girl, don't you think?"

"Her real name is Stephanie."

"Penis envy," Moshe stated.

I bit into another chip. "Penis wha—"

"Could you please not eat while we're talking."

I gulped. "Sorry."

"So what about Stevie?" he continued. "Describe her."

"Well, she smokes a lot of dope, reads Hesse, Gibran, and Castaneda, and thinks of herself as a warrior."

"Does she go to Queens too?"

"No, she's a junior at John Bowne High."

"I see." Then Moshe asked solemnly, "Have you ever smoked grass?"

"Once, but nothing happened. Have you?"

"Are you kidding! Our consciousness is what distinguishes us from animals. I wouldn't tamper with that."

He paused. "Hannah, what are your feelings about God?"

"I never had any religious experiences, if that's what you mean. But Stevie had a vision of love, as she called it, on mescaline during a Jimi Hendrix concert. I'm afraid not to believe, so I sort of do. I guess you could call me a skeptical agnostic, of Jewish descent—"

Moshe interrupted excitedly. "I've got something that will blow your mind. Have you ever eaten a Devil Dog? You know, those phallic chocolate things that look like frankfurters?"

"Sure."

"Fix the words Devil Dog in your mind. You got them? Okay. What do they spell backwards?"

It took me a while. "God lived!" I exclaimed. "Bizarre."

"I figured it out when I was seven and my mother put one in my Captain Kangaroo lunch box. It's haunted me ever since. I think it's a message, connected to the Holocaust my parents survived."

"You mean, they were in concentration camps and have numbers tatooed on their arms?"

"At the dairy restaurant where my father works, there's this guy who plays the numbers according to my father's numbers."

"That's horrible!"

"He doesn't think so. If the guy wins, he gives my father a big tip."

Just then, during such a heightened moment of shared intimacy and awe, my mother picked up the extension. "Are you going to get off the phone or what? You've been on the line for forty-five minutes!"

"Mother," I said angrily. "Please remove yourself from the phone."

"Uh-uh. No one can call, and I can't call outside. I'm not getting off until you hang up. Who are you talking to anyhow?"

"*Get off!*" I raised my voice imperatively. "Do you hear me? I'm talking about something very important."

"Hannah, I need the phone. Do I have to beg to make calls? You're not the only one with a social life, for your information."

"I'm sorry!" I screamed at her. "Terribly sorry. Wait till you have a private phone call. Then I'll interrupt you so you'll know what it feels like. Moshe, I've got to go."

"Don't worry. She's just competing with you because she's afraid of losing her own youth," Moshe declared knowledgeably.

"What!" Bella yelled into the phone. "Who the hell is this?"

The phone clicked.

"Listen, Moshe. Don't mind her," I apologized.

"Don't mind her," my mother mimicked.

"He hung up!" I cried. "It's all your fault! You spoil everything so nothing good ever happens to me."

7

I even wore a Tampax. In case I was swept away in a paroxysm of passion, I figured, lost all reason, decided to forfeit my treasure for a moment's pleasure, I would be blockaded. But why was it a treasure if you just left it there, untouched? Did it accrue interest like the savings account my parents started for me at the Kew Garden Hills bank when I was in third grade?

"Welcome to my bachelor pad," Moshe announced, removing the police lock from the door of his fourth-floor walk-up.

Out of breath, I hesitated. Standing at the threshold. "Couldn't we go out or something?" One step could change everything.

"I told you," he said. "I'm not going to rape you. We'll have dinner here and talk. So what's the big deal?"

What was I scared of? "It's just that I'd feel more comfortable if we—" I stopped. Virginity was no longer a meaningful concept.

Moshe turned on the light.

Slowly, I entered my first male apartment. Admiral Perry must have felt this way. Janet Leigh in *Psycho.* I looked around. Disillusionment like blue hairy mold set in as I noted the peeling green paint above the radiator, the cracks on the ceiling and above the decrepit dresser and desk where a Columbia banner hung. Moshe indicated that I should sit on the couch, covered with an Indian fabric.

So it was a garret. Isn't that what I hoped for? Like in

Notes from the Underground. He was unwilling to sell out. But suppose there were roaches. Athlete's feet fungi. What do you want him to have, I scolded myself, a crushed velvet couch? French Provincial bar on wheels?

"What better way is there for us to get to know each other than for you to see where I love, how I live?" He wrapped his arms around me.

I leaped up, sweeping across the room. "God, you have so many books!" I exclaimed. There were shelves to the ceiling of books I aspired to read one day, like *The Magic Mountain,* four volumes of *Remembrance of Things Past,* the *Inferno* and *Purgatorio.* "Have you really read all of them?" I asked, running my fingertips over the spines.

"Some. I used to work in a bookstore where they gave away a lot of books."

"Just like that?" I asked.

"Not exactly. But they were always ordering large stocks, so I'd help myself to a few."

"I see."

"Everyone did it. I'll be right back. Got to walk the dragon."

"Huh?"

"Piss."

"Oh."

I imagined weekends of holing up here, profound ideas wafting about the room like an aroma. We could discuss the relationship of literature to life. Did it really have healing powers? What of the surrealistic vision? I smacked my lips, feeling like my life was finally turning into a foreign movie.

Pulling out a black-spined book as Moshe returned, I called, "What's *The Lifetime Reading Plan?*"

"Oh, someone gave me that as a joke." He tried to grab it from my hands.

I held on to the book. "Can I look at it?"

He shrugged his shoulders.

"I'm just curious."

It had a chronological list of authors and their works,

from one to a hundred, everybody who was anybody: (1) Homer, *The Iliad*, which had a blue-inked page 48 next to it, all the way through (97) Alfred North Whitehead. In some places, Moshe had also scribbled dates.

I smiled as I closed the book and returned it to the shelf.

"Not there!" Moshe scolded pulling it out. "Can't you read? Fadiman. That doesn't go after Faulkner." He replaced the book.

"I'm sorry."

"It's a stupid book," he grumbled.

"I don't think so."

We sat silently on the bed. Preoccupied, Moshe pushed a cuticle on one of his nails. As for myself, I had already exhausted most of my topics of conversation during our long subway trip, so I sat like the handicapped.

"What'd you think of my mother?" I asked finally.

"Not bad looking." He grinned. "Kind of a sexy old broad."

I punched him in the arm. "She is not!"

"I wouldn't be too sure. You don't think she screws around?"

"My mother? You must be kidding!"

Moshe stood up. "Okay." He rubbed his hands together. "Would you like something to drink? I'm going to cook the house specialty, my beef bourguignon. But let's have a drink first."

All I knew was my mother's favorite, Cherry Heering, which she swilled by the thimbleful at affairs, catered ones, as far as I knew, and groaned that it went to her feet.

"I'll have a brandy and soda, old chap." Brett's drink. Liquor loosens libidinal energy, I reminded myself. Before I knew it, I'd be dancing naked, a lampshade on my *tuchis*.

"Have you ever had Sabra?" he asked. "It's an Israeli liqueur that tastes like a combination of chocolate and orange."

So Jewish, I sighed to myself. There was even a menorah with a green Elat stone on his bookshelf. And he wanted a shiksa? For what, conversion? He could be my brother, if I had one, not my polar opposite. How was he supposed to be the male principle which would call forth my female principle in a devastating sexual conflagration—several dates from now, if we got emotionally involved? "I'm not prejudiced."

Moshe returned with two long-stemmed crystal glasses. The bottle of Sabra was still wrapped. With some ceremony, he opened it and poured out brown liquid that looked like flat Coke.

"Here's to us getting to know each other," he toasted, clinking my glass.

"Thank you," I said shyly.

He studied me for a moment. "You look bustier."

I turned away.

He put his arm around me. "Is that all your own?"

"No, it's my mother's."

He smiled. I smirked. His eyes reflected the blue of his shirt.

"Cute." He hugged me.

A shiver ran down my spine like a rabbit. I moved away from him, lighting a cigarette from the Newports purchased especially for the date.

"I didn't know you smoked," Moshe said, eyeing me suspiciously.

"I know they'll kill me," I confided in a world-weary voice. "I can hardly taste anymore. But it's an addiction. I have to have them. I'm like a damn junkie." I moved farther away from him as I inhaled another puff, throwing my head back.

"Now don't get defensive, Hannah," Moshe began, edging closer. "We just have to talk about some things." He had a grim expression on his face. "I'll be direct. How experienced are you, and what am I up against?"

"What the hell do you mean by that?" I demanded.

"Listen, it's cool if you're a virgin—"

"Whatever gave you that idea?"

Even if Hymen was relatively intact, I had been extensively touched, inside and out, both by yours truly, a none too artful onanist who faked orgasms to myself, if that's what they were, and by Bobby Ginzburg, in third grade, for a month of rides on his yellow Schwinn. Did he think no one ever wanted to—with me?

"Have you performed fellatio?"

My mouth grew dry at the thought. "Of course," I answered. "Hasn't everybody?" Even if I was squeamish and waited in the drugstore until everyone left. Only when it was empty as a church did I slink up to the counter and whisper, 'A box of Modess, please. It's for a friend.' "Uh, could you recommend another book? I really liked *Nausea* and thought the characters—"

"Cunnilingus? Has that been done to you? Around-the-world?"

"What is this?" I stood up angrily. "Nuremberg? I've done everything you can imagine. With men, women, children, horses. Two men! Yes, I did. In an Olympic-size pool. At the B'nai B'rith!" My hand shook, tipping the drink all over my crew-neck sweater.

I tried to wipe the brown Sabra droppings with my hand but they spread.

"I'll get a towel!" Moshe cried, rushing into the bathroom. He returned with one marked Y.M.C.A.

"Here," he said, poised over me, embarrassed. "Should I try?"

"I'll do it." I took the wet towel, rubbing, but the spots remained. Like a case of the runs. *I* wanted to run. Once a shlump, always a shlump. That was an existential truth. There was no exit. Hell was yourself—and how were you supposed to escape that? I felt close to goddamn tears as I looked down at the splattered canvas of myself.

"It looks like it stained," he said sorrowfully. "Maybe you should let it soak in the sink. I'll give you something else to wear."

"Never mind. It doesn't matter."

"Here," he offered, pulling a sweatshirt from his file cabinet. "There's some Ivory Snow in the bathroom."

"Okay."

I took off my sweater and rinsed it in cold water. Would Lauren Bacall spill her drink all over herself? Did she ever in her whole life, even if she had a fight with Bogie? Why couldn't I do anything with *aplomb*? Just once.

I glanced in the mirror as I slipped on Moshe's Columbia sweatshirt. I always did that when I felt bad, to check that I was still there.

"How does it look?" I modeled.

"Gorgeous. Did the spots come out?"

I shrugged. "It's an old sweater anyhow." I sat down next to him.

"Okay, let's get back to the topic we were discussing. Now I definitely had the feeling that you were projecting your fantasies—"

I looked at him. "And I suppose you've done everything?"

"Well," he said modestly. "Some. I've been around. Not that I'm proud of it. What can I say? I've taken love where I could find it. Sometimes it was rather sad."

"Well, so have I."

"You have?" His horny eyes lit up.

I reconsidered. "Not that many times, though. And I had to really know the other person and be sort of—involved."

Before I could finish, he grabbed me. "Let's get involved!"

"Cut it out." I pushed him away.

"Why?" He pecked me playfully on the lips. "Don't you like to be kissed?"

Actually I had begun rather early with my Patsy Playpal doll, whose lips puckered out, a perfect sexual partner for me at age eight, enamored of afternoon Bette Davis movies. I would close my eyes, throw my head back, and sigh romantically, "I've resisted you as long

69

as I can bear it. Darling, take me. I'm yours," as I slowly descended upon her lips. But with a man, kissing led to petting which led to indirect, then direct genital contact like A to Z.

"I thought you were only attracted to blond girls with long legs and freckles," I retorted.

"Sometimes I make exceptions. Although you do look like my mother."

"I do not!"

He kissed me. "And chopped liver."

I tried to reach for my cigarette in the ashtray. Moshe pulled me to him and began biting my lower lip, sucking it with his teeth. Had he been taking lessons from Jonas Cord in *The Carpetbaggers?* I imagined tiny teeth marks forming like steps. With fortitude, I waited for him to stop.

"Sex is my forte," he whispered. "I may not look it, but you don't know how good I am. I can give a woman so much pleasure she can't stand it." He lunged at me.

"Moshe—"

"Really, one woman I knew committed herself to New York Hospital for several days. She had been driven beyond the point of frenzy."

"I really don't want to," I insisted, puffing at my cigarette like a respirator. Even if I did want to accelerate the level of my experience. I couldn't imagine seeing him naked, my body exposed, the privacy between my legs. Besides, I wanted a relationship, the touching of two souls. Not a *night stand.* And if you gave it all away on the first date, why would anyone ask you for a second and third one so they could get to know your personality too? We hadn't gone anywhere fancy like La Cave Henri IV (where Michael Weinstein had taken me on my birthday and I still had the ashtray) so I'd feel guilty and compelled to reciprocate with vital parts of my body.

"Forget it," he said. He stretched his neck, cracked his back, turning first in one direction, then the other.

He made his eyeballs levitate to the back of his head so all one could see were slits, like peering into a milk container.

"Are you all right?" I asked, tugging at his sleeve.

He opened his eyes. "I'm just doing my exercises. I've developed them from Reich's orgasm theory." But he had the look of someone not at all satisfied with his tax return.

"I don't mean to, you know—" I began to apologize, not wanting him to think I was a rejecting woman, frigid, or a ball-busting bitch like in a Harold Pinter play or that I, never wanted to, ever.

"Some music might relax the psychosexual tension. Then I'll start dinner. First dates are hell anyway. What are you into?"

Secretly and desperately, listening for hours in my room, seated cross-legged on the blue carpet between screechy speakers, Streisand. "My Man," "People," "How Does the Wine Taste?" "Gotta Move," "Free Again," "Absent-Minded Me," and "Second-Hand Rose." But I said, so he wouldn't associate me with all the homely Jewish girls in Queens who loved Barbra, thought there was hope, crossed eyes, camel-back noses, and all, "Oh, everything. I'm eclectic. Jazz, folk rock. The Stones, Doors, Janis—"

"I find current music alienating. Would you like to hear a tape I put together?"

The voice of Moshe Wozinsky. "This is a tape of some of the music that has had personal meaning for me in my life. When I met Claire, this song was playing at the Lion's Den. She was just sitting there alone. But I think the sentiments expressed are fairly universal. Sing it, Little Anthony: 'I want you to want me, I need you so badly, I can't think of anyone but you. And I think I'm going out of my head. . . .' Haven't we all felt these emotions in the violent throes of love?" he asked over the music. "Oh, the irrational power of it."

I sat and listened while he plugged the electric frying pan into a socket on the floor. Since he didn't have a kitchen, everything was laid out on his desk.

"What girl nowadays would go back to the railroad tracks to get her boyfriend's high school ring when a train was coming? Sure, it's extreme, but it's a metaphor for the sacrifices you sometimes have to make in love. If only Claire had known that," Moshe mused.

"Do you need any help?" I inquired, walking over to where he chopped onions on a plate.

"Would you fill this pot with water in the bathroom?"

I took my sweater out of the sink and hung it over his tub. Above the toilet seat, I noticed a poster of a small boy whose mouth was covered with dark chocolate pudding. Moshe had written, *Mmmm, it tastes so good.*

"This is for the rice," he said, dropping an electric coil into the pot of water. Then he took a package of chopped meat out of a half-sized refrigerator underneath the bookshelves.

The tape continued. "I first saw Ellen in Ferris Booth Hall. She was dancing with someone else. When the song ended, they played Ruby and the Romantics. She looked at me. We met in the middle of the dance floor. I'll never forget the moment."

"That's a weird poster you have in the bathroom," I said loudly so he'd hear me over the music.

As Moshe browned the onions, he looked up. "Oh, that. So many people get upset about it. That's because this society has such hang-ups about shit. Look at the way we've invented antiseptic toilets which flush it down so it disappears. God forbid we should have to deal with our own excretion."

He ripped open the plastic package and began to crumble the chopped beef in his fingers. "Other societies have a more healthy attitude about their functions, which shows that they accept their bodies more too. I mean, it's just shit. It's not evil or bad. It's a waste material, like saliva or sweat, just that it's brown and mushy." He dropped pieces of meat into the pan.

"Okay, already."

"You're shocked."

"It's not that—"

"Repulsed. I can tell. Typical Western reaction. In Sweden, they have family outhouses. Two big holes for the parents and three small ones for children. For my thesis, I'm going to do a study of it: shit. A feces thesis, so to speak, probably the first at Columbia. For a split anthro/sociology degree. That is, if they let me do it. Columbia's so conservative. Well, I'll make sure it's well documented, lots of footnotes. The appearance in literature. Chaucer. Swift. Its etiology. A masterpiece of pedagogy so they can't fault me on that. I'll call it simply 'Shit,' no subtitle to make it more palatable." He stirred the meat and onion mixture. I looked away.

Was this brilliance, I wondered, the overflowing of an original mind that would one day make him famous, me too perhaps, only after he was dead because it was so revolutionary? Like Kafka. Or was he playing solitaire with a deck of 49 cards? And was I? I glanced at him. Our eyes met for a moment. He looked down and tasted the meat.

"Mmm, good. . . There'll be a history of shit," he continued. "And descriptions of different cultures and their reaction formations to it. I want to research its appearance in the literature and plastic arts of these cultures. Question: Has it undergone evolutionary change? Was Neanderthal man's shit harder? Looser? I'm also interested in vegetarian versus carnivore shit, male and female, professors', blue collar workers', and whether there is any correlation of smell and texture to intelligence."

I groaned to myself as he opened a can of cream of mushroom soup, Bella's brand, and began to spoon it into the pan. "I'd have to study a random sample besides the control group. You could be a part of it if you wanted. Would you mix this while I do the rice?"

He poured two cups of Minute Rice into the boiling water. "Maybe we could eventually work as a team like Phyllis and Eberhard."

"Who?" I stirred the Gravy Train. The mushroom soup gave it a deathly pallor.

"Kronhausen. They write about sexual fetishes. . . ." His eyes gleamed insanely. "Coprophilia!" He waved his hands. "Do you know what that is?"

"No," I said, shaking my head. Was he dangerous?

"Love of shit."

8

Moshe poured more Sabra into our glasses after dinner.

"To the Platonic ideal of love," I toasted.

"No way," he said, putting both of our glasses down.

So the time had come. Alas. I leaned back, closed my eyes, waited for the inevitable. Pot roast on a slab. Nothing happened. I opened my eyes. Moshe was grinning at me. "What's so funny?" I demanded.

"You," he said. "You look like someone about to have root canal."

"I just get really self-conscious sometimes," I muttered, embarrassed. "Let's get on with it already." I reached over to him, determined not to seem inexperienced.

He kissed the tip of my nose. "You know, you're very funny," he said. "Sweet, too."

"Oh, yeah?" I wanted to be taken seriously, at least partly as an object of lust and desire. I screwed my face into an expression of: I'd seen my share of pain and bitter disappointment, I had loved if not wisely, too well, and it was better to have loved and lost than not to have loved at all.

He looked still more amused.

I was a regular scream. *Ha ha*. "What's so damn funny?" Was he laughing at me or with me, a distinction that was never clear anyway.

"It comes through. It really does. Your sweetness and how hard you try to hide it." He kissed my nose again. "And your ingenuousness kills me." He laughed out loud.

"You don't really know me," I declared. "That's why you think I'm so—sweet." I spat the word. "I'm not, you know. I can be promiscuous and sleep around unscrupulously."

"Inscrutably—"

"You may not believe it, but I'm going to, one of these days."

"Is that so?" he teased, taking me in his arms.

"Yes," I insisted. But as I relaxed in the lair of his arms I lost the conviction of my conviction. His eyes were a cool, Pacific aquamarine. White gulls cruised over a smooth surf. I wanted to lift my petticoats to wade but feared cold water, an undertow which would keep me so I couldn't return to shore.

"You have beautiful eyes," I whispered.

He smiled. "I was just thinking how much I liked looking at your face."

"How come?"

"Because you ask dumb questions."

For the longest time we just sat there, studying each other. And it was all right. You didn't have to be sneaky about it. I imagined the mirror of his eyes becoming a window that allowed me to peek inside of him. How decent he was, smart, and even—was I just projecting my desires?—emotional.

"Did you have your nose fixed?" he asked, examining it.

I covered my nose with eight fingers. "Not exactly."

He removed my hands from my face. "What do you mean?"

"Does it matter?"

"I want to know everything about you."

"Really?" I peered into his eyes for a moment. "You really do? Okay, it was—uh, repaired."

He leaned away from me, squinting. "I'm wondering what you looked like before"

"It was something like yours," I informed him. "Only smaller and not as hooked."

Moshe touched his nose. "Mine doesn't hook, does it?"

It blared Semite, oversized, hunchback, curving southward as if some special magnetic pole exerted influence on all our people's shnozzes.

"Well, I wouldn't hang a winter coat from it."

He frowned. "Anyway, I think they did a good job. But you can always tell by the bridge between the nostrils." He rubbed his nose against mine, a Mack truck attempting to parallel park next to a Volkswagen bug, mouth on mine in a soft, curious kiss.

I felt awkward, untutored, not knowing where this was going, whether it was just making out, as I had done many times before, or a prelude, *foreplay!* to more serious activity. The sweatshirt rode up my back as I lay in Moshe's arms, and with my free hand I tried to tug at it. He pulled it firmly over my waist. "Thank you," I managed.

He kissed me around the circumference of my mouth. I thought of Magellan, or was it Balboa? His tongue flicking ever so lightly in and out of the fold of my lips.

As in the movies, I opened my mouth to receive his tongue. "Close your mouth," he said softly. I clamped it shut like a door in the summer so the air conditioning doesn't escape. He rubbed my neck, shoulders, and upper back.

A sigh escaped from the rock-bottom basement of my soul. I bit my lip to stifle it. My mind was taking leave, a noisy, bothersome parakeet, flying out the window to some other girl, walking down Broadway with her dog. I tried to move away from Moshe, but he held me.

"You feel nice," he said.

"You do too," I answered. Were you allowed to talk at a time like this?

Now he thrust his tongue deep into my mouth, curling it, then pulling out slowly as I teased him with my tongue. God, I was yielding, opening up like a flower to the sun, a begonia that had spent its life in a window box on a dark courtyard ledge. My body hot and tense, my heart pumping, pounding as if it might rise out of my chest to the ceiling and just sit there, next to the overhead light. *And then I asked him with my eyes to ask again yes. . . .*

Our mouths and tongues intertwined in a cat's cradle, the string pulling as his hand traced the curve of my breast, cupping it. Then he did the most extraordinary thing. He kissed me on top of the sweatshirt.

"Don't, Moshe," I whispered.

"Shhh." His mouth circled my breast, his teeth nibbling ever so lightly. Then he kissed my other breast.

I writhed, trying to force his body away from mine, grabbing the bolster behind me. But he only came closer, taking me with his most persistent tongue. With every wiggle and curlicue of it, I felt *undulations.*

Did I have to stop? Who said so? I gritted my teeth so I wouldn't coo as I wanted to, crow, cockadoodle doo! My body was awakening from an eighteen-year sleep. But this was it. No further. I could ruin my life if I continued. An illegitimate child, have to drop out of school. Mentally I constructed a Stop sign but he continued, lifting my sweatshirt and nuzzling my breasts with his nose and mouth through my Carnival lace bra. I felt almost feverish, my brain spinning like a coin about to drop: head, tail, no, yes, yes, tail.

"Moshe," I said, trying to push him away.

He did not stop kissing me as he unsnapped the back of my bra. *I put my arms around him yes and drew him down to me so he could feel my breasts all perfume yes. . . .* Was this my id, which I imagined as some evil nymphomaniacal force located somewhere near the section of the cortex which controlled sexual desire, nudging me onward? Everything in me which only a few moments before had been cranky and stubborn now felt soft, milky, generous. The urge to ask if he really liked me or whether this was just sexuality evaporated like dew. I do!

Helping me out of the sleeves of the sweatshirt, Moshe then slipped my bra straps off. Half naked, I stared down at my own breasts as I did when by myself.

They were a very pale pink-orange with almost mauve nipples whose tips were no larger than pimples, staring out like unseeing eyes.

Moshe interrupted my meditation. "Unbutton my shirt," he said.

I did. I was curious to see him but frightened too. His skin was very white, covered with dark fur. Flesh on flesh, chest to chest, we embraced like lovers. But no further.

When he started to open the zipper of my jeans, I twisted my body away from his. "Don't!" I cried. "Please, Moshe."

Like the domino theory, once you started, soon everything fell. It had already gone much farther than I intended. But he only came closer, his fingers probing, his tongue. *His heart was going like mad. . . .*

And I didn't want him to stop. I wanted him to continue kissing and touching me. *Yes, I said yes, I will—* But to stop there. Next week, same time and station. He didn't. I fought for my pants but lost them. I don't believe this is happening to me! And my *samedi* French panties went too. *On a first date!*

No one had ever seen me like this. I was totally, unequivocally naked. My clothes discarded in a pile on the floor, all I could cover myself with was my hands. I didn't even lie around so intensely fleshy in my own room. Moshe stood up and took off his pants.

Then he removed the bolsters and cover from the couch and unfolded it. Now it was a large double bed with red, white, and blue striped sheets. I stared at his face as we lay next to each other. I was afraid to look farther.

Moshe smiled as he studied my body. "You're lovely," he said finally. "There's nothing to be ashamed of. Let me see." He removed one of my hands, then the other. "Look at yourself."

I did, reluctantly, and spotted the white string of my protective Tampax. How could I have forgotten all about it? I looked like one of those dolls that, if you pull the string, they cry or pee. I crossed my legs tightly, but Moshe had seen it too. "Do you have your period?" he asked.

I shook my head stupidly.

"You mean—?" He grinned. "Don't tell me—"

"I'll just go to the bathroom," I said, trying to get up. He held me. "Don't. Let me."

"No!" I screamed.

In a flash, he yanked the string and pulled out what looked like a dead baby mouse. I was numb, all sensation gone out of my body. I couldn't even make love with dignity.

Moshe lay down next to me and began kissing me again. I didn't stir. He put my hand on his penis. Then he started to stroke my thighs.

"No, please don't. I don't want to."

"Hannah—"

"I'm not ready yet."

"It's okay," he said soothingly.

"No!"

"Just let me make you come," he said, continuing to gently touch me.

It sounded so graphic, so purely sexual. I balked. "I don't know if I want to—"

"Close your eyes and relax," he whispered. "You're going to like this very much." He turned off the overhead light and switched on a red light near the bed. It made him look Mephistophelian.

I opened my eyes again and saw the darkness outside through the slats of the venetian blinds. The room was undisturbed except for our clothes on the floor.

Moshe's body lay wrapped around mine. I stroked his hair, which was thin and gave him such anguish. Moshe. Who was he? Was it true that in love we searched for our lost half? Could he be mine? Could I be Moshe's? Or had it just been sex?

But he had known. His fingers finding the skin that

80

lullabied a lonely child asleep. How did he know? He tapped a sunburst. The birds sang gibberishky. I chortled with all my teeth.

We had come so close, then stopped. Why? I wondered. Was he afraid of making me pregnant? But couldn't that be taken care of? Perhaps he wanted to save this final knowledge for another time. And how much more was there to know? I imagined days and weeks, maybe even years of nestling in the bow between his neck and shoulders, across his waist, and then, perhaps, one day knowing all of him.

He slept soundly. I thought of my father falling asleep in his recliner, the newspaper dropping from his hand and fanning across the living-room carpet. Sometimes he snored, his mouth open, which made Stevie and me giggle as we tiptoed around him. The pair of red Buster Brown shoes my mother had bought me for the first day of school. How my father had lifted me high above Stevie and my mother, who shouted, "Stashek, let the child down!" He was the monster who dangled me between danger and love. "You're not afraid, big girl." I pulled down my dress, leaned away from the stubbles on his face. "More, Daddy, I want more."

A part of my life had ended this night and another, I felt, beginning. Moshe stirred as if he had received an electric shock. I held him tightly. Had it been important to him too? Would he cherish this evening, press it in his mind like a rare leaf? Men didn't think like that. Across the courtyard, I had seen the unearthly blue light of a late movie and now it was dark. I must wake him.

I raised myself slowly, leaned over, and kissed him on the mouth. Shyness and affection, both equally intense, mingled. How like a teenage boy he looked, his face relaxed in a way that I hadn't seen. I kissed him again. "We have to go, my love."

He opened his eyes and seemed not to recognize me for a moment. "What time is it?" He turned the light switch on. "Oh, two."

"It'll take us quite a while to go back," I said softly.

He looked at me sleepily. "What do you mean?"

"I have to go home," I said.

"You could stay over here," he suggested. "Then we could be together all night and have coffee in the morning."

"My parents would have a fit."

"Look," he said, sitting up. "You're a big girl. They can't run your life forever. Tell them I took you to your girl friend's."

"I've really got to go." I stood up, gathering my clothes. "It'll take us some time to get back to Queens."

"Hannah," Moshe said quietly, "you're not really expecting me to go all the way back with you, are you? I went to pick you up, but I can't go out again and then have to travel back here."

I panicked. "How am I going to get back?"

"I told you. Why don't you stay here?"

I shook my head. "I can't."

As I put on my clothes before him, I felt ashamed. My panties that were gummed up, my bra. It was like the reverse of a strip act, not sexy in the least.

"Okay, then I'll walk you out and put you into a cab. There won't be any problem. Do you have enough money?"

"I only have a dollar and a half," I said. "I thought you—"

"You should always have money with you, in case of an emergency. I'll spring for the cab, but—"

"We've been so close," I said, tears forming in my nose and behind my eyes. "Why can't you take me home?"

"That's unreasonable and you know it, for me to spend an hour and a half to take you back and then another hour and a half to come home."

While Moshe was in the bathroom, I memorized his room. There was a Horowitz-Margareten Jewish calendar hanging on the wall above his desk. It was full of symbols and letters that he had inked in. On certain dates there were initials, girls' names, movies, and as each day passed, he put a bold cross through it. H. W.

written in pencil was entered on this Saturday, the 3rd of Elul, 5727. Didn't I rate ink? Maybe after tonight, I thought snidely. His bulletin board had a schedule of Columbia basketball games, mixers at Ferris Booth Hall, tickets to Homecoming Ball, and a football game against Princeton. Would I ever share any of these with him? I put on my jacket.

"Don't forget your sweater," Moshe said, carrying it as he came out of the bathroom.

"Couldn't I wear your sweatshirt?" I implored. Collateral. "Please."

"It's the only one I have," he said.

I turned around, took off the sweatshirt, and slipped on my sweater, which was damp.

As we walked to Broadway, neither of us spoke. I wanted him to say *something*.

Moshe hailed a cab.

"Here," he said, giving me a five-dollar bill.

"Moshe—" I began.

"This should about do it, with a fifty-cent tip."

"I guess so."

Then he pulled out a printed card from his wallet. It said: MOSHE WOZINSKY: PROFESSIONAL GIGOLO, DOG WALKER, PLANT TENDER, APARTMENT SITTER, TYPIST with his phone number underneath; CALL EVENINGS.

"I sleep late, so if you want to call, don't try till after one."

I put the card into the zipper compartment of my pocketbook.

He kissed me hastily.

"*Ciao,*" I said.

He walked away without turning around.

As the cab sped across the upper level of the Queensborough Bridge, Manhattan faded behind me like the aftermath of a fireworks display. Something cold and sticky leaked out between my legs. Did I have an orgasm? The five-dollar bill wouldn't stop shaking in my hand.

9

I should never have gone to his apartment. That was the
critical error of judgment. I had hesitated, but by then it
was too late. I was a prisoner of the situation. Vulnerable. But how could I have been so *ni-eve*? Didn't I know
what he wanted? What every man wanted? And yet, I
didn't think he would take advantage. Did he? When
Moshe lay down next to me on the red, white, and blue
striped sheet, it felt real. He had propped himself on his
elbows and looked into my eyes. It was an intimate moment. I could almost swear to that. Then he kissed my
breasts and took the nipples in his mouth. I now tried to
do the same but discovered they were too short to
reach. Four A.M., I sat in my hot sacrificial tub, scrub-
bing.

And afterwards, he couldn't wait to get rid of me,
dumping me into a cab with five dollars like some mini-
mum-wage slut and it wasn't even enough to cover the
fare and I had to add the rest. When the driver opened
his window, I wanted to kill myself. I could smell it, too.
Did Moshe take one whiff of his finger and, like the ra-
ven, say "Nevermore"? I soaped myself again.

Earlier, I had dealt with the incriminating evidence,
using Mr. Clean on my *samedi* panties (even though it
was stupid, I still rejoiced that I had worn the right day
of the week), but the shadow of Cremora remained.
"Out, damned spot!" I was like Lady Macbeth, crazily
rubbing—"Out, I say!"—or one of the women in a
Cheer commercial. Finally, I had hidden them at the

84

bottom of the hamper along with the other casualty of the date, my stained sweater.

Then I had checked myself like a medic examining a car accident victim, making sure there were no concussions, broken organs, blood vessels, especially around my neck, which had a way of blaring, even through a layer of Covergirl. So far, no physiological signs of mutilation. But maybe there were psychological scars which you couldn't see or feel immediately but could give you problems later in life, the way bad toilet training made people sew their savings into pillowcases.

Look, it wasn't like he pinned my arms down and held a switchblade to my throat. I could have said no. I did, but he wouldn't stop. All I had to do was say no and mean it. I let him. I had to face that. My id had defeated the censure of my superego. Even if we didn't exactly consummate, it was the spirit, not the letter, that killeth, and I had panted to myself.

I knew I should feel devastated. Even if I wasn't Catholic. After all, what was supposed to be the Matterhorn of human experiences, besides death, had just occurred a few hours earlier. But I still felt like myself. Wouldn't anything ever penetrate?

I felt like the person who thought he ate poisonous mushrooms. He called all his friends, left a farewell note for those he couldn't reach. Then blotto. He didn't even get cramps. So he had to call them again. "Listen, I escaped within an inch of my life, but here I am, without a single thing in the fridge. . . ." I tried on guilt, remorse, sexual despair, to see if I felt any of them. But I discovered, sadly, they were either too large for me, too tight, or just not my style. Maybe it would all change post-coitus. Then the walls of my callowness would crumble, Humpty-Dumpty like, and I would be penetrated by life.

I had lain there on his bed completely naked. Nude! The only other time I had ever done that was on my bassinet with the yellow chicks where I posed, toothless, smiling provocatively at my father, who held a Leica which shook while the shutter clicked, leaving me with two and a half arms and legs, and three eyes.

I looked down at myself, at how I must have looked to Moshe. It was as if a compass had started at the belly button, drawing breasts, the arc of a stomach, thighs which were conical cylinders like bullhorns, kneecaps. I remembered how I had stood at the full-length mirror, praying for breasts, an hourglass shell for a twig.

My nipples resembled rubber erasers sticking out of the water. They were tender as I touched them to see if I could make them erect as Moshe had. Well! I got so excited thinking of it all that I had to turn on the hot water again, trying to scald some of this wanton sex out of me. Slut, I scolded, haven't you had enough for one night? Finally, with my second and third fingers, I pressed as hard as I could and—snap, crackle, and pop! Was that all there was to an orgasm? Scratching an itch? Clitoral or vaginal? How was I supposed to know these things?

Somehow, when Moshe was touching me, it was different. I got excited, more, and more, and then the feelings petered out and his fingers started chafing me. Maybe I had had the orgasm before that and hadn't realized it. And my foot had fallen asleep so I had to shake it.

As for my doing it to him, I knew even less. I had no idea what to do. He kept readjusting my hand. Exactly where were you supposed to hold it, on the top or bottom? It was like searching for someone's pulse. Inside or out? I wanted it to be sensuous and unique so I started very gently, climbing tiptoe, my feather torture, planning to build to a grand crescendo, but he grabbed my hand and said, "Harder." So I pulled for all I was worth, tugging and shaking, helter-skelter, my wrist cramping, terrified that I was castrating him. When he finally ejaculated, it was I who sighed from relief. I had done it right.

I had been waiting a lifetime for something real and

important to happen. And now it had. What could be more real than sex? But I had to put it into perspective with the rest of my life. I climbed out of the tub to check my expression in the mirror. Had something changed?

I cleared the steam with the back of my hand. Yes, in a way. There, right on my face, was a knowing expression, as if I'd been let in on a secret women have known since the dawn of man. Venus of Willendorf and me, Hannah Deborah Wolf. That was the reason Mona Lisa smiled mysteriously. I had a lover. He had an apartment in the City. Kisses no longer had to be spun by the bottle, shared with a pillow warm for tears. They were free. I could have a lifetime supply. An exaltation of lovers. Wayne. Strange men with mustaches. Could I? I sank back into the tub.

Even if I knew the earth didn't move, you didn't turn into a pillar of salt, I still clung to the Mickey Mouse Club idea of sex and love—never mind marriage; I believed in free love—going together like ham and Swiss. Deep, passionate love was a prerequisite for fornication. Like Gudrun and Gerald in *Women in Love*.

Even if I knew girls like Stevie and her friends lost it in junior high, guilt and recrimination free. (But how could she do it just like that? What was the difference between a whore, pronounced *who-ah*, and being free? I imagined my baby sister as a groupie who lined up after a Moby Grape concert, offering blow jobs in a phone booth, just as I once opened the cream-colored pages of my autograph book to a Righteous Brother.) Did Moshe really like me? Tears welled up in my throat.

Before, I had always been the bookkeeper in the family. Doling out prescribed amounts and no more on the first date, a pinch added to the second date, and a smidge on the third. Counting buttons opened, snaps, zipper teeth, figuring kisses as opposed to soul kisses, tongue counted extra, a shoulder, bra strap, one finger, a whole hand—like some yellow-gummed usurer. Guarding the blood-engorged membrane of myself.

I let the tears pour, salty down my cheeks, dropping

like pennies into the tub. The skin on my fingertips had pleated as if suddenly I was old, in love. I pulled out the stopper. *Do you want to be a stupid, inexperienced girl forever?* There was a loud whooshing sound as the water drained.

10

I slept late. In fitful dreams, I got pregnant, contracted syphilis and gonorrhea, and he never called.

I sat at the kitchen table, drinking my freeze-dried coffee black even though I hated it that way. Asceticism after the hedonistic debauchery of the night before. So no one would suspect, I toasted an English muffin too.

Bella, in a red wrap-around lounging robe, came up behind me. "So, Sleeping Beauty has finally opened her eyes. It's only one o'clock. What time did you come in?"

I bit loudly into the muffin, ignoring her.

"Am I talking to the wall or do you hear me?"

"I don't want to discuss it."

"What do you mean?" she demanded. "As long as you live in this house and I am your mother, I have a right to know where you go and when you return."

"I didn't look at the clock," I said, staring into my coffee cup. Nothing like this ever happened to Lady Brett. *You went with the bullfighter and didn't come home. I was so worried, I almost jumped out of my mind. . . .*

"You could look up at me when we're talking. It's only polite."

"Probably around two," I answered.

"And where did you go, if I may ask?"

I imagined telling her, 'You may think I'm still the good daughter and honor student; well, I'm not! For your information, I lay naked with a man last night. So there. And I might have even had an orgasm. I bet you never had one.' Instead I said quietly, "If I went to a sleep-away college, I'd never have anyone bothering me."

"Bothering." She repeated the word.

"What I mean is that I'm entitled to some privacy."

"Maybe then," she said, "you can tell me why I found your sweater at the bottom of the hamper with brown spots. Did you drink something?"

I panicked at the thought of her examining the crotch of my *samedi* panties. "That's just what I mean! You're always snooping around in the—"

"If you want to know, I was putting the laundry together. I see a sweater ruined and I can't ask about it? You treat me like I'm some sort of horrible monster."

"I'm sorry," I apologized, relieved that she hadn't mentioned the panties.

"That's better." She nodded, sitting down across from me. "So this Moishe—"

"Moshe."

"Moishe, Moshe. It's the same in my book."

I didn't answer.

"Moshe, huh? What's he trying to be, fancy? Moishe is Moishe like Moishe Pupick, what a *paskudnik*. Ha-ha."

"All right," I said. "Leave me alone already."

"How old is he?" she asked.

"How am I supposed to know? Twenty-one or two, I guess."

"He looks older. Mature."

"So?"

"A very nice-looking man, I think," she observed.

"You really think so?" I asked, pleased.

"Oh, yes. Tall. Good built. Handsome, in a European way," she said, nodding approvingly.

"He's very well read too," I added.

"But . . . " She paused. "No, it doesn't really matter."

"What?"

"I'm not criticizing because it's not important at all. But you know, after all these years, your father still has every hair on his head he was born with."

Before she had finished, I stood up. "You see? Every time I try to talk to you! I can't even eat around here." I walked out of the kitchen.

"Hey, big *megillah*," she called after me. "What, you can go out, come home late, but you can't wash your own cup? I still have to clean up after you? Who's going to clean up after you when you get married?"

I passed Stevie as she was stepping out of the bathroom. It was the only time she came upstairs, and for supplies from the refrigerator. Otherwise, she entered and left through her own door in the basement.

"Damn her!" I cursed under my breath. "She can be such a bitch."

Stevie shrugged her shoulders. "Is that supposed to be news?"

I followed her downstairs, wondering how come she had had the good sense to become alienated before me and thus lay claim to the basement while I was stuck upstairs, next door to their bedroom.

"So what else is happening?" she asked, switching on the light at the bottom of the stairs.

"Shit and more shit," I mumbled, sitting down on her bed.

I looked around the wood-paneled *finished* basement of the house we had grown up in. The mirrored bar which once displayed Bella's memorabilia—toothpicks of the world, crystal decanters, an ice bucket covered with fake leopard fur—now held empty wine bottles with multicolored wax drippings and a brass incense burner shaped like a coiled snake; hand-lettered in a careful calligraphy, the Desiderata was taped to the mirror.

"Did you go out last night?" she asked as she bent over her turntable, playing the Jefferson Airplane's *Surrealistic Pillow*. Then she plunked herself on the yellow beanbag chair across from where I sat.

I nodded, blasé, as if it was a trifle. Stevie twirled a strand of her long dark hair absentmindedly.

Was it fair that in one family, two daughters born to the same parents, one should be, well, interesting-looking, while the other, eighteen months younger, was beautiful? I came out of the Bella mold, while Stevie had the bones, flawless skin, and ocher eyes of Sophie, my father's mother, who stared implacably from a photograph in the red vinyl album, coiffed, in a high-collared lace gown with a cameo brooch around her tapered neck. When we went out together, Stevie was admired, eyed, while I, the elder who had to buy a new nose and still wasn't quite in the running, expounded on what Bob Dylan meant when he said the vandal stole the handle.

What made Stevie bearable was a weight problem, give or take ten to fifteen pounds, depending on the ferocity of the past week's munchies and whether she could find a deli open to buy brownies and ice cream; her diets—Dr. Atkins', Stillman, high protein, carbohydrates, eggs, grapefruit—and the amount of speed she could score. So she favored flannel work shirts and loose overalls with embroidered butterflies and doves. But her hair spilled over her shoulders in ribbons of India ink.

"Did you go anywhere?" she asked.

"He has an apartment in the City," I mentioned casually. "We went over there."

"Where?"

"115th Street."

"Oh. Phil's brother used to live around there."

"Great."

"So, you balling him?" she asked.

"It was our first date," I said, looking up at her.

"That's right. I forgot you really believe in that crap, don't you?"

"What's it to you?"

"Don't tell me," she said, shrugging her shoulders. "It's not such a big deal, you know."

"Well, it is to me."

Stevie looked bored. "If that's the way you feel, forget it. I'm not that interested." She examined several hairs in the light. "God, I have so many split ends."

You were smaller than a pearl button; I threaded you around my ring finger. When it snowed, I cast spells of thimbles and toadstools. I was the one who introduced Stevie to her first dirty word: "vagina," from Webster's *New World Dictionary.* Also coitus, prostitute, anus, and semen. She contributed bowel movement and enema. When I got my first bra, a 32AA treasure of puckered cotton, she filled the cups with wet kitty litter. When I started shaving, she informed our boy cousins that I had a crewcut under my arms. Then somehow she scooted ahead of me, skipped several grades, graduated.

At fifteen, she lost it and never counted again. I remained the staid C.P.A. Could I help it if I had learned my mating rites from the Dick Clark show, assuming that all Kenny and Arlene, Frankie and Roberta did were the Pony and danced slow? Annette and Cubby were my role models. By the time the Beatles and Stones came, it was too late for me. I wasn't supposed to get any satisfaction. While I didn't believe in the concept of sin, and the only burning I feared was vaginitis, true love was what I wanted with a wild-eyed messianic fury.

Eighteen months made me a Future Journalist of America who met Adlai Stevenson (a framed photograph of us shaking hands sits on top of the TV), an honor-roll student who painted the scenery for the Senior Sing, and who didn't know my clitoris from a hole in the wall. Meanwhile, Stevie went to rock concerts at the Fillmore, felt more, balling like a pink-assed Spalding, and tried every drug known to the high school set.

"Do you ever have orgasms?" I asked, half swallowing the word.

"Sometimes."

"How are you supposed to know if you have them?" I asked as indifferently as I could. "I mean, is it obvious?"

"You can tell."

"How?" I asked.

"Look, I don't have them that often," she said.

"Why?"

"Because I don't, that's all." She looked annoyed.

"I don't think I do either."

"I didn't think you did that sort of thing," she said sarcastically.

"Lay off," I snapped.

"You think you and—" She looked up at me.

"Moshe."

"Is he Jewish?" she asked, making a face.

I nodded. "But he's not that way."

"Oh."

"He's older, too," I added.

"So you think your're going to have a thing?"

"I don't know," I said, feeling a clogged-up sensation in my chest as I thought of the date. There had been spiritual rapport between us. We had communicated besides sex. At least it seemed like that.

"Remember, just because you go to bed with someone doesn't mean they're going to marry you, Hannah."

"We didn't actually go to bed," I said.

She looked weirdly at me.

Quickly, I added, "But I touched him."

"You mean you jerked him off?" She made a gesture with her hand.

"Kind of," I admitted.

"So what are you getting so hysterical about? You didn't even fuck."

"Who's getting hysterical?"

"Never mind. You just seemed like you might."

I turned away to study the mauve record jacket. After a few seconds, I asked, "Have you ever thought—uh, been in love?"

"Of course," she said.

"You have?" I exclaimed. "What's it like?"

Her eyes brightened. "Oh, it's terrific. You want to see something?"

I nodded eagerly. "Do you have a picture?"

She walked over to the closet. I could hardly believe that she was going to share a secret of hers with me. "I know it's somewhere here," she murmured, lifting several shoeboxes from behind hangers.

"If it's dope, I don't want any," I said.

"Wait. Here it is." She removed the top of one of the boxes.

"What is it?"

"Just a minute." She took out a brown paper bag. "Open it," she said, handing it to me.

I don't know what I expected, but I unwrapped it cautiously, like it might explode. "Give me a hint," I pleaded.

"You'll see." She smiled.

The first thing I saw was the red and white lid of a jar. "Skippy Peanut Butter?" I asked, my voice dropping in disappointment.

"Take it out."

What looked like a deflated beige balloon caked with glue was locked air-tight inside the glass jar. I began to shriek. "If this is what I think it is, I don't believe it! Is it? Oh, shit!"

She nodded gravely. "I was in love with Peter for ages. He was Jennifer's guitar teacher. He also played in a rock band. But we didn't get together until the Central Park Be-In."

"Some souvenir," I said, dropping the jar back into the bag.

"You don't understand," Stevie said excitedly. "It was a beautiful experience. We did it right at sunset so you could see the sun reflected on the windows of the buildings on Central Park West. Afterwards, I saw the rubber lying there in the grass. I decided I wanted to save it, so I wrapped it in a tissue and put it in my bag."

"Did you ever see him again?"

She shook her head. "That was the only time. But it was better that way...." Her voice trailed off. She looked thoughtfully at me. "Sometimes the second time can be a real downer."

Then she began to sing with the record. " 'When the truth is shown to be all lies and all the joy within you dies. Don't you want somebody to love, don't you need somebody to love, wouldn't you love somebody to love, you better find somebody to l-o-o-o-v-e.' "

An act of coition lasts a minute, and it has been anticipated for months on end. Our passions are like volcanoes; they are continually rumbling, but they erupt only from time to time.
Saturday night, 1 A.M.
Flaubert in letter to Louise Colet

11

Twenty-third and Ely Avenue: the last stop in Queens. I held my breath as the E train ducked underwater. My family was on one shore; Moshe waited on the other. Land ho! I rejoiced. Lexington Avenue.

As I climbed the stairs, I studied two men riding down the escalator. They wore suits cut as if a jeweler had honed each lapel, the cuffs, and especially the precise pleats of the legs. Would I ever know anyone like that? Would he take me out for drinks at the Brasserie? Top of the Sixes? Would I see the opera? I imagined Wayne in a tuxedo. Now why did I think of him? *Moshe.* The men on the escalator were, of course, older. Businessmen. But I felt sophisticated too. Dangling Bella's pearl earrings, clouds of Intimate cologne wafting about me, I wore a royal blue minidress with white boots and a red slicker. Worldly wise, I was, coming into the City to meet my lover at a first-run movie theater on Third Avenue.

This was it, I exulted. Where I was meant to be. The city of dreams. You could tell by the way people strutted, October in their shoes, staring ahead as they crossed, invulnerable to lights or sputtering cabbies. Everyone on the street had a million-dollar idea of their destiny.

It was the city of money where shopwindows were polished to a dazzling invisibility so it all seemed closer, those beautiful things inside, until you reached out to touch. Then only your print, a white cage which was supposed to be yourself, stared out like a cold-hearted moon.

GIRLS, GIRLS, GIRLS, a second-floor window above Gristede's blazed. The city of sex too. Neon-lit, dark-skinned, plantinum sex vibrating from marquees, the junkies and expensive girls, hooking baby-faced men whose cowboy hats balanced above enormous paunches. And the boys hanging out of bars, from windows, on the street, ejaculating the skywriting of sex.

A long line circled the block in front of Cinema I. Suppose I don't recognize him? Ridiculous thought. I searched for half a head of thin brown hairs, a clipped goatee and—the ineluctable. What if he had just told me to come, and had no intention of meeting me? I walked to the front of the line again, panic rising like steam heat, pipes clanging.

"Hey, Hannah! Here!"

I just about yelped, beagle-eager. Moshe wore a beige trench coat with the collar up, a thick plaid scarf, and a denim cap.

I wanted to embrace, Moshe lifting me, kissing passionately on the mouth, but he said as I joined him, "I know I'm going to hate this movie. Just from the people on line, I can tell." His arms were crossed.

"*Blow-Up*'s supposed to be a masterful study of alienation," I declared, paraphrasing *Cue*. I looked up at him, so winsome, hoping that our eyes might meet and the lizards would creep back under the leaves.

"Why would anyone want to see that?" he demanded. "I go to the movies to laugh. There's enough of that other shit around to depress you all the time."

"But what about Bergman?"

"My least favorite director. I don't know how anyone can even sit through his films."

How could he understand? I needed other people's emotions on large screens so that, while devouring buttered popcorn and ice-cream-filled bon-bons, I'd shudder with an *inkling*. Movies expressed what was encased behind a combination lock of which I'd never learned the numbers. Try as I might: turn left twice, right, do not pass go, 30, 17, 25—I tried all combinations—no access. Except when certain movies pointed a beam of light like a laser so I felt raw and jelly-knee'd.

"I'm sure it's well done," I said.

"I couldn't stand *Red Desert*," he added, as the line began to move. "But since you wanted to see it and I'm the guy and I'm supposed to take you out and pay—"

I took out a twenty-dollar bill from my wallet. Moshe waved his hand and paid for both of us.

"Thanks," I said, trying to catch his eye, smiling.

He peered ahead, shaking his head. "It's going to be pretentious and asinine. I just know it."

I sat riveted, not wanting it to end. True decadence! A voluptuous universe where everything was pronounced with an English accent, and you could do what you wanted without neighbors squinting from their decks where they sat in rocking lawn chairs. Oh, I longed for such freedom. When Vanessa Redgrave took off her blouse in front of David Hemmings, just like that! and revealed no bra, little breasts, I loved it. Dare I go bra-less? And she wore a man's watch with a thick band. Would anyone ever look at me the way David Hemmings did besides men sloshing Thunderbird out of paper bags?

Next to me, Moshe sat twitching in his seat. He cracked his back several times in both directions and rotated his shoulders. He didn't even put his arm around my seat, which then might have led to putting it around me.

I nudged him, whispering, "Are you enjoying this at all?"

He didn't answer.

I moved closer. After all, we were lovers. But he wasn't acting that way. Would we go back to his apartment? Would we make love? I assumed that once you did it, you did it each time. Suppose he didn't want me? I vowed to act aloof, enigmatic and interesting like Vanessa.

"You hated the film, didn't you?" I confronted him boldly, once we were outside.

"What a piece of exploitation shit!" he said, making a face. "Awful."

"Why didn't you like it?"

"You don't know? You have to ask?" He turned to me. "It's got the whole English mod scene but examined in a totally superficial way: parties, dope, group sex.... Oh, and the metaphor of an invisible tennis game, how profound," he scoffed. "It doesn't add up to any kind of cogent point of view."

Moshe turned to a couple about to enter the theater. "Don't waste your money," he said. "It stinks. It really does."

As they walked past, ignoring him, he said, "They'll see I'm right. Just you wait."

"But it captured a feeling that many people have," I argued, determined to stand up for what I believed. The movie had inspired me. "That it doesn't really matter what you do, that maybe the answer is living for pleasure."

He looked sternly at me. "You believe that?"

"No, not really," I said, intimidated, "but I still thought it was a powerful movie. It created this mood of emptiness."

"That's just what I mean," Moshe fumed. "You know all those artistic-type directors say they're making a statement, like about alienation, self-concern, whatever. But they don't make a statement. They just do what they're supposed to be attacking. It's like pornography. There wasn't a genuine spark of feeling in the whole film."

"What about the romance?"

"Are you kidding? They were just using each other. Couldn't you see that? Neither was faithful or gave one shit about the other. Your typical contemporary loving relationship."

As we walked up Third Avenue, Moshe fought the

wind for dominion of his cap. He did not take my hand. I tried to keep up with him.

"Do you want to stop for some coffee?" he asked.

"Sure."

We sat down at a table in a Greek coffee shop, the Athena. "I just don't know how you could stand that film," Moshe continued. "Can't you see that it's just exploiting a popular sentiment?"

"All right." I gave up. "I see what you mean."

"Don't agree with me if you don't feel that way."

"It's not that I agree with you," I argued. "I just figure everyone's entitled to their opinion."

"There are intelligent opinions and others that aren't—" Moshe looked at the waiter. "Two coffees."

"One tea, please," I said, then turned to Moshe. "That's not fair, what you said."

"Look, maybe we're just really different people with very different values. . . . " His voice trailed off.

"Moshe," I pleaded. "Could we please forget the movie already?"

He stared at me. "You don't understand me, do you?"

"I do," I insisted, fearing that he might walk out and I'd never see him again. "But it's just a movie."

"Just a movie!" He looked at me in amazement. "Do you know what you're saying? If you don't care about art or what they're pawning off and calling art, then there's no reason for us to see each other."

I burst into tears. "Goddamn it, Moshe!"

"What the—?" He took my hand and began stroking it. "I didn't think you were that sensitive."

"Never mind," I said, grabbing a napkin to wipe my eyes.

"What's the matter?"

"Nothing," I said nastily. And then, because his voice was gentle and he looked like he felt sorry for me, I really started crying. I tried to gulp the rest of my tea, not looking at him.

He didn't let go of my hand. "Were you upset after last time?" he asked softly.

"Aren't we intuitive," I said, trying to control my voice between sobs.

"Tell me."

"The way you were talking about the movie and saying we were too different—"

"Is it a crime? I get excited about movies."

"But you were attacking me and saying I was stupid."

"I never said that."

"You implied it," I insisted.

"I don't think you're stupid, but you are oversensitive and very insecure."

I blew my nose loudly. "I am not!"

"Shhh," Moshe whispered, looking around. "Do you want everyone to know what we're talking about?"

"I don't care." I glanced at him. "It's just that after the last time . . . "

"Didn't I ask you that before?" he demanded.

I shook my head miserably. "And then I didn't know . . ."

"Let's go to my place."

"Why?"

"So we can talk."

"I didn't know if you'd call or how you felt," I began. "I was so unsure."

"It came as a surprise to me too. A nice one. Look, let's go, please." He signaled for the check.

"I don't know."

"Godjesus, are you going to start that again?"

"And then all you cared about was your opinion of that damn movie. I wish we'd never seen it."

"Who's idea was it? Huh?" Moshe stood up and put on his coat. "I don't want to talk about it here."

"Well, I don't really want to go back with you," I said, not stirring. Then I added softly, "Yet."

"Okay. You want to go home?"

I thought of the trip back to Queens. Twenty-third Street and Ely Avenue. "No."

"You want to stand outside in the cold? Or maybe you'd like to see another movie."

"Moshe, it's just that—" I stood up next to him. "Never mind."

"You're afraid if we go back to my place, I'm going to tear off your clothes."

"No, I'm not, damn it! You just don't understand."

"What?"

"You might be used to older women who are free, who go to bed with anyone and have diaphragms. Well, find yourself one of them," I blurted.

"Hannah, I told you, I like you."

"But do you respect me?"

"Somewhat."

"How can you say you respect me? You were just calling me stupid and saying my opinion wasn't intelligent."

"That's not what I said."

"You don't even know me," I insisted. "All you want to do is use me for sex."

"I resent that," Moshe said angrily.

"Well, so do I. The way you've been acting—"

We walked out through different doors of the restaurant. Neither of us spoke as we crossed Third Avenue.

"Do you want a cab?" he asked, looking at this watch.

"It's still early. I can take the subway."

"Suit yourself," he said. "I didn't want it to end like this."

I waited on the fourth step of the subway entrance, following Moshe with my eyes as he walked up the street. He held his cap down with his hand. When I could no longer see him, I entered the station.

The subway platform was empty. I walked to the center, stared at the clock, then turned back. It was 10:30. *Do you know where your children are?* I had had a date. Someone had esteemed me enough to take me to a first-run movie and to a coffee shop. *Do you know where you are?*

It was all his fault. Moshe had totally ignored my feelings and just kept arguing about that movie. He didn't say one emotional thing. And I had thought him so sensitive, with a mind like a 17-jewel Bulova, that he was FM, not AM bubblegum. He wasn't. He was crass and self-centered.

But he had called me up to ask me out. On Wednesday night. For a second date. That said something. And we had gone to see *Blow-Up* because I suggested it, even if I now wished I could eat and blow it out the other end. Afterward, Moshe hadn't said *anything*.

Why did I always need to have things stated, block letters on the dotted line, when looks and gestures sufficed for most people? More, my insecurities screamed. I needed talk, to sputter how miserable I had felt at first, and scared, worried that he wouldn't call, that he thought I was promiscuous, and how relieved I was when he did. I had to have words. They kept me company, told me everything was okay, but screwed me in the long run.

A train from the opposite direction came first. I took it to Seventh Avenue, where I could also catch the Queens train. *L'amour est finie. Comme c'est triste.* Oh, shit.

I didn't want to go home, having finally been given a visa to leave the land of attached houses. A reprieve from my yellow room, the daisy chain of matching bedspread, curtains, and vanity, from Bella. Even when fate smiled or at least grimaced at me, I still ended up in Flushing.

At Seventh Avenue, I found a telephone. I checked Moshe's card in the zipper compartment of my pocketbook, even though I had the number memorized: KL5-5687. I took a deep breath, reciting as I dialed, 'Listen, I've realized you were right. *Blow-Up* was pretentious and asinine.' Give me one more chance, I'll be good.

As soon as the phone rang, I hung up. A failure of nerve. I would not surrender to it. I tried again, wondering what I would say. After five rings, I knew I had lost out. A freckled blonde with long legs sat next to him on a bar stool. He bought her a whiskey sour. They were talking about the movie and he was telling her that he had been stuck with this dumb girl from Queens who he had finally dumped. "Yes, let's!" she said. At that moment, they were heading for his apartment. She was on the pill.

I was desperate to halt the inevitable. It was like the scene in *A Man and a Woman* when Jean-Louis Trintignant raced to see Anouk Aimee. At Columbus Circle, I tried Moshe again. Stop in the name of love! This time I let the phone ring ten times. Still no answer. They had gone to her dorm room at Barnard instead. She was an art history major who miraculously, despite her looks, was Jewish and intelligent too.

I phoned again from the 116th Street station.

"I just walked in," Moshe exclaimed breathlessly. "I heard the phone ring and ran upstairs as fast as I could."

"Hi," I said shyly.

"Where are you?" he asked.

"At the subway."

"Oh."

"I'm sorry. . . ."

"So am I."

"Really, I am. I was just trying to—I don't know. I guess I felt pretty weird after last time and all. . . . "

"Do you want to come over?"

I nodded gratefully.

"Hannah?"

"Yes."

"Would you pick up a six-pack of Miller's on your way?"

12

Moshe took the bag from my arms and looked inside. "Did they run out of Miller's?" he asked.

I shook my head. "No, but this was much cheaper."

"Hannah," he said patiently, "don't you know that there are certain things that it's worth paying top dollar for? Like Chicken of the Sea white tuna. For the extra twenty cents, there's no comparison to chunk. And Breakstone butter in a cup. It makes an enormous difference."

"I didn't know," I said, looking around. On the Horowitz-Margareten calendar over his desk, I noticed that he had written over the penciled "H.W." of last Saturday in blue ink and put a single star next to my initials.

"Just certain things, though," Moshe continued. "I mean, I would never dream of buying anything at a department store. You know there's an automatic 20 percent markup as soon as you walk through the door."

Didn't he know what *this* cost me? And he was going on about comparison shopping. *I don't believe it.* But I was determined to be charming. Agreeable. Easygoing. I unbuttoned my coat and dropped it with a certain wild abandon on the bed. "So were you surprised—" I began.

"No, no!" Moshe cried, picking my coat up off the bed. Then he carefully laid it over a chair on the other side of the room. "This is your corner," he said. "Put your shoes underneath and your clothes—"

"You're kidding, Moshe."

"This is a very small place, and everything has to be put away or it gets very cluttered and you can't find anything."

"Right," I said, saluting him and marching to attention. I was not going to lose my sense of humor.

"You might think it's hysterically funny, but you don't have your own apartment."

He put out a plate with Ritz crackers arranged around the border and a hunk of Velveeta cheese in the center. Then he sat down next to me on the couch.

"An hors-d'oeuvre?" he asked, spreading the cheese on a cracker. "You do drink beer, don't you?"

I nodded.

He opened two cans and gave me one. "Let's start this evening all over again and pretend that none of the other stuff happened. What do you think?"

"Moshe," I began, breaking all promises to myself. "I think we should talk about it."

"What?"

"Look, I realize I was testing you before, to see if you—uh, were interested—"

"Another cracker?"

"But you were so thick, all you could talk about was that movie."

"Don't you think two people can have an intellectual discussion without turning it into a personal—"

"Never mind."

"I knew what you were after, Hannah. But I don't want to baby you. You have to stand up for yourself in this relationship."

"Oh." I clinked my beer into his. "Okay, let's forget it. To a blank slate."

"That's amazing," Moshe said. "Did I tell you about my theory of the magic slate?"

"I don't think so."

"Do you remember those slates you used to get as a kid that you could write on, and then all you had to do was lift up the page and the writing disappeared? But it didn't ever really disappear, did it? You could see everything on the back of the slate. Well, I decided that was what life was like. It turns out that Freud wrote about this but I never knew it. Anyway, you had experiences, they passed and seemed to disappear, you know, a new day and all. But I knew they were written down somewhere, just like the magic slate. That's memory, the unconscious."

"And so," I said, "There's no such thing as a blank slate."

"Exactly. That's why I can never look at liver. Because she tried to disguise it with fried onions, my mother, but I always knew it. You know, for a girl from Queens, you're not too dumb."

"Thanks," I said, half grateful, but I tried, in a last-minute switch of intonation, to turn it into sarcasm.

"Anyway," he said, standing up. "How about some music?"

I waited, sipping the beer, staring at my initials in blue ink with a star. Did the star mean he scored? How come this week I appeared in red ink? Was he more attracted?

Suddenly, loud rousing applause blasted through his speakers. Moshe bowed to me, then to the other side of the room. I joined the applause. "And now live from the Brooklyn Paramount, Murray the K!"—who made animal sounds which the audience, along with Moshe, repeated after him. Then he asked: "Okay, all you submarine race watchers out there. Are you ready?" An ear-shattering "Yeah!" "I can't hear you." "YEAH!" "I want you to all welcome Jay and the Americans." More applause. The lead singer began in a quivering baritone.

Moshe put his arm around me. "If I could be someone in the world, do you know who I'd be?"

"Sartre?"

"Murray the K."

"Why?" I asked.

"Have you ever seen him? He wears these tight knit pants with no fly and boogies on the stage like a black guy."

"Do you like to dance?"

"Only when I'm blind drunk."

"How come?"

"I don't know," he said. "I love listening to music, but when it comes to performing in front of other people . . . "

I stood up and took his hand. "Well, why don't you dance with me? Nobody will see us."

He held back.

"Come on, Moshe." I tried to pull him to his feet.

"I really feel awkward."

"It's easy." I wouldn't let go. "Come on."

He stood up shyly. "You don't know how much of an asshole I feel like. I've got three left feet."

"Moshe—"

"You lead, okay?"

I did, wrapping my arms around his neck, hardly believing my own raciness. Such nerve. I was a Patricia Neal character, moving my hips, saying things like, "Hey, big boy. I like the way you move. . . ." I enjoyed being close to Moshe, the way he held me so tightly as if he might fall. But when the song ended, he sat down eagerly.

"No more for you?" I asked, weaving seductively in front of him to the Marvelettes' "Please, Mr. Postman." I was being downright wanton. What did I want?

"Give me a chance," he pleaded.

I took a deep swig of beer. "Moshe wants a cracker?" I teased, spreading the Velveeta on a cracker.

He nodded eagerly.

I fed him. Before I could withdraw my fingers, he kissed them. "Mmmmm, good," he said.

"You know," I said, moving away from him, "I'm reading Chaucer for my English Lit class."

"A brilliant mind," he said absently.

"I love the Wife of Bath."

He grabbed me. "What's the wildest thing you've ever done?"

"What do you mean?"

"You know what I mean."

"You mean . . ." I hesitated. "Sexually?"

He nodded.

I wiggled out of his arms. "None of your business."

"Tell me," he insisted, pinning me down on the couch. "I won't let you go until you tell me."

"I don't know if I should," I stalled. "What's yours?"

"Come on," he encouraged. "Please."

"Will you tell me yours if I tell you mine?"

He nodded eagerly.

"This is probably the only thing I ever did like this—"

"Yes?" He urged me on.

"It was last summer when I was working as a counselor at camp. It was horrible there. I was dying of boredom. I couldn't stand all those dumb dances, with the guys standing on one side of the room and the girls on the other. But what could I do? I was stuck in Bucks County. One night after sitting around with a couple girls and them all giggling about their crushes and how this one was adorable and that one had a good physique—I really did do this, Moshe, as unbelievable and out of character as it may sound. Sometimes I don't even believe it myself. And probably would never do it again in a million years—"

"Get to the point," he said, nuzzling against me.

I pushed him away. "Anyway, that night I snuck out of my bunk when everyone was asleep. I didn't know where I was going; it was just an impulse. I saw the fence that separated the boys' cabins, climbed under it, and walked into the first bunk I came to. There wasn't even a moon, by the way, and I almost killed myself. But I knew the counselors' beds were the two by the door since the campers slept in bunk beds. Anyway, I sat down on the first bed by the door, and—I swear this is the truth—started making out with this guy, Joel. We had never even spoken to each other. I just used to see him across the flagpole when everyone had to sing taps. At first he was asleep and not too much happened. But then he started to wake up and said, 'What the hell? Who are you?' I didn't answer. Finally, he got into it and we made out like mad for hours. Then when he fell back asleep, I snuck out, without him ever knowing who it was."

Moshe looked disappointed. "That's baby stuff."

"Wait," I said. "That's not all. I liked it so much that I started visiting different bunks and made out with someone else every night. Well, actually, I only did it a few times but I got really good at sneaking in and out. I'd wear a scarf over my hair so no one could figure out who it was. I was like a succubus, although I never let anyone suck my bust." I smirked at Moshe. "Strictly making out. And over the loudspeaker that awoke the camp every morning, they started referring to me as the Midnight Kisser and made announcements like: 'The Midnight Kisser struck again last night, Bunk number 5, Mel Bernstein reported.' I was like Jack the Ripper and no one knew it was me."

"Did you ever get caught?"

I shook my head. "I even did it with the guy I was sort of going with up there, and we had made out a couple of times before. But did he figure it out? Nope. Stu just reported another Midnight Kisser episode. Besides, I think the anonymity gave me freedom to kiss different-ly, more expressively, than I usually did with Stu." I puckered my lips.

"That's the stupidest story I've ever heard!" Moshe exclaimed.

"I never told anyone, but it did happen, I swear."

"I know. No one could possibly make it up." He kissed my forehead, nose, and cheeks. "It gives your personality a whole other dimension—or maybe I should say dementia." Then he paused thoughtfully. "But you really didn't seem like you had promiscuous tendencies."

"Moshe, I told you it's the only time I ever did anything like that, ever."

He looked distrustful. "Frankly, it worries me," he said gravely.

"But you liked the story!" I cried, throwing him off.

"I just can't afford to be involved with another woman who can hurt me." A look of psychic pain crossed his face like a shadow.

"I didn't hurt anyone," I said defensively. "It was just fun. You understand, don't you?"

"I guess," he answered slowly. "It's not like you were really involved with anyone up there, right? But what about betraying that guy, Stu?"

"I told you, we made out a few times and that's all."

"Okay." He sighed so heavily it sounded like *oy vay.* "At least you told the truth. You've always got to be honest with me if we get involved."

"If we get involved?"

"You know what I mean. I'm not possessive, but I want to know everything that's happening. Do you promise to be honest with me?"

"I'll try."

He shook his head sadly. "I don't know if I can ever really trust my emotions with you now that I know. It's so difficult."

"What's the wildest thing you ever did?" I asked, trying to change the subject.

"I don't feel like talking about it," he said moodily.

"You promised if I told you—"

"Yeah, but this is depressing. And raunchy too."

"Moshe—"

"I'll turn the record over," he said, standing up.

When he sat down, I said, "So?"

"All right," he said, turning to face me. "You asked for it. It happened last winter. . . ." He began in a voice like he was about to recite *An American Tragedy.* Dion sang "Runaround Sue" in the background.

"I was walking from Tak-Home on Broadway where I'd gotten a hero, about one in the morning. This car pulled up on the curb next to me with a girl at the wheel. When she asked me if I wanted to go for a ride with her, I didn't know what to do. Suppose she was a hooker who just wanted to roll me? But I only had a couple dollars in my wallet. Besides, I've always been attracted to danger." He looked into my eyes. "It gets the adrenaline going, the blood on fire. . . . And she didn't really look like that type—"

"What'd she look like?"

"Real depressed. With bad skin. I'll tell you something I've found out from experience which is not very nice but true. The easiest girl to make, say, you walk into a mixer or bar is the one who looks miserable, like her mother just died. She'll go without an argument. You want another beer?"

I nodded. "Go on."

He passed me a can which he opened. "Where was I?"

"Did you go into the car with her?"

"Right. But as she drove around the corner to Riverside Drive, I got scared. Suppose she had a couple thugs waiting for her down there? Finally, after not saying anything since I got into the car, she asked me, 'Do you have somewhere we can go?' "

"What happened?" I asked impatiently.

"We came up here. She sat right where you're sitting. And I started kissing her, fondling her breasts, stroking her, but nothing happened. Zero effect. I couldn't understand it because she must have been pretty horny to just drive around and pick someone up."

"Are you sure she wasn't a guy?" I asked, having read about such things in the *Village Voice*.

"Of course," Moshe said hotly. "She was just a very weird chick. Anyway, I thought maybe if she relaxed, it might happen. So we had drinks and I started to undress her. She just sat there like a catatonic. I bent down to unlace her boots, which came up past her knees. Suddenly, when I looked up at her, I realized this was turning her on."

"What, her boots?"

He nodded. "So I made an elaborate thing about unlacing the other boot, slowly, with my teeth, my mouth, even tongue—"

"Yuck!" I exclaimed. "How did you know she didn't step into dog shit?"

"It's not going to be on her shoelaces! There you go again with your hang-up about shit."

"Go on!"

"This is grossing you out, isn't it?" He paused to take a sip of his beer.

"Not at all." I stared down at my feet.

"By the time I had both of her boots off, she was panting wildly."

"From her feet? I don't get it."

"Look, she was weird, I told you. Obviously, with a foot fetish. Anyway, she wanted me to kiss her feet, stick my tongue between her toes, suck them. It turned out really disgusting. And for all my efforts, she wouldn't do anything to me."

"Is that kind of thing a chemical imbalance?" I wondered aloud. "Did her father tickle her feet or something?"

"Who knows? Anyway, I never heard from her again. Sometimes I look for her on the street, but I've never run into her. She told me she went to Barnard."

"Barnard!" I exclaimed. "Come on, no Barnard girl's going to do that!"

"You know, you're really naive in a lot of ways. Just because a girl goes to a good school doesn't mean she doesn't fuck. Barnard girls ball their brains out. And at Smith, they're supposed to be hotter than Puerto Ricans. Those all-girl schools are the horniest! As for Jewish girls in city schools, they're wild!" He grabbed one of my feet. "Maybe you're really a foot fetishist. What do you think of that?"

I didn't have a chance to answer. Moshe kissed me softly, barely touching the rim of my mouth, like a swimmer sticking his toe into the water to see if it is cold.

I looked into his eyes. "Do you really like me?"

"You? The notorious Midnight Kisser?"

"Really. I'm not kidding, Moshe."

"Maybe a little."

"Do you think I could pass for Barnard?"

"No. More Mt. Holyoke."

"Do you really mean it?"

"Of course not."

"I hate you!" I said, punching him lightly on the shoulder.

"So you want it like that?" He pinned my arms above my head. "Do you like me?" he asked.

I stuck my tongue out at him.

"I wouldn't do that unless you plan to use it."

We unfolded the bed together.

13

"There's one thing I can't figure out," I asked as I sat up, pulling the red, white and blue sheet to my neck.

Moshe reached over for the plate of crackers.

"Shut up, Hannah," I told myself.

"Okay," he said finally. "What?"

"Does this count as sex to you?"

He looked up at me.

"Don't you want to go all the way?" I blurted. "I mean, isn't this a poor substitute for you?"

"We will. But I don't think you're ready yet. Are you?" he asked, putting his arm around me.

"I don't know. Somehow I feel we should move forward, otherwise it's like getting left back at school."

Moshe kissed me. "You pass," he said. "Here." He gave me a cracker with a huge hunk of Velveeta on it.

"No, really," I said, biting into the cracker. "How do you feel about it?"

"What do you mean?"

"Well, is it out of the ordinary? I'm aware of the fact that you've had a lot of girl friends and . . ."

"It was real nice."

"No, but is it run-of-the-mill, ordinary, just blah?" I continued, never leaving well enough—well.

"Bells went off, Hannah, and I saw the face of God."

"Forget it," I grumbled. "Could I ask you something else?"

"Shoot."

"It's embarrassing."

Moshe bit into a cracker loudly. "Yeah."

"Tell me the truth." I paused anxiously. "Do I smell down there?"

He thought for a moment. "Of course. All girls do."

"But is mine worse than the average?"

"I don't think so."

"That's a relief," I said.

"Don't you and your girl friends talk?" Moshe asked.

"Not really. I mean, we'll tell each other about our feelings but nothing like that."

"Well, you can ask me whatever you want."

"Does it look okay too?" I asked shyly.

He nodded, putting his arm around my shoulder. "Like a rosebud."

"You can be really nice, Moshe," I said. "But other times, I feel as if I don't know you. I couldn't stand how mean you were about the movie."

"I get that way sometimes," he admitted. "I'm anal and very obsessive-compulsive."

"And what's that supposed to mean?"

"I'll show you." He climbed over me to get out of the bed. Standing on his toes, naked, reaching for a book from the shelf, he said, "A classic neurotic syndrome. . . ."

I began to laugh. "Hey, professor!" I called, breaking into giggles. "Your participle is dangling!"

"Okay, it's right here," he said, flipping through the pages of a thick green text, *Abnormal Psychology*. Then he looked up and frowned at me.

I tried to be serious. "Yes?"

"Quote: 'a type of personality disorder characterized by rigidity, overconscientiousness, and a strong inhibition against self-expression and self-gratification.' I also have an Oedipal complex like you'd never believe. I once even dreamed of my mother, me, and my father in bed together."

"Come on."

"Don't you think I'm that way?" he demanded seriously.

"I don't know about being inhibited."

"But I am!" he insisted. "I was dying when you first wanted me to dance."

"But you make tapes," I said. "That's self-expression."

"In private," Moshe argued. "That's different."

"Do you think I'm *something*?" I asked hopefully.

"I do have an idea," he said. "But I don't know if it's ethical for me to tell you."

I was delighted. Maybe I had a neurosis that would add an interesting kink to my character, a breadth of complexity and ambivalence that would make it resonate like a minor chord, darkly.

"I haven't given it much thought, and mind you, I'm only a student of the mind, not a professional. This is merely a hypothesis." He paused.

"Continue."

"I think you have, and I quote again—" He turned several pages hastily. "Well, for one thing," he said, scrutinizing me, "you have no tolerance for ambiguity. You want all the answers immediately."

"But what does the book say?"

"You have what I think would be called 'a hysterical personality'—"

"Me?"

"Let me finish, please, which is, and I quote, 'a personality disorder characterized by emotional instability, egocentricity, self-dramatization, overdependence on others, and an insatiable desire for attention.'"

"That's nothing like me," I cried in disbelief. "I don't dramatize and try to get attention."

"As I said," Moshe continued, "it's just a working hypothesis, based on not knowing you very well—"

"What do you mean? You know me in the most intimate possible way, better than anyone else in my whole life."

"—and some training. But mostly intuition and what I pick up from talking to you."

"I never get hysterical!" I protested. "That sounds more like my mother."

"I was also going to say," Moshe added, "that I have the feeling that the major conflict that faces you now is with your family, how you will deal with them and define yourself as a separate individual."

"But we get along, more or less. Anyway, no one can stand their family."

"To give you an example. We're very close now and comfortable, right?"

"I know what you're going to say!" I interrupted. "How come I can't stay over. I don't want to argue about it again." I glanced at the Baby Ben on his desk. "Besides, I've got to go soon."

"That's exactly what I'm talking about."

"I can't help it."

"Yes, you can. You're a free agent. And you're going to have to start breaking the umbilical tie with your family."

"I just know they couldn't handle it at this point," I said, gathering my clothes from the chair.

"Who couldn't?" he asked. "Them or you?"

"You're not being fair," I argued. "It's just the second time we've been together, and it was almost the last. And now you want me to change my whole life to suit you." I fastened my bra.

"I don't believe you really want to stay. If you did—"

"I do, damn it!" I got down on my knees to search for my panties, how humiliating, which I found under the chair. "But it would make things impossible."

"Why don't you just try telling them you're staying with a friend?"

"We've been through that already."

"But I don't understand how you know it won't work if you don't even give it a try."

I shook my head. "I brought enough money for the cab," I said, somewhat bitterly. There were women who charged for this sort of thing. "If you'll just walk me . . ."

Moshe took me in his arms. "I won't let you go, that's all. You have nothing to say about it."

"I've got to go," I said, pushing him away.

"Let's make love again!" he said, pressing up against me.

"You'll try anything! I told you I can't."

"Do you know how nice it would be to spend the night? We'd be together for hours—until the sun came up—just holding each other." He tried to unfasten my bra. "Sleeping in each other's arms."

I pushed him away. "Don't you think I'd like to stay and not have to worry about the time and getting home?"

"Never mind." He slipped on his jeans without underwear. "I get real leechy sometimes—about good-byes . . . ." His voice trailed off, into his shoes. "Separation anxiety."

I turned to him. "I'm sorry, Moshe. I wish—"

"Drop it."

"It's not as if I don't want to stay or be with you."

"I was going to wait a while longer but I might as well bring it up now—"

"Yes?" I said expectantly.

"Homecoming is in a couple weeks."

"What's that?"

"Just the biggest weekend of the term, maybe even the year." He walked over to his bulletin board and took down a blue invitation. "There's a cocktail party on Friday night, the game against Princeton on Saturday, and then the formal ball."

"But I thought you dropped out and weren't into—"

"That's classes. I wouldn't dream of missing Homecoming. Anyway, I wanted to invite you."

I ran to hug his waist and planted a kiss on his cheek. "I've always wanted to go to something like that, straight out of *Franny and Zooey*."

"There'll be all kinds of activities because it's the first home game. But—" He hesitated. "You've got to stay the weekend."

"Oh." My heart sunk like the *Titanic*, the passengers gasping for breath, suffocating.

"This way, you have a few weeks to work on them. All you have to do is tell them you'll be staying at the Barnard dorms."

I sat down to put on my stockings. "I don't know if I'll be able to. . . ."

"Well, I have to know pretty soon," he said, reaching for his sweater. "Otherwise I'll make some other arrangements." He avoided my eyes.

"You mean, if I can't stay over, you'll ask someone else?" I asked incredulously.

"I wouldn't want to," he said. "I really want to take you. But Homecoming is very important. And you just can't keep going back and forth to Flushing. It would totally break the continuity."

"This is blackmail," I said, looking hard at him.

"You know, that's ridiculous."

"That's exactly what it is. If I don't stay over, you'll make other arrangements." I repeated his words, thinking how much it infuriated me when Bella did the same thing. "Well, forget it."

Moshe shook his head. "Don't be like that."

"Like what?"

"You put me in a difficult position."

"You think this is easy for me?" I asked.

"All you have to do is tell your parents—"

I interrupted. "You tell them if you think it's so simple."

"—that they've set up special rooms at the Barnard dorms for visiting women. That is, if you really want to come," he said.

"I told you I do."

"Then you should be willing to risk—"

"It's not that." I sat down on the bed.

"What's the problem?" he demanded. "Do you want to go or don't you?"

"You know, I've never done anything like it, and my parents are—"

"Well, there's got to be a first time sooner or later," he said. "If it's not with me, it'll be somebody else."

"Damn it!" I screamed out of frustration. "Will you stop being such a bitch!"

"Bastard," he corrected me. "A man cannot be a bitch."

"Whatever. I don't care."

He walked over to where I sat and put his arms around me. "It'll work out," he said. "Come on, smile."

"Cut it out." I threw his arms off me. "This is ridiculous. We can't part like this."

I glared at him. "Why not?"

"Let's just each say one nice thing to each other before we go, okay?"

"I can't think of a single thing."

"Don't you think I have a great ass?" He turned from me and unzipped his jeans, mooning.

I couldn't help laughing. "No," I sputtered.

"I like your pussy," he said.

"Is that it?" I asked.

"And the dimples above your ass."

14

"How long has it been?"

"Since we first met or our first date?"

"Does it matter?"

"Five weeks including our first meeting." I gave Greta my most serious look. "I think this is it."

She shook her head. "You always say that. Every time you have a date."

"That's a total lie!"

"What about Doug what's-his-name?"

"An infatuation. Before I found out that all he was interested in was the Mets." I paused. "This is *so* real."

"Should we walk?" she suggested. "Otherwise we'll never get to Ronnie's."

Greta Cohen had been summoned on an important mission: the purchase of my Homecoming dress for next weekend. I leaned into the traffic, squinting all the way to Kissena Boulevard, but still no Q65A, the vital link to civilization and the subway.

"Okay."

We walked side by side as we had since second grade, former Brownies who pitched a thousand fish-eyed marbles into hula hoops, dressed Betty and Veronica in cut-out beachwear and strapless gowns (I played Veronica by virtue of darker hair and being three months older). We had also decided upon our future husband's hair colors and whether we wanted split-level or ranch houses.

Greta was two inches shorter than me, wore mink eyelashes, and a ZBT pin on her lumber jacket. Both of us had gone to the same plastic surgeon. Thus, our noses bore the resemblance of first cousins.

The sun shone faintly. We would have to walk over a mile. Past connected houses that lined Jewel Avenue like the Great Wall of China. As we crossed the Grand Central Parkway, a black Mustang with oversized tires screeched in front of us.

"Where you going?" a boy with a cigarette behind his ear called. He had a QUEENS COLLEGE sticker on his back window. "Want a ride?"

"Not with you," I retorted.

"Fuck 'em," his friend muttered as they drove off.

On the other side of the parkway, Forest Hills began. You could tell because the houses separated, lawns and two-car garages flowering between them, and each one was different. Some were flanked by tall columns like beanstalks, white shutters. Others had enclosed porches. Black shingles hung from wrought-iron posts with D.D.S. and Attorney at Law printed in white letters.

"Jerk off!" Greta called after them.

"But do they all have to go to Queens? Jeez." Then, smiling contentedly as I thought of it, I poked her in the waist. "Did I tell you he goes to Columbia?"

She nodded. "Harvey's cousin the broker went there."

"And you know what else? He dropped out," I declared with pride. "He didn't find the work meaningful."

"Oh." Her voice lowered, a death in the family.

"Don't you see? He's a nonconformist." In an awestruck tone, I revealed, "He's even in psychoanalysis."

Horror streaked across her large brown eyes, the lashes spreading like spires of a black sun. "Is he crazy?"

"No, he's complex," I answered. "Sensitive. Highly intelligent and . . ." I paused, adding, "Neurotic."

"He doesn't sound that great to me."

"Are you kidding?" I exclaimed. "He's fascinating.

God! Last Saturday night, we spent four hours talking about time. In a Greenwich Village café."

"Four hours?" She closed her eyes. "About time?"

"Moshe discussed how the concept of time is created by man. That it doesn't actually exist. It's true people and things decay—mortality, if you will. So the idea of time has been propagated to deal with that—and so you can catch the beginning of a movie."

Greta stepped off the curb, peering behind us, hand shading her eyes. "No bus."

"We're almost there."

"My lens is killing me." One of her eyes started to water. "Shit. I hate these contacts." She lifted her eyelid with her forefinger. The eyelash shook like a helpless caterpillar on a waterlily, starting to fall.

"You're losing your eyelash," I said.

She blinked several times, then pressed the lash to her lid. "Is that okay?"

I nodded.

As we crossed Yellowstone Boulevard, I continued. "And you know what? We're totally honest. I have to tell Moshe everything, even what I think about. Do you and Harvey do that?"

"Not everything."

"Moshe demands it. He says he wants to know my soul." I stopped, searching for words. "Greta, he brutalizes me with his mind."

"Harvey just wants to make it all the time. Ever since we got pinned."

"Have you ever spent the night with him?"

"Almost every weekend. There are rooms at the frat house."

"I didn't know that!" I exclaimed, pointing naughty-naughty with my finger.

"There's a lot of things you don't know." She smiled secretively.

"Like?"

She looked me in the eye. "I'm on the pill."

"No!" I squealed. "You're not! You've been to a gynecologist? And you didn't even tell me. What was it like?"

"Horrible," she answered, dropping her voice as we passed a covenant of religious Jews strolling in the opposite direction. "This old man sticks his finger up there and you can't even see what he's doing 'cause the nurse is holding a sheet over you."

"Did it hurt?" I asked.

"No, but it was real disgusting. He put this white glove on with jelly gook and stuck it inside of me. Then he played with my breasts—"

"I can't believe this." My cheeks burned. "Was he sexy looking?"

"He was an old fart."

"And you let him touch you, just like that?"

"Hannah! He's a doctor."

"God. I had no idea." I shook my head. "Did you tell him your name?"

"Look, it's not that bad," she said. "I closed my eyes and pretended that Harvey was doing it to me."

"Did that work?"

"Well, I really got into it until he stuck this metal clamp all the way up and looked inside."

"How big was it?"

"Like a plumber's wrench."

"I'm never going," I declared. "I swear. Not on your life."

"I told you, Hannah. It's not that bad."

"Can he tell how many times you've done it— and if you ever touch yourself?"

"He didn't say anything."

As we came to the gray stone-faced Ridgewood Savings Bank on Continental Avenue, I stopped. "But what do you tell your mother?" I asked. "When you're—"

She grinned, lashes aflutter. "That I'm staying with you."

"You don't."

"Sure. I've been telling them that for five months."

"And Bella gets hysterical over one measly weekend. You're lucky. Hey, maybe I can *stay* with you sometime."

"Anytime. Just tell her. They never call."

"How come?"

"Because they don't want to know," Greta counseled. "This way they can hope that's where you are. Nobody says anything."

While we waited to cross Queens Boulevard, the Q65A rattled by. It was noon but the lights in Ronnie's windows glowed like a movie star's mirror. Greta patted her face with a waxed square from a packet in her shoulder bag.

Although I had been inside Ronnie's before, I had never considered buying anything. My desert boots sank into the thick brown carpet as I contemplated patent leather bags with gold chains, belts, silk blouses draped across the wall. It was like the library, a museum, F.A.O. Schwarz. Look, perhaps finger gently, furtively, but do not want.

I thought of Bella taking me to Ohrbach's for my sixth-grade wardrobe. She had looked around herself suspiciously, like any minute someone was going to hold us up. "I want you to be careful," she said, grabbing my hand. "They make everything look like you have to have it, it's so beautiful. But don't be fooled." She had dragged me through the first floor, stopping in front of a display. "You see," she said, tugging at a violet sweater with a lace collar. "Junk. That's what it is. Let's see how much they want for this *metsieh*." She turned over the blue price tag. "Twenty-five dollars. Is that all?" she asked. "How cheap. Only twenty-five dollars for a junky little sweater. They should be ashamed."

"Look at this!" Greta called, pulling out a cream-colored chiffon with a high bodice and long sleeves. "It's only forty-two dollars."

I shook my head. She had charge cards at Macy's, Gimbels, and Alexander's. I started at the beginning of the size eights. Whenever I saw a color, a fabric, something that held promise, I pulled it out, first checking the sleeve for the tag.

"Oh, I love this one!" Greta cried, her face flushed with excitement. She held up a black and white minidress with a geometric pattern down the center. "Very mod."

"Nope," I said, looking up momentarily, then continuing to leaf through the dresses like a magazine rack. Above all, I was wary of designer labels.

"Well, is there anything you like?" she asked, holding a dusty rose angora sweater and skirt outfit to her shoulders, staring in the mirror. "I'm going to try this on."

I didn't answer, concentrating. I had fifty dollars in my pocketbook, withdrawn the day before from the Kew Garden Hills Savings Bank. So, I scolded myself, stop looking for a $10.99 miracle. Money talks, bullshit walks—or rides the Q65A.

My heart sung out for it. A simple black slip of a dress with thin spaghetti straps. The top, I knew, would cling, revealing the tiniest hint of cleavage. I'd wear my gold locket, heart dipping between the auricles of my breasts. I held the dress to me. The hem was mid-thigh—with slits up the sides! I had to have it. I held my breath as I turned the price tag: $34.99. *For a dress?*

I carried it over my right arm to the dressing room in the back. "Greta?" I called.

"In here. One sec. I'll be right out." She split the maroon curtains. "What do you think?"

"Fair," I answered, it being too pink, dowdy, and Easter-egg-like. "How do *you* like it?"

Her eyes narrowed as she scanned the ebb and flow of the rose angora in the gold-leaf mirror. "It doesn't make it."

"I'm glad you said that," I told her.

"Would you watch my things? I'll see if there's anything else." She saw the black dress on my arm. "What's that?"

"What does it look like?"

She lifted it by the hanger. "You and Moshe going to talk about death at Homecoming?"

"Did anyone ever tell you you have no sense of humor?" I retrieved the dress. "Wait till you see it on"

Unlacing my boots, I took off my jeans and green flannel shirt, throwing them on top of Greta's things. I stood before the reflection of my white cotton bra, yellow from too many washings, white underwear, and gray knee socks. I removed them. Then, slowly, I slipped the dress over my head.

It felt like a christening, the black sheer against my skin, a blood oath of all the parties I would gambol into, the people I would play with, oh, the devastating conversations, their eyes darting across the room to know me, the Queen of Spades. The dress fit like I was born to it. I stepped out of the fitting room in a chiaroscuro of sensuality.

Greta held several coin belts in her hand. She dangled one of them against her waist, a golden three-tiered chain with half-dollar coins. When she turned around, I motioned to her.

"Well?" In suspended motion, I spun around, on tiptoe to simulate heels.

"Hmmm," she scrutinized me. "It's different."

"From what?" I demanded.

"I wouldn't dream of wearing it—"

"So far, so good," I said.

She continued to examine it, touching the skirt. "Slinky, isn't it?"

"Yeah—"

"Okay, you want the truth?"

"Greta—"

She shook her head. "You look sensational!"

"Really?"

"How much is it?" she asked.

I looked at her. "I want this dress."

Greta smiled. "I never thought I'd hear you say that."

"Isn't it beautiful?" I whispered, close to tears. As we hugged, the price tags of our dresses entangled. The young salesgirl had to unravel them.

15

My yellow mustache of La Jolie Creme Bleach for Unwanted Hair burned as I shaved my legs with Bella's Lady Norelco. The goal was consummate hairlessness except where every woman, even *shiksas*, had it. And I sang over and over because it sounded sexy, "Goldfinger, he's the man, the man with the Midas touch— Such a cold finger, beckons you to enter his web of sin. . . ." I didn't know all the words. "But don't go in. Golden words will pour in your ear, but his lies can't disguise what you fear. For a golden girl knows when he's kissed her, it's the kiss of death from Mister . . ." I prepared for my first weekend of love as if it were the last supper, immaculately.

I had bought a white peignoir especially for the defiling, which I packed along with cosmetics and my toothbrush in my blue overnight case with the mirror. Homecoming would be my coming home to Moshe, at last. A whole weekend of embraces, bodies joined, our dreams *tête à tête*. My black dress hung in a plastic bag from the closet door. I could hardly wait.

It was only four hours away, two hundred forty minutes. Soon we would make love. Moshe had shown me what we would use. Emko, which came in a blue plastic pouch, and Extra-Sensitivity Trojans. "When you're ready," he'd said. Like the coming attractions of a movie. "It's the safest method of birth control." Would he take off my white peignoir? Would the vestal virgin be divested of her *vaginity*? Finally?

Just a few weeks ago, I had been a girl. Protected as a

132

glass slipper. How had I existed before this? My life was hurtling ahead at the speed of love.

"You're not sleeping at the Barnard dormitory to-night," Bella said as I walked out of the bathroom, my hair wrapped in a towel. "Do you hear me? I don't care what your father said."

"What do you mean?" I asked.

"You think I'll believe any story you tell me? I wasn't born yesterday."

"But they've set up these rooms—"

"I heard already," she said, lighting a cigarette.

"Well, I am."

"Hannah, I know exactly what you're up to. Your father may believe anything you tell him. All you have to do is smile sweetly, and he's eating out of your hand."

"I don't want to discuss it," I said, beginning to comb my wet hair. "I'm going whether you like it or not."

"I know you're not a little girl anymore. And I'm glad you have a boyfriend—" Her eyes fixed on Moshe's Columbia jacket, which hung on the door of my closet. "Did he give you that?"

"It's on loan."

"We've never talked about boys and such things. Sometimes I worry." She paused. "I don't know what you know. . . ."

"Don't worry," I said, covering my face with my hair so I could part it. "I can take care of myself."

"Do you remember, Hanny, how I used to part your hair?"

I didn't answer.

"Your hair was long then. I'd ask you where your nose was and you would show it to me. Then I would start from the middle of your nose, up your forehead with the comb, and part your hair. It always came out straight that way. Do you want me to do it for you now?"

I shook my head, watching her through the shrubbery of my hair. Her expression was wistful. Finally, she crushed her cigarette in my Aquarius ashtray.

"You do not have my permission to spend the weekend in the city. I don't care about this—Home-thing."

"It's my business," I said. "Not yours."

"You're my daughter, and if you want to live in this house, you have to follow the rules."

"But what do you have against me sleeping in a dormitory room with other girls?"

"Hannah—"

"You never stop Stevie from doing anything."

"Your father will gladly pick you up from the station if you want to come home a little later."

"That's not the point," I said.

"What is, then?" she asked, staring at me.

"That I'm not a baby anymore and you can't tell me what to do. I'll go where I want to and come back when I want to, too!"

"Is that so?" she asked, crossing her arms. "I forbid you to not come home this night. If you don't, you'll feel very sorry."

She slammed the door as she walked out.

"Daddy said I could!" I called after her. "I don't care what you say."

"Morningside Heights—"

"Hi, Flushing."

"Moshe," I whispered into the phone. "I don't think I can come tonight. . . ."

"Why not?" he demanded.

"Did you hear a click?" I asked. "Did anyone else pick up the extension?"

"I didn't hear anything," he said.

"It's hard to tell," I said, listening intently.

"What's the matter?" he asked.

"Dangerous to talk," I said softly into the receiver.

"This is ridiculous," he said. "You want me to call you back?"

I didn't answer as I listened to hear if anyone else was on the line.

"Hannah—"

"She doesn't believe me," I said.

"Who?"

"Who do you think? Bella."

"What'd you tell her?" Moshe asked.

"Everything. About the dormitories and chaperones. I can't do it. Not tonight, anyway."

"I don't believe you," he said irritably.

"I'm sorry," I said, "but you don't know my mother."

"This is just your own ambivalence which you're projecting on her. You probably want her to find out."

"I don't!"

"Do you want to come or don't you?" Moshe insisted.

"You know I do."

"Then just tell them you're coming and that's it."

"But she forbade me," I said.

"Don't you think you're a little too old for her to forbid you to do anything?"

"I know," I said.

"Then—"

"I can't. Not tonight. We had a fight and—"

"Hannah, the cocktail party's tonight."

"I'm sorry."

"You should have told me before," he said.

"I didn't know she was going to have a fit about it."

Moshe paused thoughtfully. Then he said, "What about tomorrow?"

"I don't know what to do."

"How can you do this to me? You said you were coming."

"Don't you know I'm dying to come? How about if I meet you tomorrow morning?"

"I still don't see why you can't come tonight."

"Moshe, I told you why."

"I'm very disappointed. I want you to know that."

"What time does the game begin?" I asked.

"Noon," he muttered.

"Okay, I'll meet you at your place at nine."

"You know I sleep late," he said.

"Then what time?" I asked. "Ten?"

"Ten forty-five."

"I'll be there," I said, "and at least we'll get to spend one night together."

"I would have to be involved with a girl who lives in Queens with her parents."

"I can't help it."

"What are you going to wear for the ball?" he asked.

"Why?"

"I want to know."

"You're afraid I might embarrass you or something?"

"Paranoid! I just wanted to make sure. You've never been to this kind of ball, right?"

"That I don't wear gold lamé and look like a lady from Miami, don't worry. I'll look as good as any of the girls from the sister schools." I glanced at my new dress which hung shroud-like.

"Aren't we sensitive!"

"I am not. I just don't see why you have to ask me what I'm wearing, like you're afraid—"

He interrupted. "Maybe I'm a little curious."

"Well, it's a surprise."

"So's mine."

"What?"

"I have a surprise for you too."

"You do?" I exclaimed. "What is it?"

"You'll see when you get here."

"I'll tell you what I'm wearing," I coaxed.

"No deal."

"Animal, mineral, or vegetable?"

"Haven't you ever heard of suspension of disbelief?"

"Moshe—"

"All you know is instant gratification."

"Forget it."

"Can't you come tonight?"

"Is it something that smells nice like a corsage?"

"Don't be any later than ten forty-five. It'll take us a while to get to Baker Field by subway."

"Until then, my love," I whispered.

"Will you cut the romantic bullshit? If you were so in love, you'd come tonight."

I laid down my blue overnight case on top of the vinyl checkered suitcase at the bottom of the stairs but kept my pocketbook strapped over my shoulder.

"That's the way you go to a ball?" Bella asked as she rushed out of the kitchen to inspect my white cable-knit sweater and jeans.

"First, they have a football game. I told you."

"Yes?"

"I'll change there later."

"Where's *there*, exactly, if you'll tell me?" she asked insinuatingly. "I still don't know where you'll be staying or with who?"

"How many times do I have to go over it? Look, I didn't go to the cocktail party because of you. Isn't that enough?"

My father, his napkin still tucked in the belt of his pants, joined her. "It just doesn't seem right. Maybe we're a little bit provincial, but—"

"Dad," I said, looking into his eyes with complete conviction, "since a lot of Barnard girls go away on weekends, there are empty rooms in the dorms which are being given to girls visiting Columbia for Homecoming. It's done every year."

"But what about some kind of supervision?" he asked. "Is there a curfew?"

"Of course. And they have chaperones too. You have to sign in and out—"

"I don't like it," Bella said.

"Will you stop treating me like I'm three years old!"

"It's just that we're concerned," he said gently.

"I'm sick of it," I said, taking my coat out of the hallway closet.

"What about some breakfast?"

"I've got to go or I'll be late."

Bella looked imploringly toward my father. "Don't you have anything to say to your daughter?"

"Hannah," he began unsurely, first looking at her, then me. "We want you to have a good time. It's good that you have a date. I'm sure Moshe is a very decent boy."

Bella interrupted. "Sure, I went to parties and balls all the time. But I came home afterwards." She studied me for a moment. "You set your hair?"

I nodded, avoiding her eyes.

"You used to have such tight ringlets all over your head, like a *shvartzeh* baby. Such a big girl now. She doesn't even come home anymore. And me, I'm almost middle-age."

"That's not true," my father said, putting his arm around her waist. "Look how skinny your mother is."

"I got to go," I said, picking up my suitcase.

"Let me help you carry it," my father offered.

"No, I can do it." I lifted the overnight case with the other hand.

At the door, he said, "I want you to remember that your mother and I trust you."

"Don't worry," I said.

Bella shook her head. "Wait till you have a daughter."

"Have a good time," my father said, putting his arm around me. "She's a good girl. I'm not worried about that."

"But be careful," Bella instructed. "Don't drink too much. You never know what can happen then. Boys nowadays, even from good families, don't have any respect, if you know what I mean."

"Bell," my father chastened her. "Hannah's been brought up to know how to behave."

"I got to go," I repeated, opening the door.

"They think they can get away with anything," Bella muttered.

A gust of wind blew in as I stepped outside. "Bye-bye."

"That they can have the milk without buying the cow—"

"Your mother's just concerned about you."

"So when will you come home, if I may ask?" Bella called from inside the doorway.

"Tomorrow, I don't know what time." I carried everything down the brick steps carefully. "Don't worry."

"If you want a lift from the subway, call from the station," my father shouted. "Don't forget. . . ."

"Bye," I said, not turning around.

I knew they were standing there, watching me from the living-room window as they had when I began school, making sure I looked in both directions before crossing. When I turned around, my father raised his hand as if to wave but didn't. Partly down the next block, I remembered the cleaner's bag with my dress hanging on my closet door.

"Stashek, drive her to Continental Avenue," Bella pleaded as I came downstairs with the dress bag draped over my arm. "This way she won't have to *shlep* all her junk to the bus stop."

"I'll take the bus," I said, hastily picking up the suitcase and overnight case.

"Come on," she insisted. "It's five minutes."

"But the car's in the garage and look, I'm not even wearing shoes," he said, lifting one of his feet.

"So you can drive in slippers. Who's going to see?"

"You don't have to," I said. "The bus comes every few minutes."

He grumbled as he put on his black coat with the brown alpaca collar. "You ready?" he demanded, picking up my suitcase.

"You really don't have to," I said, following after him.

Neither of us spoke as we drove down Jewel Avenue. Out of the window, I stared at Flushing's only landmark: the remains of the World's Fair. You could still see the Unisphere, a steel skeleton of the world, its oceans drained.

"Have a good time," he repeated as we stopped in front of the Continental Avenue entrance of the subway station.

He passed the dress to me from the back seat while he carried my suitcase.

"Can you manage all right?" he asked, setting it down on the sidewalk.

"Sure."

"Honey—"

"Thanks, Daddy."

I kissed his cheek, which was smooth. He had just shaved and I could smell his Aqua Velva. He put his arm tenderly around me.

"Don't forget—" he began, but changed his mind. "If you want a lift, call when you get to the station."

"I will."

"Have a good time. . . ."

16

"Isn't this great?" Moshe asked, squeezing me as we sat in the bleachers of Baker Field. "You do understand what's going on, don't you?"

It was so all-American, like sitting on a star of the flag. "Sure. But which is Columbia's end-plate?" I asked, pointing. "The right or the left one?"

As Moshe launched into a detailed explanation of the rules and strategy of football, Princeton's lineup, I stared around me.

It was like being one of *The Group*. The girls wore no makeup. Nor any jewelry except tiny gold posts in their ears. Camel, taupe, gray, brown virgin wool sweaters and straight-leg pants, blazers, tweeds, just like Villager advertisements in the Sunday *Times*. I was fascinated, couldn't unglue my eyes. They did *nothing* with their hair. It just hung limp and straight with maybe a plastic barrette. Was that what class was, confidence that even if you were plain as a pill, you would be loved? As for the guys, several actually wore raccoon coats. Tennis sweaters, tweeds too, and they waved pennants.

"Do you know a lot of the people here?" I asked after he was finished.

"Some. We're sitting in the Columbia section. Over there," he pointed to our left, "is the opposition."

"Oh."

"Not too many Jews there, huh?" he said, poking me.

"I was thinking that."

"Columbia has quite a few. Harvard does too. But not

Princeton or Yale. And," he looked proudly below, "we're slaughtering them!"

During half time, the Columbia band led the crowd in several songs. "Roar, Lion, roar," I yelled along with Moshe, who stood up as if he were pledging allegiance. "Oh, who owns New York? Oh, who owns New York? Oh, who owns New York, the people say? We own New York, We own New York. C-O-L-U-M-B-I-A!" God, I was where the elite cleat, no small feat.

"How are you, old man?" A dark-haired boy with thick glasses approached Moshe. "I haven't seen you in ages." They shook hands.

"Not bad," he said. "Good game, huh?"

"Where've you been?" he asked.

"I'm not taking too many courses this term," Moshe said casually.

"I've got eighteen credits. So I haven't been hanging out much."

"Well, see you around."

After he left, I asked Moshe, "Who's that?"

"Just someone I used to know," he said.

"Is he a friend of yours?"

"I don't have friends," Moshe said, looking seriously at me. "Don't you realize I'm a loner? Besides, he's a creep."

"He didn't seem like that."

A silence followed. "Do you think the girls are pretty?" I asked, looking around us.

"Are you kidding?" Moshe exclaimed. "They're beautiful."

"I don't think so. They're not at all interesting looking."

"Who do you mean?" he asked.

I indicated three girls sitting behind us with a twitch of my head and shoulders.

Moshe turned around.

I nudged him. "Don't make it obvious."

"I wouldn't throw them out of my bed," he said.

142

"You wouldn't throw an orangutan out of your bed."

"That doesn't speak very well for you," he said, grinning. "Let's watch the game."

At the Gold Rail Tavern, we, the victorious, drank beer by the pitcher. The glass mugs sparkled against the dark wood walls. All of a sudden, the jukebox stopped playing.

"A toast to Princeton," one young man shouted, standing next to a boy in a Princeton jacket. "Hymn..."

Others joined him. Moshe watched longingly, raising his glass.

"Why don't you go over there?" I whispered to him.

"If I feel like it, I will," he said.

They began a barbershop medley."Hymn ... hymn ..." they sang in unison. Three more boys joined them, surrounding the Princeton boy. Moshe twitched nervously. At last, he got up and joined them too. "Hymn ... hymn ... hymn ..." he sang loudly.

Hymen, I thought. Hi men?

They stood on chairs, climbing the long table, clanging glass mugs. "Hymn..." The Princeton boy stared down into his beer. Everyone was patting him on the back. "Hymn ... "

Finally, a rousing overflow of voices screamed, "FUCK HIM!" Pause. "FUCK HIM!"

When Moshe returned to our table, I was staring miserably into the bottom of my glass, which was empty.

"What's the matter?" he asked, pouring beer into my glass.

"Nothing." I took a large swill.

"Are you upset about something?"

"Does it look like I'm upset?"

"Damn it, Hannah."

"Remember what we were talking about on the subway?"

"What?"

"You know...."

"Will you cut this out already?"

"The way they looked at me. I could tell by their expressions. Especially my father's. They know."

Moshe took my hand. "It's got to be that way. Sooner or later, you've got to break free."

"That's easy for you to say. You didn't have to have them looking at you like that," I said.

"You're here, and we finally have some time together. Now you're going to spend the time feeling guilty?"

"I can't help it," I said. "They trust me and I lied to them."

"You would have told them if you could. Wouldn't you?" he asked.

"How could I? 'Mom, I just wanted you to know that I'm going to sleep with Moshe at his apartment tonight. You don't mind, Dad, do you?' "

"A lot of girls do that. Look at Linda Le Clair and Peter Behr."

"Who are they?"

"Jesus, you don't know anything! They're the ones living together at Columbia that the *Post* had an article about."

"Yeah?"

"They started with her staying at his place. Peter was in my Humanities class."

"I can't help it. I feel horrible."

"The Gentiles have original sin and we have original guilt. Frankly, I prefer sin."

I ignored him. "You should have seen them. There was this awful silence like they felt they had lost me, or something had changed permanently."

"It has and that's natural," Moshe counseled. "You're beginning to lead your own life. That's bound to threaten them."

"Well, I don't know if I really want to yet," I said, looking around the bar. "How do you think that Princeton guy felt?"

"Come on," Moshe said, reaching over the table to kiss me. "Aren't you even a little bit curious about your surprise? I mean, if you don't want it, we can forget about it." He casually planted a white box with a gold plastic bow on the table.

I went for it.

"Uh-uh," he said, grabbing it and stuffing it in his shirt pocket. "Are you dying of curiosity?"

"Moshe!" I leaped up from my chair and tried to reach into his pocket and grab the box. "I'm curious, look at me. Yellow! Blue! Let me see it!"

"Well, all right. You women are so demanding. . . ."

He handed me the box.

As I slipped the bow off, Moshe said, "Happy Homecoming."

"What is this?" I asked as I lifted the white tissue.

"Don't take it out here."

I examined the box underneath the table. "Where'd you get this?" I asked, staring at a black satin garter with red ribbon woven through it.

"Near Times Square."

"Let's go back so I can see it on you."

"Over my pants?"

"No, silly. Without them."

"Moshe, isn't this what prostitutes wear? I don't know what kind of perversions you have in mind just because I'm sleeping over."

"It's going to look very sexy on you. I want you to wear it tonight, under your dress."

I lifted the cotton in the box. "I don't get it. How come there aren't two of them?"

"Erotica," he explained. "Sometimes I can't believe how innocent you are. A virgin. You're an endangered species, you know, about to become extinct like the dodo."

"Thanks a lot," I said. "Is that why you're attracted to me?"

"Whoever said I was attracted to you?"

"Seriously. I sometimes feel that you've got some funny ideas like you're the sugar daddy, only I don't know who I'm supposed to be."

"The sweet potato," he said smiling. "I do like your body. You know where my favorite spot is?"

I thought of them standing at the living room window, my father about to wave. Why didn't he? "I'm starting not to feel right about any of this."

"The inside of your thighs."

"Moshe, please don't talk about it."

"That's the softest place. It feels like baby skin."

"Okay, already."

"Listen, you've still got to get your Columbia tour, so we better go. But . . . " He whistled softly and make a pumping gesture with his hand. "I promise I'll get you later."

"You're embarrassing me."

"You like it," he said.

"I do not."

I looked behind us at a nearby table. A couple sat across from each other, holding hands. He reached over to push a strand of hair from her face.

"Sex, sex, sex." I protested. "What about love?"

"What do you think sex is?"

"Physical."

As we walked up Broadway, I stopped to look into the window of a travel agency. In it was a red sign with white letters.

IF YOU'VE GOT THE HONEY
WE'VE GOT THE MOON.

Couples walking on the beach in Antigua, Guadaloupe, Nassau, St. Croix were pictured on the covers of brochures. A wedding dress, white and lacy, hung nearby.

"Isn't this corny," I said. "Who goes on honeymoons nowadays anyway?"

Moshe shrugged his shoulders. "One of these days you'll be dying to get married too."

I turned to him. "How do you know?"

"You're a nice girl from Queens, that's why."

146

"I'm not so nice anymore," I said, looking pointedly at him. "Am I?"

He nudged me with his elbow. "Corrupt flesh."

"Well, I won't be after tonight."

He shook his head. "You don't think so, huh?"

"I don't know."

We entered the Columbia campus at 113th Street.

"Ferris Booth Hall." He pointed. "That's where Homecoming will be tonight. The Lion's Den is inside. I met Ellen there. Did I tell you about that?"

I nodded. "More than once."

"Well, it's important that you know these things. How else can you know me." He pointed to our right.

"Furnald. I lived there freshman year."

"That's a nice building."

We continued to stop at each building like Christ's stations of the cross.

"Butler Library," Moshe indicated with a sway of his head. "You can find almost anything here. They have amazing stacks."

I looked up at the names carved in stone like a marquee. HERODITUS, VERGIL, SOPHOCLES, HOMER, DEMOSTHENES, ARISTOTLE, PLATO. In smaller letters below: BENJAMIN FRANKLIN, GEORGE WASHINGTON, ABRAHAM LINCOLN.

"Alumni, huh?" I asked, pointing above our heads. "Very impressive."

"You can be sarcastic all you want, but the best minds in this country and abroad attend Columbia."

"I wasn't being sarcastic," I said.

"Everyone here has college boards in the six and seven hundreds," he said. "You can meet people of the highest intellect who really do something and not slouch through lives."

"Great," I said, exaggerating a slouching posture.

"What's yours?"

"What?"

"College board scores."

"They're above average."

"But what are they?"

"I don't remember the exact number."

"Well, were they in the six hundreds? Seven hundreds? Just a ballpark figure."

"I think they averaged to about five-fifty."

"Oh," he said. "Well, it doesn't really matter."

"But I scored in the ninety-second percentile on my Iowa's with a ninety-nine on the English part."

"I want to show you something," he said excitedly, grabbing my arm.

"Slow down," I implored as we tripped up the steps to Low Library, passing a young couple. The girl carried an overnight case just like mine except hers was paisley. "I don't see why I need this tour," I complained.

"I though you'd be interested," he said, hurt. "Do you know what kind of columns these are?"

"Doric?"

"Right. You can always tell. Doric is plainest."

He stopped in front of a statue. "This is Alma Mater," he said. "Our mother."

I stared at the laurels around her hair and the scepter with the crown of Columbia. "I can see the family resemblance."

Moshe looked at me. "Since you're such a smart ass, there's an owl hidden somewhere in this statue. Whoever can find it, will find wisdom . . . so it's said," he challenged me.

"Okay." I began my search. In the stony folds of the dress. Under the arm. In the back. Between the shoulder and head. Inside the folds of the bosom. Once around again.

"Do you give up?" Moshe asked after a few minutes.

"No." I continued walking around the statue slowly. "You're sure that damn owl is somewhere—"

"I'll give you a hint," Moshe offered.

"I don't need any," I said, examining the many folds of the dress again.

After several more minutes, Moshe became impatient. "We don't have that much time left and I've still got to shower and wash my hair, which takes a while."

"I'll find it," I said firmly. "I know I can."

"Hannah—"

"Okay. Just tell me which side it's on."

"Right."

I examined it minutely. "Are you sure there's an owl here?"

He nodded. "It's over—" He bent down. "Wait a second. I always find it. . . ." He broke into a smile as he pointed under one of the folds of the dress, near the left foot. A scowling beady-eyed owl. "Do you see it now?"

"How could I have missed it!"

"I couldn't find it the first time either," he confessed, taking my hand. "Let's *vamos*."

We walked down the steps, Columbia's expanse at our feet. At the sundial, he held me in his arms.

"Do you think how deep a person is is related to their intelligence?" I searched his eyes.

"I guess."

"You're really introspective, aren't you?" I asked.

He nodded. "So?"

"What do you see when you look inside? I mean, do you really see something?"

"*Edge of Night*. That's the most idiotic thing anyone ever said to me." He looked perplexed.

"Never mind."

I sat down on the sundial. Moshe stood before me. "This is a magic place for lovers," he whispered in my ear.

"How so?"

"Close your eyes."

As we kissed, I imagined a cave of tongue paintings and teeth. A body of water awaiting the diver to split its mirrored skin. When I opened my eyes, Moshe was staring unhappily at me.

"Time is incredibly transient," he said, drawing away from me. "The laughter of today will be just echoes in the passageway of time."

"But you said that time doesn't really exist. Just decay." He wasn't listening. "I'll remember this moment."

"Today will soon be long ago and all this will be dust." He turned away mournfully.

"Moshe, don't say that!" My voice was plaintive. "It doesn't have to be that way."

"We'll both be old and yellow—"

"Everybody has to die eventually," I added softly.

"Hannah, you have to make me a promise." His eyes flashed.

"Yes—"

"In five years, you'll meet me here. October 21. No matter what. Even if you're married with ten kids or I'm a rich businessman," he cried passionately. "Do you promise?"

I nodded, watching the shadows spread over the sundial.

"What if you live in Boston or New Mexico or Timbuktu?" he demanded. "Will you be there?"

"Yes."

"You're not like the rest of the world. Cold, unfeeling, amnesiac," he said, examining my face. "You won't forget. Five years, no matter what."

"I'll be there."

I put my arms around his neck. The sun dropped behind Ferris Booth Hall.

17

After about forty-five minutes, Moshe walked out of the bathroom with a brown towel wrapped around his head, wearing a short yellow terrycloth robe.

I looked at him curiously. "I thought we didn't have much time."

"This shampoo has to be on my hair for at least fifteen more minutes. I can't help it."

"How come?" I asked.

"Psoriasis."

"Oh."

"Do you know what that is?"

I shook my head.

He unwound the towel, bending toward me. "Take a look at my scalp."

"I believe you," I said, backing off.

"No, come here. There's nothing to be afraid of. You should know these things about me."

"I don't see anything," I said, peering intently. A bald crescent near the center of his head was rapidly expanding into a full moon.

"You see the pimples?"

"Yeah."

"And the rash by the hairline?"

I moved away from him. "I see what you mean, Moshe."

"It's not contagious or anything," he said, drawing me closer. "Not like leprosy. Just nerves. When I get uptight, it's a lot worse. Can you tell if I'm uptight right now?"

"I don't know."

"I'm not. I'm having a good time. Otherwise," he said, pointing, "this would be a lot pinker."

"I see."

"Does it repel you?" He asked, wrapping the towel again. "You can tell me if it turns you off."

"A little," I admitted. "Not that much."

"Hannah," he said seriously, "I want to be able to share the reality of my life with you, not just the good times. It's a very important part of intimacy."

"I don't see why we have to share things like that."

On the bathroom shelf under the mirror, his ointments were lined up like soldiers. Psorex shampoo, "ends itchy scalp, rashes, the painful embarrassment of flaky skin," extra hold hairspray, and a tube of Max Factor Erase for "unsightly pimples and blemishes." I reddened my cheeks to a rosy glow, borrowing a dab of Erase for the tip of my nose.

"I still think it's revealing," Moshe complained after we checked our coats. "Couldn't you have worn something more—"

"I thought you'd like it," I protested, looking down at the billowing of breasts in my dress, my locket lodged between them.

"I do, and if you weren't my date, I'd be coming on to you! But it's a bit much, if you ask me." He wore a dark suit with a Columbia pin in his lapel. "I was afraid this was going to happen."

When we'd walked into Ferris Booth Hall, the crowd parted like the Red Sea—for me—worth the $34.99 plus tax. The other girls wore tasteful gowns in muted pastels. Mine was deafening, a slice of black forest cake *à la mode* in a batch of oatmeal cookies. Moshe's garter was wrapped around my left thigh and I hobbled in black patent stiletto heels.

Tables covered with royal blue cloth, Columbia's color, were set up around the large room. A black group from the Apollo, in yellow turtlenecks and shiny green pants, sang "Up on the Roof." Couples danced in the center.

"Do you want to sit down?" I asked.

"No, let's find the bar." He took my hand as we walked to the other side of the room, glaring at anyone who looked at me.

I downed my vodka and orange juice in a few gulps, as did Moshe his Tom Collins. "It's a free bar," he said. "I had to pay ten bucks for each of us. So you can drink as much as you want. Another round," he told the young student working behind the bar. "Let's get high," he whispered in my ear.

This was it: the life I was meant for, had hoped for and read about. Fast music, alcoholic beverages, my lover, and me in my black slinky sheath. Oh, what a heady, enormous feeling, the lights above in a beneficent glow for me, their star, blazing in the night like a nebula. As the band started to play "Mickey's Monkey," I took his hand. "Shall we mosey on over to the dance floor?"

"Not yet," Moshe said. "I want to see if anyone I know is here." His eyes moved slowly through the crowd like searchlights. "Let's get another drink and take a walk."

I swallowed what was left, feeling like a brunette version of Lee Remick in *Days of Wine and Roses*. "Do you have Dubonnet?" I asked the bartender, winking at Moshe.

"That could be lethal," he said.

"I'm bored with orange juice," I said, adding, as I'd heard it in the commercial, "With a twist of lemon, please."

"If you barf later, you better aim in the other direction."

I kicked him lightly with my knee.

As we walked, Moshe pointed. "That's guy's name is Harrison Alexander, believe it or not. His father served with Eisenhower. He was in my chem lab.... Oh, I don't believe it! Look at the dog he's with. Some ladies' man." He chuckled. "And there's Charlie Diggs. He's on the basketball team. And that guy over there, the one with the thick glasses and mustache—"

"In the blazer?"

"No." Moshe turned my head. "You see the four guys talking?"

"Yeah."

"The one with the glasses works on the *Spectator*. Allen Meisel. He's a pretty nice guy."

"Do you want to go over and talk to them?" I asked.

"Of course not," he said quickly. "I don't know them that well. I mean, I just know them to say hello and all. . . ."

"Let's dance," I said, looking restlessly around.

"With that dress of yours, you could probably find a partner—"

"But I want to dance with you. It's our first night to be together for the whole night." I put my arm around his waist, serpentine, I hoped, as opposed to clutchy, insecure, which I wasn't, tonight.

"Couldn't you lift the straps with safety pins? I'm sure you could get some in the bathroom."

"Moshe," I said angrily. "All you talk about is this and that being sexy. You give me the garter, but when I want to—"

"That's private. Between us. Everybody can see your dress. Do you know what they're probably thinking?"

"No, what?"

"It doesn't matter." His eyes swept the room. "Oh, okay."

We walked into the center of the room. I put my arms around his neck. He took my right hand and held it. I thought of my parents dancing to the "Anniversary Waltz."

" 'I don't like you, but I love you, seems like I'm always thinking of you.' " Moshe sang along softly with the band as we danced.

" 'Wo wo wo, you treat me badly, I love you madly.' "

I joined him. " 'You really got a hold on me.' "

He grinned, harmonizing. " 'You really got a hold on me. . . .' "

" 'Oh yeah, you really got a hold on me. . . .' "

" 'Just hold me—' "

" 'Squeeze me. . . .' "

" 'Oh, baby. . . .' "

Suddenly, Moshe froze in my arms. "My God!"

"What's the matter?" I asked, startled.

"She's here."

"Who?" I followed the direction of his stare.

He jerked me with his hand. "No, don't do that. She'll see you."

"Who are you talking about?"

"Let's dance and pretend we don't see her. I know the way Ellen's mind works. She just came for spite," he said furiously. "She knew I'd be here."

"The one with the boyfriend at Cornell that you read the letter and your psychiatrist said she wanted you unconsciously to find it—?"

"Shhh," he whispered. "She'll hear you!"

"How can she hear me? She's all the way across the room."

He continued to stare across the room as we danced. "I wouldn't want to give her the satisfaction."

"But which is she?"

"In beige," he muttered. "She looks like she's getting fat."

"The one with the tall guy in the white jacket?"

"She just wants to upset me. That's the only reason she came." Several ice cubes fell on the floor as he cracked the plastic glass in his hand. "I won't let her get to me."

He stopped dancing.

"Moshe—"

He ignored me—stood *rigor mortis*, staring. Finally, he said, "I've got to talk to her."

"You said it was over between you."

"There were a lot of unresolved things when we

broke up. It was so sudden. Besides, Ellen still has a couple of my books." He glanced at me. "I'll be right back."

"But this was supposed to be our night. . . ."

As he walked to the other side of the room, Moshe patted the top of his hair in place.

For several minutes, I stood there, in the exact spot he had left me, a dose of Novocaine shooting through the cavity of my body. I watched them.

He started talking to her. Ellen looked up, lit a cigarette. She introduced her date to Moshe, who nodded to him, then they shook hands. Soon he walked away. Now Moshe took a seat at her table, moving his chair closer. She lit another cigarette. Moshe lit his cigarette with hers. *But he never smoked!*

She had a cool manner in the way she spoke, never flailing her arms, leaving them placed gracefully on the table like cucumbers. An assurance about her looks, the color of her dress, her brown straight hair worn with a part on the side. She didn't have to flaunt anything. After all, she went to Barnard. I was beginning to submerge, a dark squid, tentacles tangled, leaking vital ink into a sea of goldfish.

This time, I ordered a martini, *dry.* I sipped it slowly, shifting my weight from leg to leg. I understood why people drank. No one loved them. The band was playing a rousing "Do Wah Diddy." I tried not to look at them, studying the ceiling, the walls, EXIT signs around the room. I also recited multiplication tables and the phone numbers of everyone who liked me.

Now he was making her laugh. Laughing too. How could he do this to me? *It was our night to be together for the whole night.* He never even once glanced in my direction. Between two fingers, I held my locket. Bella had given it to me. My fingers stroked the filigreed surface as if it were Braille.

I trembled as I weaved in and out of dancing couples until I finally made my way across the large room. If he wouldn't talk to me, I'd take off the garter and return it, right there. What to say? I had given Moshe my emotions, my body, most of it, more than I'd ever given anybody else. And he just left me standing there like a weed. It wasn't right. I thought he liked me.

He was so involved talking, he didn't look up until I stood next to him. I cleared my throat.

"I'm sorry to interrupt," I began uncomfortably. "But, Moshe, I have a—uh, headache and was thinking, if you wouldn't mind very much—"

"Oh," he said. "Ellen, I want you to meet my friend, Hannah."

And what was that supposed to mean? She scrutinized me like sale merchandise.

"I just love the band," I said in an effort to be conversant. "Don't you think they really sound like the original groups? Especially on the Drifters, the Miracles—"

"Hannah," Moshe broke in. "We've still got to settle some things. I won't be long. . . ."

No self-pity. I won't, will not, I told myself as I stumbled back across the room, muss my makeup. I returned to the bar for another martini.

When a brown-haired boy in a navy blazer asked me to dance, I nodded, gazing into his hair and past it to where Moshe sat, smoking still another cigarette, a drink in his hand. The band was playing the Shirelles' "Tonight's the Night."

Abandoned on the eve of my deflowering. My first coed sleep-over, wrested from my parents' steadfast grasp. I thought of how they stood at the living room window. How could he do this? They had tried to protect me. We were to be together for the whole night. Skin wrapped inside of each other, our bodies rapt. Asleep. Waking to make love again. *I won't.* I exploded like a hernia on the dance floor.

"What's your name?" he shouted, trying to grab me by the waist.

The music was breaking through me at fantastic velocity. "I can feel it!" I cried, disengaging myself. "I really can!"

By the fifth song, I danced by myself, spinning in a divine drunken bliss. The room whipped half a lap faster than me.

18

Something was beating against the drum of my forehead. I needed air. *Let me the hell out of here!* I grabbed my purse and attempted to bolt. But the crowd kept swelling, more and more two-headed monsters with similar interests pushing to get on the dance floor. Eyes fixed on the wall in front of me, I tried to squirm through them and not spill my drink.

I felt a hand on my shoulder.

Was I under the influence, like Ray Milland in *Lost Weekend,* who saw elephants on the wall? "Wayne?" I said his name incredulously.

He smiled. "Was that you dancing?"

I nodded modestly, having lost my partner after the third song. "One and the same."

"It was wild!" he exclaimed, shaking his head. "How ya doing?"

"Uh, not too bad." I toasted his beer mug with my martini and down the hatch, a haze misting my eyelids. "Do you remember me?" I asked.

"Sure." His face was alcohol-flushed, smile incandescent. "We were in Humanities together."

"Uh-uh."

"Do you go to Barnard?"

"Nope."

His eyes narrowed; he scratched his head. "I know I know you. . . ."

"Try the bookstore on Broadway," I suggested. "You were reading Plato's *Phaedo.* Then we went to the College Inn. You ordered a chocolate milkshake. . . ."

"You have some memory."

"And," I added pointedly, "we were supposed to meet the following week."

"You were reading—" he began. "Wait a minute. The cover was blue, right?"

"Wrong." I gave him a hint. "*The Great*—"

"That's it! *The Great Gatsby*. And you go to Queens College although you"—he grinned—"lied."

"You do remember!" I rejoiced like meeting a lost uncle from Upper Volta.

"Of course," he said. "Hannah Wolf. I always meant to meet you, but something came up and I didn't know how to get in touch with you."

I shrugged. "Oh, well."

"No, I really did," he insisted as he gave me a good long once-over. "You look different."

I took another sip of my drink.

"I almost didn't recognize you," he continued, starting from the top again. "You really look sexy."

"Thanks." I smiled wryly. "So do you." I was admiring his herringbone jacket with suede elbow patches, honey-colored corduroy slacks.

"You here with anybody?"

I glanced to the other side of the room where they still sat talking. Moshe was laughing. He never laughed like that with me. *What's so damn funny?* I thought *they* didn't have a sense of humor. She whispered something in his ear. I turned to face Wayne. This could be a major turning point in my life.

Hadn't I imagined him, his face, when I knew I shouldn't, as Moshe kissed and touched me, wondered what it would be like with one of them who papered the walls of my dreams? Golden as taxicabs. Would it be different? Extraterrestrial? What white teeth you have. Such a smile. The better to kiss you. No psoriasis.

"What about you?" I asked.

"No way." He shook his head, a golden lock springing across his forehead.

That was the talisman I wanted endlessly to twirl

160

around my forefinger. Would it change my luck? Moshe, I couldn't help but notice, was standing up.

"I'm crashing," he said. "I didn't buy a ticket or anything."

"Oh." He was about to dance with her. She put her arms around his neck. "Let's get out of here!" I pleaded.

"Okay, follow me." He held my hand as he pushed through the crowd. I stumbled on several toes and knocked over a chair.

The night air rippled my arms and legs in waves of goose-bumps as we stepped outside.

"Are you cold?" Wayne asked.

"Kind of," I said, shivering.

"Do you want your coat?"

"I can't go back in there—"

"Should I?"

"No, don't leave."

"Here." He spread his jacket over my shoulders. The herringbone felt soft.

"What about you?"

"You'll keep me warm." He wrapped my arm around his waist. "Won't you?"

I nodded. The band inside played the Four Tops' "Reach Out." "Can we split?" I began to walk.

"Are you okay?"

"Considering I drank two screwdrivers, a Dubonnet, and two martinis including a double?"

"I had five beers," he admitted. "In as many minutes."

"So in other words, we're both looped." Gales of bubbly laughter floated up. I belched softly. "Oh, no!" I gasped. "Excuse me."

He laughed. "It's okay."

I squeezed my eyes shut, shaking my head back and forth. "I'm so dizzy."

"Don't worry," he said. "I'm holding you."

I opened my eyes. "How'd you get in anyway?"

"Tom, the guy at the door, is in my dorm."

"Which one is that?"

"John Jay." He pointed to an old stone building in front of us. "You want to see it?"

"I don't want to go inside," I said. "I like the air."

"Me too, actually."

As we walked away from the campus lights, the night sky gathered stars. I traced the Big Dipper with my finger, beginning to giggle.

"What?"

"Nothing."

"Come on." He squeezed me.

"I was just wondering if you could use it for wonton soup?"

"Huh?"

"As a ladle." I pointed to the long-handled Dipper.

"Oh." He smiled, looking up. "Have you ever been to the Harbin Inn?"

I nodded, flashing to Moshe's chopstick lesson of the week before. "Keep one stationary," he taught, crushing my finger with his. "And the other one does all the moving. Like this." En route to my gullet, the beef lo mein dropped, landing on the cloth napkin in my lap. He had slipped under the table, threatening to lap up the noodles with his tongue. "That's lewd!" I whispered, loving it, him. *I won't muss my makeup.*

"They have the best shrimp with lobster sauce," Wayne said. "I could live on just that and some pork rolls. Have you ever had them?"

I shook my head.

As we walked toward St. John the Divine, the music disappeared. Still more stars studded the sky, and a niggardly slice of moon.

"Where are you?" he asked.

"I was thinking," I turned to him, "of when you winked at me. It was the first time anyone I ever knew winked at me."

"Did I?"

"Right before you walked out of the College Inn."

"I guess I did." He grinned.

162

"But what did you mean by it?" I asked. "I was trying to figure that out."

"Just friendly, I guess."

I winked at him. The left eye first, then the right.

"What do you mean by it?"

"That I want to see what it feels like to be kissed by you," I said, closing my eyes.

Before I finished, Wayne's mouth pressed mine, soft, cushioned. Mine was flush, stirring to meet his. He drew me closer to him, his lips parting. An aperture. I licked the inside of my mouth, tidying up before company. Slowly, his tongue slipped in, his arms moving to grasp my waist.

I flung my head back. "Do you realize that each star up there is a sun and they have their own solar systems and planets . . . ?"

His lips caressed my neck, climbing to my ear, across my face to my mouth, which he filled with a galaxy of kisses. I held on tightly, curling a lock of his hair around my finger.

As we pulled apart, sucking the air to replenish our breaths, I gasped, careening backwards.

Wayne snatched me. "What's the matter?"

I jerked out of his arms, running to Moshe, who stood at the corner in the shadow of the cathedral.

19

"How can you say that! You're the one who walked away from me!" I screamed.

"I couldn't even trust you for fifteen minutes."

"Make that an hour."

"It was not."

"Yes it was."

As we argued, we bumped drunkenly into each other. It took Moshe five tries to unlock his door. I dropped on the bed, burying my head under the pillow.

Popping open a can of Miller, he seated himself in his desk chair like the Grand Inquisitor. "We were *just* talking. . . ."

I looked up at him. "If you wanted to talk to her so badly, why didn't you take her instead of me. You just left me standing there." I replaced the pillow over my head.

"Well, you seemed to do all right for yourself. I saw you and that guy. . . ." His words slurred.

So did mine. "What about you and Ellen?"

"You knew him from before, didn't you?"

"We met once," I admitted.

"When?"

"Why should I tell you?"

"Hannah—"

"Right before I met you."

"Did you go to bed with him?" he asked.

"Sure," I answered. "While you were dancing with Ellen."

"I mean before."

'You're not serious."

"You were attracted to him. That was obvious."

I kicked off my heels. "What about you and—?"

"Admit it," Moshe accused, turning his chair away from me. "You thought he was better-looking than me."

"You're both different."

"But wouldn't you prefer to be with him?" he demanded, swiveling to face me again. "You can tell me."

"Look, you're the one who said you're never attracted to Jewish girls because they remind you of your mother. Your blondes and redheads with long legs," I taunted him. "Like Ellen, who wasn't anything special, in my opinion."

"Are you kidding!" he exclaimed. "She's so refined."

"You see?"

Moshe took a long sip of beer.

I turned on my side, smoothing my dress over my legs. "You're still in love with her, aren't you?"

"That's not what we're talking about," he said.

"What is?"

"Shaking your boobs in that dress of yours, which was totally inappropriate, and the way you danced."

"What was wrong with the way I danced?" I demanded.

"You wanted to give every guy in the room a hard-on!"

"I did not!"

"It was crude."

"You just left me standing there alone. Do you think that was right?" I punched the pillow.

He crossed his arms. "Everyone was watching."

"Look, I'm not the one who walked away. And you said you'd be right back."

"I told you I had to talk to Ellen. We hadn't seen each other in months, and I had to get some things off my chest," he said. "It was important."

"Sure. Like dancing together?"

"When you've been with a person for a while, you have some shared things between you—"

"I bet," I said sarcastically.

"I felt that I couldn't really give myself to you until I saw her again. That's why I went to talk to her in the first place."

"Come off it! Don't lie to me, Moshe! You talked to her because you wanted to. It had nothing to do with me."

"You're wrong. I told her about you, our relationship—"

"How I was"—I stressed the word—"your *friend?*"

"It's too corny to say girl friend. And how hopeful I was about it."

"You just left me standing there," I repeated unhappily. "You didn't give a damn about me. For all I knew, you were going to take her home."

"You didn't really think that, did you?" he asked, standing up. Then he came over to where I lay. Taking my hands in his, he kneeled by the bed. "You *are* insecure, aren't you?"

"Don't start that sweet stuff with me again." I pushed him away. "Forget it, Moshe. It won't work." My voice quaked.

"Hannah—"

"You're selfish and don't care about anybody but yourself." I stood up. "I think it's better if I go home."

"Do you know the time?" he asked. "It's almost four."

"I don't care." I hid my face in my hands as tears started to ooze out of my eyes. "Not one iota."

"I didn't mean to—"

"Never mind." I began to gather my things. "Just walk me to Broadway, okay?"

"You can't leave," he said, grabbing me around the waist.

I threw his arms off. "Yes, I can."

"Why do you want to leave?"

"Because everything's turned out so bad. And it was supposed to be beautiful." I sobbed. "Our first night together."

"I swear I didn't mean to hurt your feelings," he cried, reaching to embrace me. "Sometimes I just can't help it. But you must know how important you are to me, how I"—he paused—"don't want to lose you."

"You don't have to say any of it. I'm still"—I wept—"still—going home."

"Don't," he pleaded. "I'm sorry. I really am."

"When I came over to where you and Ellen were sitting, I felt like a stranger. You didn't even know me."

He shook his head guiltily. "You're right."

"Nothing I do is good enough. You criticize my dress, the way I dance, that I'm not smart. Everything about me."

"I won't do it again," he implored. "I'll try not to. You have to believe me."

I wiped my eyes with the back of my hand. Black mascara stained it like an ink blot. "Why should I?"

For several moments, we watched each other. Moshe stood up. "Got to water the hose," he said.

I took a sip of his beer.

He was pushing a cuticle with his finger when he walked out of the bathroom. "I want us to be close," he began. "That's why I showed you my psoriasis." He grinned sheepishly. "Even though it turned you off. I know that. But it's my way of sharing something.

"That's not being close." I sat on the edge of the bed.

"I have a hard time," he admitted. "I always have. Remember that first time when I put you into the cab?"

I nodded grimly.

"I wanted to kiss you, to run after the cab and wave until you couldn't see me. But I walked away without turning around."

"It was awful." I stared at my shoes.

"I kept wanting to turn around but I couldn't do it."

"Why?"

"Would John Wayne act mushy over a girl?"

I looked at him. "I don't understand."

"You didn't have to take the subway to yeshiva every day, wearing a crocheted yarmulkah. My mother made it. It looked like a bull's-eye so any maniac on the train could take aim and shoot if he wanted to. Attached to my head with a fucking bobby pin."

"What does that have to do with—"

"You know," he broke in, "I've spent every New Year by myself. Just to be festive last year, I went to Orange Julius on 110th Street." He laughed bitterly. "Me and the bag ladies sang 'Auld Lang Syne.' "

"What about Ellen?" I asked.

"What about her?" he demanded, bolting to his feet. "Did I ever show you any pictures of my parents?"

I followed him with my eyes as he opened his desk drawer. "They're all in this folder," he muttered, slamming it. "I don't know where I put it."

"I still don't see—" I began.

"If I could find the pictures, you'd see how much we look alike. I'm just like my father. He can never say the things he really wants to. All he does is work. Sometimes ten, twelve hours, even on Saturdays. At fucking Kupferman's Dairy Restaurant. Then he eats something at home and goes to sleep. That's his life." He turned from me. "I don't know how he can stand it. He never takes a vacation or anything. He's so alone." He sat down on the bed next to me. "I'm telling you this because I want us to be close. Don't leave—"

"It's late anyhow," I said softly.

"We've never talked." He stared at me. "Can you imagine that? We couldn't. Every time we were around each other, neither of us could think of anything to say. Except—" He stopped himself, biting his lip.

"What?"

"Last April. I want you to know. So you'll understand." He studied me for a moment, running his finger over my face. "I was supposed to have my second physical for the draft. I had dropped out a few months before and my classification had changed. I was terrified. I didn't know what I'd do if I was drafted. That's when I went to the shrink, David, to get a note from him: *Neurotic anxiety with episodes of paranoia.* I saw it. But we didn't know if it would get me an exemption. Anyway, the night before the physical, he came over. In all the time I've lived away from home, neither of them ever came here. But my father left work, which is something he never does, to see me. He thought I might get shipped off to Vietnam. He was worried about me. That's why he came."

"Did you finally talk?" I asked.

"It was strange to see him here. He tried so hard, but he didn't know how. We talked about the war when he was in Poland, how he lost his younger brother escaping to France. He told me—" Moshe took a deep breath. "He told me he loved me, that he didn't want anything to happen to me."

"So you did communicate." I squeezed his hand. "Didn't you?"

"Don't you see? Neither one of us could show anything to each other. When he was finished, we shook hands and he left. We couldn't hug. He took his hat and went back to Kupferman's. He didn't even know if he would ever see me again."

Moshe picked up one of my shoes and held it by the strap. "I'm trying to change. I don't want to be like him."

I stood up, putting my arms around his neck. "You're not. You're you."

"I've always been so alone. I just can't stand it." He closed his eyes.

"You're not alone now," I said, kissing his forehead.

"Ellen just played with me. She never even wanted to see me. And I followed her around like a puppy dog." He pulled me to his lap. "Do you think you could love me?"

I nodded. "I might already—"

"With how much of yourself?"

"What do you mean?"

"What percentage of your total being?"

"99.9."

"I need you," he said. "Sometimes I get so terrified..."

"So do I, Moshe."

"... and I don't know what to do, there seems no way out."

From the fourth drawer in his desk, Moshe took out a blue plastic case and a foil-wrapped Trojan, which he laid side by side on the table. We unfolded the bed.

"Sometimes I feel as if I'm all alone and that's how it'll always be," he said, taking off his shoes. "If I dropped dead, no one would know or care."

"I know the feeling."

"Then I get frightened."

Each of us undressed in our own corners of the room. I hung my dress carefully in his closet, making sure not to move his clothes on the rack.

Turning away from him, I dropped my white peignoir over my shoulders. It was time. I slipped under the red, white, and blue striped sheet. Moshe came to my side, putting his hand on my stomach.

"Is this mine?" he asked.

"Yes."

"And this?" He stroked the nape of my neck.

"Si, señor."

"You know," he said, stepping out of his boxer shorts, "tonight I don't want to screw or ball or fuck."

"You don't?" I stared at his penis, which stood facing me like a loaded pistol.

"No. I don't ever want to do that with you."

"How come?" I demanded.

He looked into my eyes. "I want to express love. To you, with you, upon, beneath, suspended above you. So that it's real, from the heart. Do you?"

I nodded.

"For hours."

20

While Moshe threw up in the bathroom, my worst fears congregated on a platform just above my hairline. Suppose I couldn't figure out how to move my hips. Pretend you're dancing. More critical: I was tiny, impenetrable, and he couldn't get in without an operation. *Two-four-six-eight. Time to copulate.* I had read about that. Then what would I do? My hymen, a steel trap, snapped as he entered. And I guillotined him. I had read about that too. Suppose, on the other hand, it was like sticking your pinky into a shopping bag.

"I'll be right out," he called. I heard him flush the toilet. He was brushing his teeth. "One more minute."

"You look better," I said as he walked out, his hair freshly combed. "You were really green."

"God, I haven't gotten sick from drinking since I was a freshman." He sat down unsteadily on the bed.

"Do you feel all right?"

"I still have a terrible taste in my mouth."

"Do you have orange juice or something like that?"

He peered into the refrigerator "Beer and a Hostess Twinkie."

"Ugh."

"Well, well." He returned to the bed, rubbing his hands together like a maestro. "Shall we?"

I grinned, lifting the sheet to my chin.

"Are you ready?"

"For what?"

"You know. . . ."

"No, I don't."

He lay down next to me, playing with the straps of my peignoir. What now? I thought in panic. It would have been so much easier to go with the passionate flow of the moment, whoosh, when he said he wanted to express love suspended above me. Puking, he had broken the mood. I felt cold, as I had that first time.

"Yes, you do."

He kissed me, tenderly stroking my forehead. I kissed back but kept my mouth shut, as he had instructed me, until his tongue tapped its secret signal.

"Show me," I whispered.

He rolled closer, stroking my right breast through the gown; then, slipping his hand under it, he alternated between my right and left one.

I kissed his neck, following its curve until I could reach and blow into his ear. I played with the hair that grew in sculptured clumps across his chest and down his stomach, burrowing in and out with my fingers. But I scrupulously avoided anything lower because I knew there was supposed to be a decent period of time allotted to foreplay which was pre-genital.

"Relax," he whispered. "It's all right. You've touched my body before."

"I'm trying to," I answered too loudly. "I really am, but you see I always knew we'd stop. Now that we don't have to—"

"Just a second." He reached up to turn off the overhead light. "This'll help."

"Much better," I said. As he was about to switch on the red light, I grabbed his hand. "Please don't."

"Why?" he asked. "Don't you think it's erotic?"

"Couldn't we"—I dropped my voice—"do it in the dark for the first time?"

"Anything you want," he said, leaning back.

"Anything?"

"Yes."

He took my hand in his and placed it squarely on his penis. I resisted, reaching to touch his stomach. Ten more minutes of foreplay. It was only decent: not to rush things. He replaced my hand, moving back and forth. At first, it was a rubbery vegetable stalk. Then suddenly it grew, Clark Kent's spectacles and suit cast off in a phone booth, transmogrified into Superman, rising, able to leap tall buildings in a single—*shlang!* I crossed my legs demurely.

He returned to my breasts, probing, pushing, pinching, pressing the left nipple between his fingers, the right, *honk*, like Clarabell's nose. I wiggled restlessly.

He landed, starting to touch me.

"Not so hard," I whispered, pulling away from him.

"Okay." He drew me closer. I resisted. "Relax," he coaxed, trying to part my legs with his leg. "Wait, let's do this right. Sit up."

"Why?"

He pulled off my gown, flinging it on the floor. I was completely naked except for my white lace underwear. He tossed them too. I shivered slightly.

He began again, his fingers soft, wings beating. I could feel myself opening up. It was automatic, like a camera's lens. Soon I was wet as a swamp where turtles dove off pearl ridges. My mind was floating.

Moshe lowered himself on top of me. I braced myself, holding on to the edge of the bed. He poked around until he entered.

"No!" I screamed. "That's my asshole!"

"I'm sorry," he said, buckling. "Open your legs wider."

I did. In a moment, he was inside. I could feel him, moving to fill me.

"Is it all right?" he asked.

I nodded. "It doesn't hurt at all."

"Good," he said, mucking around a bit. "Let's get ready, then." He filled the Emko applicator while inside of me, then withdrew, shooting its whipped squiggle like a Roman candle in my vagina. I ripped open the foil. He slipped the condom on, raincoat-like.

"Do you have your seatbelt on?"

I nodded.

He entered slowly, moving back and forth and around again. "This doesn't hurt, does it?" He bunted lightly.

"I love it!"

"It's 190 degrees in there, and so juicy," he said, plunging deeper. And deeper. I didn't know I went that far. Like discovering an extra wing of a house.

"You're hot," I whispered in his ear, bucking colt-like.

"Oh, you want it like that." He leaned forward, rubbing against my lips, which puckered to be caressed by his body. I pressed to hold him, deep within me.

"I love you!" I gasped. "I really do."

"So how come you're knocking me off the bed? Could you move?" He nudged me.

I protested. "How can I move with you on top of—"

"One, two, three." We gripped the mattress and moved in unison. "That's better."

This time he dove into me, jackknifing through the darkness, 20,000 leagues under the sea. I held my breath, trying to grind against him as hard as I could, faster and faster, my arms gripping his shoulders.

"Wrap those beautiful legs around me," he cried, lifting me by the buttocks. "Come on, Hannah!"

I was startled to hear my name. As I climbed up to join him, I thought of playing horsie on my father's knee. Again and again, I climbed, falling back against the bed. Somehow we kept missing each other. Too far left, right. Wrong! I dropped my legs, trying to press them together.

Moshe lifted them again, holding my legs with his arms, pinned to his back. I couldn't move. Our stomachs applauded.

"Let me down!" I cried as I had, finally, when my father lifted me in his arms high above my mother and Stevie, struggling to get loose. Reluctantly, he released my legs so they fell across his waist. I bent my knees, slapping myself against him with all my might.

I was whirling blindly in a labyrinth. There were doors at the end of each passageway. I wanted Moshe to open them. I threw myself against him as I felt a tightening. As if all of my being was honed to a spot the size of a pea, diamond-hard. I tried to reach it, gritting my teeth, squeezing my fingers into Moshe's back. My body battered itself hungrily against his.

All of a sudden, I feared I might drown. Gasping for breath, I started to spin. I heard a loud rumbling. Was it my own breath? It was coming closer. Would I fly? I opened my eyes to see them rush, a stampede of animals. They didn't stop. I tried to contain all of them.

I was still gasping when I knew it was over. He thrust a few more times. I tried to hold him. He grew soft as a flower and slid out of me. I felt as if I'd lost one of my own vital organs.

I wanted tears because this was it, what I'd been promised by every book, movie, Liz and Dick, eyeshadow. Was that all there was? I curled up next to Moshe, hiding my face in his shoulder.

Several minutes passed. I bent over to look at him. His eyes were closed. "Are you asleep?" I asked.

"Just resting," he said, turning away from me. But he held my hand.

I thought about it all. How there was no hymen to guard the door. It had been slashed. The world would flow through me now.

Is *that* what was meant by an inner life? The dark continent inside of me that had been cordoned off from experience, waiting out childhood to live. Did I finally have one? But it wasn't intellectual. I didn't contemplate philosophy or a white whale or the heart of the jungle or war or *madeleines*. A private bedrock of myself?

"Moshe," I said, "can you hear me?"

"What?" he muttered.

"I really love you. Do you know that? I've never been closer to anybody. I mean, I've had friends but this is different. I never thought anyone would love me. . . ."

He turned around and laid his head on my chest. "Just a few more minutes."

Gently, I stroked his hair. "I know I sometimes act

real stupid and say things that don't turn out the way I mean them. But I try hard, and one of these days, I swear I'll become an interesting woman."

I shook him lightly. He didn't stir.

"Are you sure you're not asleep?" I demanded. "I'm articulating something important."

"Don't, Han," he grumbled. "I told you, just a few minutes."

Our bodies had been one. Miss Vagina and Mr. Penis. I laughed softly to myself. It would be better the next time. Post-coitus, everyone got depressed as hell. I had read about that. And men had to rest.

Outside the window, the sky was a deep gray down, streaked with salmon and rose. Much of night country had already been cleared. Even Broadway's derelicts slept, curling inside their dreams like pearls, scratching the walls to become beautiful. But I was awake to an eternity of thoughts about life in general, the nature of love, male and female, eros, even thanatos, which Moshe had explained. I stirred, trying to push him off so I could steal away to the toilet. He awoke.

"I'm leaking," I said softly, trying to get up.

"No!" He held me. "Don't leave."

"I'll be right back, I promise."

As I climbed over him, I discovered a spot of blood which looked like a tomato slice. I stared at the sheet, embarrassed.

"I'm sorry."

"Don't worry," he said happily. "It proves you really were a virgin."

"Didn't you know?"

"You can never be sure."

"Now you know."

"I took your virginity," he declared. "I'm the first."

"Our bodies are wed," I said, taking his hand. "Did you hear what I was saying to you before?"

"When?"

I looked into his eyes. "Do you really care about me?"

"Are you kidding? This face?" He pulled me to him. "These shoulders?" he asked, kissing each blade. "I'm crazy about you."

"That's what I was saying before. I love you," I said. "I really do." I kissed his chest hair. "I really do."

"I really do too," he teased. *"Really!"*

I stood up, pointing in the direction of the bathroom. "But will I be the last?" he asked.

I stared at the blood. People made babies this way. All over the world. Since the beginning of time. *God.*

21

The morning after, I hid in my corner of the apartment like a ghost. Moshe scowled as he picked up a Kleenex from under the bed. "Do you leave things on the floor in your own house?" He held the guilty tissue between two fingers. "I don't see why you can't clean up after yourself."

"Come on, Moshe," I said, taking it from him. "You can really be a pill sometimes."

"If you want to stay over, you have to—"

"I thought you invited me. You know, it wasn't easy for me to lie and—"

"It's just not right for you to mess things up this way." He crossed his arms. "I live here, you know."

"What did I mess up?"

Solemnly, he pointed to one of my stockings hanging from the refrigerator door. "That."

"I'll pick it up," I said, starting to reach over for the stocking. Then I felt sick again. "Ugh, Moshe. My stomach feels horrible." I held it to show him.

"Mine too," he said. "You want we should make an Alka Seltzer cocktail?" he asked, imitating a Yiddish accent. "For both of us? I feel like hell."

I nodded.

Running the water, he filled his toothbrush glass and a plastic mug that said WET MY WHISTLE, then dropped one tablet in each. It fizzled noisily. Moshe handed me the mug.

"Okay," he declared. "A toast to not feeling nauseated, sick to the stomach—"

"And to a beautiful night," I added. "It was worth it."
I placed my hand on his arm, smiling suggestively.

"And no more dizziness." We bumped glasses and drank.

"Vomitacious!" I made a face, rolling my eyes. "I think I'm going to be even sicker."

"Relax," he said, bending down to tuck in one of the corners of the stained red, white, and blue sheet. I took the other side.

"You know, you haven't said a single thing about last night," I began, turning to watch him unsurely. "How you feel—"

"I told you, I get very uptight in the morning. I haven't even had my coffee. And I don't usually get up this early." He looked away from me. "I just want to straighten things up before you go. Let me do this." He pulled the sheet from my hands.

"No, I'll help." I picked up a corner again.

"Look, I have my own way I like to do it." He tucked the bottom sheet in tight hospital corners. "You see?"

"Oh."

"Have you packed yet?"

"I've just got the stuff in the bathroom."

"Why don't you do that. So we can leave soon."

"You're unbelievable," I said as I walked toward the bathroom. Passing Moshe's desk, I picked up the top page from a stack of handwritten pages.

"What's this?" I asked, reading aloud. " 'The ability to love another grows out of the patient nurturing of one's own ego first—' "

He spun around. "Who said you could look at my writing!" Furiously he snatched it from my hand. "Just because you stayed over doesn't mean you can go through my things."

"I was just wondering what it was."

"You don't have respect for anybody's privacy. The way you leave all your stuff around—" He held my white peignoir by the straps. "How'd this get here?"

"You're the one who took it off!" I said, snatching it.

"Then you go looking on my desk. . . ."

"Okay, already," I said defensively. "I'm sorry."

"My mother's like that. She'd go through my books and letters, look at my underwear to make sure I was wiping properly."

"Moshe!"

"I can't stand that sort of snooping around."

"I wasn't snooping. It was sitting there, so I thought—"

"Well, now you know how I feel." He threw my panties over to me. "These are yours too, right?"

"Why are you in such a bad mood?" I asked finally.

He climbed over the bed to tuck in the other side. "First of all, I feel hung over," he said. "I didn't get enough sleep because you were talking to me all night. And thirdly, I really want to take you back already."

"It isn't even one-thirty," I said, staring at his Baby Ben.

"I can only be with one person—and this is nothing against you, Hannah—for a short time. Then I get antsy."

"Oh." I swallowed quietly.

"And I feel like my space is threatened with all your stuff thrown around."

"You found one stocking," I argued, dropping my toothbrush in the blue overnight case.

He picked up the Emko applicator and washed it in the bathroom. Then he slipped it in the blue plastic kit, returning it to the fourth drawer of his desk. "I find intimacy a grating experience."

"Is that why you've been picking on me ever since we woke up? We were so close last night." I nudged him in the waist. "Weren't we?"

He recoiled. "I wish you wouldn't do that."

"Moshe—"

"I've already turned myself off," he said, looking away miserably.

"What do you mean?"

"So the pain of being alone again won't be so intense.

180

As far as I'm concerned, you've left already."

"But how can you do that? I'm right here."

He stooped to pick up the foil of the used condom. "No, you're not." He threw it across the room, missing the basket.

We stood in front of the 116th Street I.R.T. station on Broadway. Moshe laid my suitcase down with a heavy thud. "It's crazy for me to travel all the way out to Queens just to come back here again."

"You said you'd take me back."

"I know I did. But it seems unnecessary."

I grabbed my suitcase and started walking down the stairs. He followed after me. "Don't be like that."

"You said you would."

"Under coercion," he complained. "Because you insisted."

"I don't want to travel all the way back by myself." I stared down at the suitcase. "Please, Moshe."

"It's not my fault you live in Queens."

"And leave you," I said, putting my arms around him.

"All right, already. I'm a mere mortal." He picked up my suitcase. "I can't take the guilt."

He bought two tokens, dropped them in the turnstile, and we went through. "Thanks," I said.

As we stood on the platform, he said, "I'll go down as far as Seventh Avenue and that's it."

"It was such a beautiful day," I said mournfully. "The best in my life, with a football game, the Gold Rail, walking around Columbia—"

"I really don't want you to get all mushy here."

"I won't."

As the train came in, I whispered, "I love you, Moshe." No one heard it.

He put his hand over mine on the pole in the middle of the subway car. I counted stops. Five more and he would be gone. "I'm going to miss you," I said, eyes fixed on a Speedwriting advertisement.

"We'll see each other soon."

I nodded bravely. IF YOU CAN READ THIS, YOU CAN LEARN TO SPEEDWRITE. Four stops. "How much of yourself do you love me with?" It burst out of me, my eyes suddenly runny.

"Not here," he said. "For God's sake, don't—"

I began to cry.

"Hannah! You said you wouldn't."

"I told you when you asked me what percentage," I sobbed.

"You promised." He looked around. "Please try to control your emotions." Finally, he fled to the other side of the train, sitting down next to a black teenage boy with a green and red pick lodged in his Afro.

A white-haired woman who stood nearby, a Macy's bag at her feet, was watching sympathetically. Moshe turned to stare out the window. I covered my face with my hands. "All men are bastards," she told me.

At Columbus Circle, I carried my suitcase off the subway. "How could you leave me standing there?" I demanded as we waited for the D train. "It was inhuman."

"You embarrassed yourself and me. That's not fair."

I hid my face in his shoulder, starting to sob again. "I'm going to miss you so incredibly much."

We took the subway one stop. Seventh Avenue. Moshe carried my suitcase to the lower level where the Queens train would come.

"I'll wait here," he said, "but I'm not going all the way back with you."

I nodded. "Will you call me?"

He squeezed my shoulder. "If you stop crying."

I hesitated, searching his eyes. "Do you love me?"

"It's impossible for me to talk about these things here." He took my hand. "Please don't cry."

"Okay." I sniffled.

"I want to tell you something."

"What?"

He leaned over to whisper in my ear. "I've still got you on me. I didn't wash because I wanted to have it for later."

"Don't!" I said, my cheeks burning. "How come you can talk about those kinds of things but not emotional feelings?"

"I can smell it right now." He rubbed against me. "You .. "

"Will you quit it!"

As the subway pulled in, I lifted my overnight case and dress in one hand, the suitcase in the other. "I guess this is it."

Moshe took me in his arms and kissed me on the mouth, his tongue plunging like a parachutist.

"Wow!" I said breathlessly.

He helped me on the train. "You have everything?"

I nodded, placing my suitcase by my foot, and the overnight bag on top of it. "Moshe—"

"I'll call later," he said as the door closed.

I leaped forward, forcing it open. "This was the most beautiful night of my whole entire life. Even though we had some fights." I rushed to finish. "It was so beautiful ... I mean it. . . ." I stared meaningfully into his eyes. "I love you."

"Will you let the door go!" A man in worker's overalls demanded loudly. "Je-sus!"

"99.9 percent!" I called as the doors closed.

Moshe turned around to look at me. As he was about to walk away, he stopped, raising his hand to wave.

I studied the women on the train. If they wore wedding bands, I figured they must have, at least once. But I couldn't quite believe it in some cases. They looked so well-mannered. Urbane. *Clean.* Did they grow wet, everything opening like an umbrella? A pale girl wearing a navy wool suit, with a briefcase in her lap? The fat woman next to her whose legs were hams in support hose, her cheeks glazed with rouge? I tried to imagine them making love. The black woman with a mustache, holding the hands of two boys reading comic books? I undressed them, one by one, trying to visualize them sighing on a bed, a man touching them, their bodies hot, panting. I turned to a red-haired woman with a large mole on her left cheek which she tried to conceal with makeup. She wore an engagement ring. Someone loved her too.

I thought of Bella on Sunday mornings, how she wore her red wrap-around bathrobe. There was often a smell of vinegar in the bathroom, as if she had just prepared a salad. In a revelatory flash, I understood. She douched. Was that why? She too had sex, with Stashek Wolf. Women with watchbands, leather gloves, pocketbooks, babushkas, who went to college or didn't, read *True Romances* and *Watchtower,* were freckled, pimply, Golda Meir, with makeup, without, frosted hair, flat-chested, obese, Oriental, religious. Women who bit their fingernails angrily, read *New York Times* classifieds, wore corrective shoes. All had moments when they too lay naked with husbands, lovers, *someone,* writhing, their bodies arched against stomachs, chests, hands grasping waists, penises rumbling inside of them. Even my mother—and father too!—galumphing in each other's arms ecstatically. And I was one of them now, penetrated. No longer a remote satellite, beheld every night but never touched.

There was passage now. Hymen slaughtered. Witness the blood. Added to the legacy of all the others piled like torn screen doors. I had lost my virginity and the absolute belief in innocence. Everyone did it! Sluicing, golden with sweat. Nothing at all immaculate in the conception, knees bent, legs buckling, a blustering fandango.

But couldn't a randy palomino, bicycle, roller coaster do the trick? So that all the years of saving, of waiting and praying, would be wasted. I could have been a courtesan spinning tricks in a great Milky Way across the universe. Across the car, a young girl with curly dark hair, about thirteen, chewed gum, staring dreamily. Soon hers too would be flung, a useless key to a forgotten lock. She was already in the throes, her mouth hungry to be kissed.

•   •   •

184

At Continental Avenue, I laid my things in front of the phone booth. My father would come, pack my suitcase in the trunk along with my overnight case. We'd sit side by side in the Oldsmobile. I would tell him about the football game. He'd grin, saying, "So now you like football. Better than the Mets?" Or he'd mention an editorial in the newspaper. Often he quizzed me on the names of LBJ's cabinet or the Prime Minister of South Africa. But I knew he wouldn't ask anything. He'd never think of me that way, that I'd have sex and even use birth control. Suppose he somehow whiffed it, even if I did shower—that something had changed. I carried my dress, overnight case, and suitcase to the bus stop.

The Q65A turned the corner. Climbing the steps, I tried to chasten my facial expression. I hadn't seen anything, done anything. I swear. Could a person tell? Slut! That I had mated in the flesh, and now, forever, a placard had been erected: Moshe slept here. What would I say to them? Was my mouth suddenly hard and cruel?

I stared out of the window as the bus headed up Jewel Avenue. Yes, I decided, I'd tell them about the football game, how Columbia and Princeton rammed into each other like bumper cars. That was good. I'd even seen blood. And about the ball. Ball? Would I tell Stevie? My stomach clenched.

It wasn't my father. I was his: Hannileh. He'd gouge his eyes before seeing. But *Belladonna* made me shudder, want to run away as I had, at eight, riding the train by myself to Brooklyn until a policeman brought me back. She would know. No secrets could be kept from her. Even if I rehearsed in front of the mirror. She was psychic! When I cut classes, my knee and wore long pants to hide it, ruined my graduation dress with ketchup. She would look at me in that witchy way of hers. That Michael Weinstein had broken up with me. Somehow she knew, even why, and tried to talk to me. But this was different, so very private.

As I walked from the bus stop, passing houses I knew,

their doors and mailboxes like characters in a childhood book, a neighbor called me.

"Is that you, Hannah?"

"How are you, Mr. Fein?"

"Been away for the weekend, huh?" he said, raising his eyebrows. He looked at my suitcase. "You're getting to be quite a young lady."

My face burned.

"What grade are you in now?" he asked, leaning against a broom which he used to sweep away leaves in his driveway.

"I go to college," I told him.

He shook his head. "Wait till you get to be my age. The years zoom by. I remember when you were a little puppy."

I smiled, starting down the street.

"Say hello to your parents!"

I could tell by the way he looked at my suitcase, the insinuating tone of his voice. He knew my legs had quivered above a man's head.

As I turned up 71st Road, our semi-attached house came into view. The picket fence grimaced, teeth sparkling white. Except for a light in the kitchen, the house was dark. They left it on so thieves would think they were at home. Maybe I could steal inside.

They'd probably gone for a drive as they often did on Sundays. I wouldn't see them until evening. The car was in the garage. Could they have taken a walk?

I glanced upstairs. For an instant, a silhouette passed across my bedroom window with the blue tasseled shade. I recognized the beauty-parlor set of Grecian curls like snakes, hissing.

*The tragedy of sexual intercourse
is the perpetual virginity of the soul.*
Yeats

22

My hand shook as I fit the key into the lock. Before I could turn it, she opened the door. "Well, well. Look who's come home," she said, placing her hand on her hip. "Stashek, she's here."

I brushed past Bella quickly.

"How come you didn't call your father to pick you up? We were worried." She scrutinized me, head to shoes. "Then you wouldn't have had to wait for the bus."

"I didn't want to bother him."

"What else does he have to do so much? He's reading the newspaper. So he'd put it down for a few minutes. It wouldn't kill him."

"Hanny!" he cried from the kitchen. "Why didn't you phone from the station?"

"Hi, Dad!" I called, still holding my suitcase. "The bus was right there when I got out of the train."

"Let me help you carry," Bella offered.

"No, thanks," I said, starting to climb the first step.

My father took off his glasses as he walked in the room. "There she is," he said, putting his arm around me. "Did you have a good time?"

I nodded, looking at him, then my mother. How come they acted so innocent? As if they never lay together, sighs of pleasure muffled in pillows so the children wouldn't hear, my father erect as the Empire State.

"I went to a football game. Columbia against Princeton. It was very exciting." I stared at the stalks of the avocado shag rug. "Columbia won."

"You're lucky," he said. "It was such a nice, warm day."

"Yeah," I agreed, digging my shoe into the pile, making small circles. "It was a beautiful day."

"Don't do that!" Bella scolded. "You'll ruin the rug."

"There were so many people there, and the Columbia band played. . . ." I started to walk upstairs. "I had a great time."

"That's good." He nodded. "I'm glad. But you should have called. We were concerned." He put his glasses back on, returning to the kitchen. "As long as you're home and everything is all right."

My mother trailed after me upstairs. "What about the ball?" she asked. "Was it wonderful?"

"Very nice," I said.

"Did you feel good in your dress? And Moshe liked it?"

The door to my bedroom was open. I turned to her. "Were you in my room?"

"Sure. I looked out your window if I could see you. I told you, we were worried." She pushed my closet door shut with her foot.

I dropped my suitcase on the bed. "You worry about me like I'm a baby."

"No," she said, sitting down on the bed. "I worry because you're not a baby anymore."

I began to unpack my overnight case, placing my shampoo on the dresser.

"I don't want anything bad to happen to you, that you should be hurt." She shook her head. "It's not such a nice world."

"I can take care of myself."

"If I don't worry about you, who should?" she declared. "The President?"

"All right," I said, taking out my cosmetic bag. "If it makes you feel better, worry as much as you want."

"You think it's such a pleasure? Neither of us could sleep last night." She lit a cigarette.

"Will you stop trying to make me feel guilty!"

"It's true. Your father won't tell you, but all night he was tossing and couldn't sleep. Finally, he had to take a pill."

"Other girls go to sleep-away colleges. I leave for one night and—"

"The ball was nice, Hannah?" she continued. "They had drinks and a band playing?"

I nodded.

"Did you dance?" she asked.

"Almost every dance." I thought of Moshe sitting with Ellen.

"So he can dance?"

"Yes."

"That's good," she said. "In my book, a man should know how to dance."

"I'm taking a bath."

"Aren't you hungry? There's cheese and bologna in the refrigerator. You want me to make a sandwich?"

"Maybe later," I said, taking my bathrobe and shampoo.

As the water filled, steam coated the mirror. I traced HANNAH + MOSHE, circling the names in a silver worm of a heart. Soon it began to unwrite itself. As I sat down in the tub, the water rose dangerously.

It was mine. Moshe had taken my virginity but it belonged to me. No one could take it away. Not even Bella. No matter what happened. Flaring like a lightning bug, it beckoned. *Come hither, come hither.*

At least, any physical manifestation had been purged. I was semen-scoured. *Pareve.* My hair, Breck; my body, Ivory; talcum everywhere. I tied the belt of my bathrobe.

She was waiting for me when I came out. My suitcase gaped. I slammed it shut. "Who said you could go through my suitcase?"

"What's this?" she demanded, dangling the garter between two fingers. I tried to grab it from her. "How dare you go into my stuff! It's mine!" I tugged at her sleeve. "Give it to me!"

She held it stiffly above my head. "I was just trying to help you unpack—"

"Who asked for your help?"

"—when I found this thing. Where'd you get it?"

"You just wanted to look into my stuff!" I shouted. "I can't have any privacy around here."

"What do you need privacy for?"

"Would you like it if I looked through your things?"

"You act like I've never cleaned for you, washed your stinky underwear, straightened your drawers."

"I'm moving out!" I cried furiously. "Just wait and see."

"Where'd you get this?" she repeated.

"None of your business." I lowered my voice menacingly. "I demand that you give it to me."

"Hannah, I want to know."

I ignored her, picking up my dress from the bed. "That's private property." I hung it in the closet.

She stood up. "I guess I'll just have to show it to your father and see what he has to say about it." She tucked the garter in her pocket.

"It's mine, damn it!" I screamed.

"It looks like something a street walker would wear," she said. "Do you want me to tell—"

I turned to her angrily. "For your information, I won it." I paused. "It was a prize."

"For what?"

I thought fast. "There was a dance contest at the ball. Moshe and I won, and that was the prize."

"Why didn't you tell me?" she asked suspiciously.

"I would've if you didn't go through my things." I approached her. "Can I have it back now?"

"I just don't know when to believe you anymore." She reached into her pocket and returned the garter.

I wrapped it around my wrist. "Thanks," I added sarcastically.

"Did you know that your father and I won a champagne ball at Grossinger's? Not just a local bungalow colony. There were maybe a hundred other couples. I wore my green flapper dress and we danced the cha-cha. We did all kinds of fancy steps like the double turn and dip." She stood up. "I think I can still do it now."

I glanced at her. "You've shown me already."

"You see?" She demonstrated. "Once you know the basic rhythm, you can vary the steps. There are a million varieties. Here. The double dip." She leaped to one side, dipping twice, then the other. "We won hands down. A unanimous vote by all the judges. One of them was from Arthur Murray. So I thought maybe I could teach. That would be fun, a real career." Her enthusiasm dropped like a hand-painted porcelain cup. "But when I came to the school in Manhattan, the treated me like a nobody. Like I hadn't won. And they put me in the beginner's class. Even though I was one of the best."

"Maybe they had their own style—"

"No, they just wanted young girls as teachers. I was fatter then," she admitted. "Like a blimp."

"But you're not anymore," I reassured her. "I bet you could dance circles around Arthur Murray."

"We were given a bottle of excellent champagne, New York State, I think. It's still downstairs."

I groaned. "It must be vinegar by now."

Suddenly I thought of her douching; her bush, apricot-hued.

"We're saving it for an occasion." She looked at me. "Is it serious?"

"I don't know."

"A woman knows such things. Does he like you? Does he respect you?"

I raised my shoulders, dropped them, then raised them again. "It might be."

"He seems like an intelligent man." She paused, tapping her finger on her Newport pack thoughtfully. "You know, maybe it would be nice if he came to supper. So we could get to know him a little."

"He wouldn't come."

"Why not?" she demanded. "I'll ask him, if you like."

"Don't!" I exclaimed.

"Then you ask him. For Saturday evening."

"Mom, he hates to come out to Queens."

"What is he, a prima donna?"

"It's a long trip," I said. "Over an hour, and then he has to go back—"

"Your father travels for almost two hours every day, to that *farshtinkener Baking Times.*"

"Okay," I conceded. "I'll talk to him."

"I'll make my roast!" she said excitedly.

After she left, I thought: no matter how Flushing crushed my very soul, another life awaited me where there was vitality, intellectual stimulation, and sexual intercourse. I could see Manhattan in Moshe's genitalia: the spired tower of the Pierre and, across the Hudson, the Palisades' mighty boulders.

"It's me."

"Oh, I was going to call you. How you doing?"

"I had a close call with Bella."

"What do you mean?"

"She found the garter."

"How'd she do that?" he asked,

"She unpacked my suitcase while I was taking a bath."

"How could you allow her to do that?" he demanded, raising his voice. "That's outrageous."

"I didn't exactly let her."

"Yes, you did. She wouldn't do it if she didn't think she could get away with it."

"Moshe—"

"I can't believe it. Your mother unpacking your suitcase! You're a grown woman."

"I know. Look, it's not my fault."

"What do you mean? Relationships are an agreement between two parties. Your relationship with your mother allows her to go through your things," he said angrily. "Mine too. What happened with the garter?"

"She wouldn't give it back to me until I told her where I got it."

"What did you tell her?"

"That I won it in a dance contest."

"Oh." He sounded relieved. "But it's despicable that she would go through your belongings like that."

"I know."

"You've got to do something about this, establish new rules. How can we have an affair, which is an extremely intimate thing, when she—"

"That's the way she is. There's nothing I can do about it," I said miserably. "Moshe, don't make me feel worse that I already do."

"Okay, I'm sorry. But one of these days she has to wake up to the facts of life—"

"It'll be so traumatic for her," I groaned.

"For whom?"

"I don't know what you mean."

"You're just as tied to being her little girl as she is to treating you that way."

"You don't know what you're talking about!"

"Listen, everyone has to go through it," he said. "Do you think it was easy for me to move out of my parents' house? God, they had shit fits for months, calling me all the time, begging me to come home. My mother even told me that my father was going to have a heart attack. You can't imagine the crap I had to deal with."

"But you escaped," I said.

"So will you," he assured me. "One of these days."

"You know, I never had anyone that I could talk to about these things."

"Sometimes I worry that I'm being too directive with you," he admitted. "The best kind of analysis is when the patient finds out for himself."

"What?" I asked.

"Do you want a list?"

"No, seriously. Just tell me one thing you've found out."

"That I sometimes emotionally transfer on you," he

said. "Without even being aware of it."

"Me? What do you mean?"

"Remember how mad I got when you started crying on the subway? I wasn't really reacting to you, but to my mother and how she used to embarrass me in public. Once we were on a bus going down Fifth Avenue. I sat several seats behind her. Suddenly I heard her voice: 'Moshileh, lift your suit jacket so you don't get it wrinkled.' I nearly died."

"But what does that have to do with my crying?" I asked. "Maybe I embarrassed myself, but I wasn't doing anything to—"

"You know what?" he broke in. "I found one of your pubic hairs—"

"Don't say things like that on the phone!"

"It was black and very curly, like a ballpoint spring."

"Okay, already."

"I bet your pussy is blushing."

"It is not!"

"In that case, maybe I should tell you my plans for next weekend," he threatened.

"I've got to ask you something, but you don't have to—"

"We are going around the world," he declared.

"Moshe, my mother wants you to come to dinner this Saturday. I'll think of some excuse to tell—"

"I'd love to," he interrupted.

"I thought you hated coming out to Queens."

"I have a couple things I'd like to discuss," he said. "Set things straight."

"Don't you dare!"

"I'll be perfectly polite," he assured me. "And charming."

"Do you promise?" I insisted.

"Listen to this," he recited, " 'Today, when I was taking a pee/I thought, Hannah, of thee./There upon my hot pink member/Was your pubic hair, remember?' I wrote it after you left."

"But you won't say anything to them—about anything. . . . Do you promise?" I demanded. "Otherwise I won't let you through the door."

"I had a great time," he said softly.

"So did I."

"And you're really a good person. I want you to know that."

"You are too. . . ."

"No, I'm not. I try to manipulate you, and then I can't show any emotions when you're leaving—"

"But I could tell you felt bad and didn't really want me to go. You just had to do that. Besides," I paused. "You did wave. . . ."

"99.9," he whispered.

"Double ditto."

"It'll be just fine," he told me. "I even know what I'm going to say to her."

"You won't!" I protested.

"Parents always love me."

I could see it: Godzilla meets King Kong. Telephone poles sparking. The whole army powerless.

"Moshe, you promised."

23

He brought Bella pink gladiolas. Dressed in turquoise double-knit, she smiled demurely. "Let me find a vase. I'll be right back."

"Where's the funeral?" Stevie murmured as my father took Moshe's black coat. He wore a dark pin-striped suit with a navy tie, his Columbia pin on the label.

"Jealousy," I said under my breath. "Moshe, you haven't met my sister, Stevie. . . ."

"Hannah's told me a lot about you," he said.

"Oh, yeah?" she challenged. "What did she say?"

He leaned over and whispered, "That you give fantastic head."

She was taken aback for a moment, then grinned. "A wise guy, huh?" She stuck her hands into the pockets of her jeans.

My father returned to the living room. They shook hands. "I'm glad to meet you, Moshe. Would you like a drink before dinner?"

It was a trap. If Moshe accepted, God forbid, they'd shake their heads, concluding that he drank and was not *serious,* my mother's phrase for unacceptable marriage material.

"If you have J&B on the rocks," he said. "Thank you, Mr. Wolf." My father's brown slippers flopped as he walked to the basement door. "I think we have a bottle downstairs."

Upstairs, in the kitchen cabinet, they kept what was actually imbibed: Creme de Cacao, Cherry Heering, schnapps, and Stolichnaya vodka, which my mother cautioned, "Watch your liver, Stashek. You only have one. It's too strong for you. . . ." Down in the nether zone of the basement, there were other, more pernicious bottles. Every Christmas, my father received one, packed in a box with silver foil which he never opened, storing it near the boiler. They were piled on top of each other like cardboard cinder blocks, what Gentiles who went to bars drank, and in case one visited, or a profligate Jew, my parents would have something to offer.

Bella returned with the gladiolas in a glass vase. She set it down on the coffee table, placing herself next to Moshe on the Saran-wrapped avocado sofa. "Oh, I love flowers so much. But the only time you ever get them," she complained, "is when you can take the centerpiece from your table at Bar Mitzvahs and weddings. You should see how the women fight over it."

I stared down at my shoes. Stevie laughed, saying softly, "What a pisser."

"So, Hannah tells me that you go to Columbia and went to yeshiva too," Bella began, straightening her dress over her knees.

He nodded. "I've had a lot of religious training. I used to work as a rabbi, running Passover services in the mountains to make some extra money."

"No!" my mother exclaimed. "She didn't tell me."

"I didn't know either," I added doubtfully.

"Sure. I did it for three years. It was fun, in a way. I got to meet a lot of people. The men would offer me jobs, and the women, especially the grandmothers, would give me the phone numbers of their nieces in New York."

"Really," she said. "How forward."

"Did you ever call any of them?" I asked.

He shook his head. "Uh-uh."

"Lucky them," Stevie grumbled.

My father walked up the stairs, carrying two glasses. He looked apologetically at Bella. "I thought I might try some too."

"Stashek," she said, dropping her voice. "You know you shouldn't—"

"Here we are."

"Shalom," Moshe toasted. "Next year, Jerusalem."

"Have you ever been to Israel?" my father asked.

Bella interrupted excitedly. "He was just telling us that he used to work as a rabbi in the mountains."

"That's something," my father said. "But you never considered it as a vocation, a calling?"

"For a while, I was really religious, wearing phylacteries—"

I spun to face him. He couldn't have said prophylactics.

"And I'd go to *shul* every day," he continued. "Save my fingernail clippings as it said in the Talmud. I even had an automatic switch device for the lights on *Shabbus*."

"What changed your mind?" my father asked.

He swallowed a generous gulp. My mother and father glanced at each other. Clearing his throat, he went on. "You see, I didn't know about my parents' concentration camp experience until I was in high school. They kept it from me. So all that time, I was a good yeshiva *boychik*. But when I found out about it, everything changed. My father was in Auschwitz, the worst camp of all. I read as many books as I could find. What I feel now is how can any Jew possibly believe in God or in being a chosen people after the Holocaust." He downed the rest of his drink.

My mother nodded. "I can see why you feel that way."

"It's a guilt that we American Jews live under the shadow of," my father confided. "That all Jews feel even if they weren't in Europe. . . ."

"I don't believe this conversation." Stevie groaned.

"But your parents are—all right?" my father inquired.

"They—"

"They're functioning, if that's what you mean. But it's been terribly difficult for them. My father was an intellectual in Warsaw, a very respected man. When he came here, he didn't know the language or have a trade he could work at."

"What does he do?" Bella asked.

"For fifteen years, he's been a waiter in a dairy restaurant downtown." He shook his head. "It hasn't been easy."

"Oh, that's a tragedy," my mother said. "The poor man."

"At least, he works," my father added. "Many of them can't get jobs and go on welfare. We have one of them working with us."

"I'm hungry," Stevie exclaimed. "When are we going to eat?"

"Can't you see that we're discussing something?" Bella demanded. "If you listened, you might— Oh, God! The meat!" she screamed, lifting her skirt and running to the kitchen.

"But at least he can be proud of his son. That he attends Columbia University," my father concluded, pointing to Moshe's button.

"It was very important to them that I get a good education," he said. "They made a lot of sacrifices."

"Ready!" Bella called from the kitchen. "Everyone go to the dining room. Hannah, can you help?"

As I entered, my mother grabbed me, putting her arm around my waist.

"He's very nice, Hannah. Intelligent. Feeling. And better-looking than I remembered. With such a good vocabulary."

I nodded.

"Here," she said, "you carry the *latkes*. I wonder how it's affected him. No, I'll take the roast."

I laid the dish in the center of the table. My mother brought out the meat platter and her electric knife. "Stashek, please slice. But thin pieces. If they're fat, no one eats it."

"Okay," he said, poising the electric knife over the roast.

I sat down next to Moshe. "How are you feeling?" I whispered.

"Fine, fine," he said. "How am I doing?"

"My mother likes you. She told me."

"So far."

"I want a rare piece," Stevie said.

"Just a minute," my father said, slicing rapidly. "It's not running away."

Bella returned, seating herself opposite Moshe and me. "Don't slice the whole thing!" she exclaimed. "Then what's left over will be dry as a dog's bone."

"Everybody get started," my father declared, sitting down at the head of the table.

Stevie was at the opposite end. "My friend's brother used to live near Columbia," she declared.

"What's his name?" Moshe asked.

"I don't know. I never met him." She reached across the table for a slice of the meat. As she carried it back to her plate, she left a trail of blood on the tablecloth. "But he's supposed to be a nice guy."

"Why can't you be careful!" my father cried, raising his voice. "Stevie, you always do this."

"It was an accident," she said. "I couldn't help it."

"Yes, you could," Bella scolded. She turned to Moshe. "Will you have some meat?"

"Thank you," he said, taking the platter. "God, I haven't seen *latkes* in ages."

"That's her specialty," my father proclaimed. "And she makes a great gefilte fish too. A masterpiece."

Moshe squeezed my knee under the table as he turned to Bella. "This is delicious. Thank you for inviting me."

I smiled contentedly. So did my mother.

Stevie pouted, her lower lip turned inside out. "Too much." She stared ahead of herself.

"You were the first one to grab the meat with no manners, and now you're not going to eat?" my father demanded. "What's the matter with you? I just can't understand—"

"Leave me alone!" she cried, raising her knife and fork. "Everyone picks on me around here!"

Moshe studied her curiously. I watched him, aware of her hair, which she brushed so it tumbled over her shoulders, sparks flickering in its strands. She wore a red corduroy shirt with a Dead button on the pocket.

"What year are you in school?" he asked.

"Ju-niah," she answered sullenly.

"Have some more," Bella urged, noting that his plate grew empty. "You want another *latke*?"

"Sure." He served himself two more slices of meat too.

"Bachelors don't know how to cook, huh?" she asked, her eyes twinkling. "They eat cornflakes every meal."

"Oh, I can cook a few things. But not like this."

"I make brownies," Stevie added. "With nuts and other things. . . ."

After dessert, a lime Jell-o mold in the shape of a still life, my mother announced, "We'll have coffee and cake. But let's wait to digest a little. Why don't you kids go out for a walk?"

We looked at each other. "Let's, Moshe."

He nodded, bowing his head. "Everything was delicious."

Bella beamed.

With Moshe's arm coiled around me, we strolled down 71st Road. When we came to Park Drive, we stopped to watch the Grand Central Parkway below. Car lights flashed in the dark like a starry night. He took me in his arms. As we kissed, I felt the quirk of love like a pinprick. "Moshe—"

"You see," he said, rubbing noses. "I told you I could deal with them. Parents always love me."

"I don't know. Why'd you have to tell them about having been a rabbi and your prophylacteries. Was that true?"

"Phylactcrics," he corrected me, laughing. "It's a good thing you didn't say that!"

"Were you really a rabbi?"

He shrugged his shoulders. "Does it matter?"

"They believed you. So did I."

"I figured it was a good story. Why do you have to take everything so seriously?"

"You were talking about God," I said.

"That's what they wanted to hear. That I was a good Jewish boy. I'll tell anyone what they want to hear."

"But that's not right," I protested.

"Like this queer guy, Bob, at school. We'd talk sometimes. So I'd tell him stories about how I was kept by this aging queen, Alexander, who gave me money, bought me clothes. Bob nearly died of jealousy. As a matter of fact, Hannah, Alexander gave me this suit. I could never afford it. It's a Pierre Cardin."

"Come on!" I said doubtfully. "You wouldn't."

"Look at the label." He turned over the collar.

"Will you stop bullshitting already."

"I'm sorry. Don't get upset," he said, grabbing me around the waist. "I got it at Sym's for fifty dollars on sale. Now does that make a good story? No."

"Damn it!" I punched him on the arm.

"You're so funny-looking. . . ."

He kissed me. I kept my lips pressed together. "No, you don't."

"Hannah," he whispered. "I want to lick you everywhere tonight. So I'll know how you taste. . . ."

Soon his tongue found its way into my mouth, hiding behind teeth, seeking mine. A giddy, private school of fish swimming around each other, diving off rocks, playful. "Come back with me tonight," he said.

"You know I can't, and don't start."

He nibbled on my neck. "Why not?"

"Them."

"I want you."

"I do too." I looked into his eyes. "I really do."

"Let's go back to your room."

"We can't, there."

"Yes, we can." He kissed me again. I was dizzy.

When we returned, my mother greeted us. "Did you have a nice walk?" she asked. "Beautiful evening, isn't it?"

"Lovely, Mrs. Wolf," Moshe said. "So many stars."

"You can call me Bella," she said. "Or Bell. That's what my friends do."

My father looked up from the paper. "It's not too chilly outside tonight?"

"No," I said, still breathless. "It's beautiful." Not looking at either of them, we climbed the stairs to my room.

Moshe placed my desk chair against the door.

"I'm scared," I whispered.

"There's nothing to worry about. We'll hear if they come upstairs." He took off his jacket.

"I don't know," I said. "I've never done anything like this. Suppose they find us—"

"Shhh." Moshe started to unbutton my velour bell-bottoms.

"I can't." I struggled out of his arms. "Not here. I grew up in this room."

"That'll make it more exciting," he said, pulling them down. "Undress me."

"Moshe—"

"This is what's known as Jewish foreplay. Two hours of begging." He took off his tie, unbuttoned his shirt, throwing it on my desk.

"I just know there's going to be trouble." I slipped off my turtle-neck. "What happens if she wants to come in?"

"We'll make it a quickie. Besides, I don't have any prophylacteries with me," he teased, undoing his belt.

"Then what'll we do?" I stepped out of my panties.

He sat down on the bed, unlacing his shoes. Then he stuffed his socks into his shoes. "I'll use my mouth on you."

"Where?" I asked, startled.

He grabbed me between the legs, pressing his finger. I was afroth. I made a fist around his penis, winding up, down, around it like a Maypole. As he grew hard, I held on—whee!—and swung, my thighs wrapped around his arm. He began to lower himself, his tongue trekking from my mouth, licking my chin, neck, making a figure eight around my nipples, my rib cage, belly button. Just as he was about to land—his tongue, the *Pinta, Niña,* and *Santa Maria:* welcome to the New World, my unexplored vagina, *that way*—we heard someone mounting the stairs.

I froze, digging my nails into Moshe's shoulder.

"Hey, kids!" Bella called. "Why don't you come down. The coffee's ready, and wait until you taste this Rumpelmayer's cheese cake! It's the best in all of New York."

Moshe whispered, "I am going down—on your daughter!"

"Shhh! What should I say?" I covered his mouth with my hand. "We'll be right down!" I yelled. "Moshe is reading one of my papers." I dropped my voice. "I knew this would happen."

She turned the doorknob. My heart boomeranged, crushing my lungs. She pushed the door. "Don't!" I cried. "Please! Wait."

"What did you do to the door?" she demanded, heaving it.

"I'll be right out, Mom," I pleaded, covering myself with the blue blanket. "Just a minute." The chair rocked unsteadily.

"Why won't you let me in?" She tried it again, shaking the door.

"Goddamn it," Moshe muttered. "When is she going to leave?"

"She'll hear you," I whispered.

"I don't care. What does she have to come up here for? It's like she doesn't trust us. My balls are killing me."

"What?" Bella asked. "Moshe, what did you say?"

"I'm reading Hannah's paper on the medieval influence of iconoclasm on the iconography—"

"If you don't come out this minute, I'm going to call the police." She shook the door one more time. "Do you hear me?"

24

We leaped off the bed, searching for underwear, socks, under the desk, at the speed of panic, mine. "Hurry!" I cried.

"I can't do this," Moshe said, pulling his tie out of his collar and folding it in his jacket pocket.

"She'll see it!" I exclaimed. "She notices a button missing."

"Everything will be cool," he said.

"What makes you so sure?" I demanded.

"I can handle it," he told me. "Don't let your anxiety take over."

My parents sat at the dining-room table, silently, as at a concert.

I quaked in my clothes, still wet. "Where's Stevie?"

"She said she was going to see some of her friends," my father answered, looking up. "Those hooligans."

"Here," Bella said, pouring coffee into each cup. "Do you want milk?" she asked Moshe. "Sugar?"

"Thanks," he said, taking the cup and saucer.

I sat down next to my father, avoiding both of their eyes.

"I didn't know it was so warm," she said, staring at Moshe, "that you have to take off your tie."

"Bell," my father said. "It's not comfortable to wear a tie all evening."

"Actually, I had a crick in my neck. It really hurt," he said. "Hannah rubbed it for me."

"She rubbed it for you," my mother said sarcastically. "How nice."

"It wasn't anything really, I just moved it around a little," I explained, blushing furiously. "His neck and shoulders where he had a crick ..." I paused, meeting her eyes for a moment. "In his neck."

"I didn't know that you knew how to give massages." She peered at me. "Maybe you can give me one too." I felt her eyes burning cigarette holes in me.

I shrugged. "Sure."

"Here, have a piece of cake." My mother passed a plate with a slice of cheese cake, strawberries on the side. "Rumpelmayer is twice as expensive but they use real butter. *Extraordinaire,*" she said, licking the knife. "I really shouldn't, but you only live once, right?"

Moshe looked down at his plate. "Oh." His voice dropped in disappointment. "Taste this—"

"What's the matter?" Bella asked, turning to him. "It's delicious."

"No," he insisted. "Taste it."

"Moshe," I intercepted. "You haven't even tried it."

"Here," he said, passing the plate to my mother. "Please taste it. Do me a favor."

"Okay," she agreed. "Where's the fork?"

"Ah!" he exclaimed, pointing sagely to the ceiling.

My mother shook her head, smiling. "That's from the joke about the customer and his chicken soup. Hannah, get Moshe a fork in the kitchen, please."

"Say the word 'wing' three times." He turned to Bella. "Go ahead."

"Actually I wanted to know why the door to Hannah's room was—"

"It's just a joke," he interrupted. "Say wing three times."

"Okay," she reluctantly agreed. "Wing. Wing. Wing."

"Hew-wo!" He grinned. "How are you?"

My father chuckled softly.

"A regular joker," she declared, watching him through narrowed eyes. "You still haven't told me—"

"That's what he is!" I exclaimed, passing Moshe a fork. "A joker."

"Did you hear about the Frenchman and the Polack who go hunting together?" he asked. "Suddenly, as they're climbing down this steep hill, they see a beautiful girl lying naked near the water. The Frenchman cries, 'Oh la la! Let's have her for dinner.' So the Polack shoots her."

"Ha-ha!" I laughed loudly. "How can you tell the bride at an Italian wedding?"

My mother and father looked at each other.

Moshe thought for a moment. "Mozzarella breath?"

I raised my arm. "She's the one with braided armpit hair."

"What about an Italian bath?" Moshe asked.

My father turned to him. "You know a lot of jokes, don't you?"

"Chef Boy-Ar-Dee?" I suggested, smiling at Bella.

"A couple drops of—" Moshe began to laugh. "This is cruel but those *goyim*—" He bent over, cackling. "A couple drops of holy water! That's their idea of a bath."

"What I want to know," she said suddenly, "is why the door to my daughter's room was blocked."

"I have another one for you," he pitched rapid-fire. "This is a real pisser—"

"God, it's already ten o'clock," I said, pointing to the kitchen clock. "Maybe you should—"

"It is late," my father agreed.

"What's the difference between a pizza and a Jew?" Moshe asked. "This is the last one."

I looked at him. Something about his expression made me fearful. He stared ahead of himself, in the space between my parents' chairs, unseeing.

"There've been enough jokes," I cried, standing up.

"Let him finish his cake," Bella said, her eyes fixed on Moshe. "Go ahead."

"The difference between a pizza and a Jew . . ." He hesitated. "Maybe I shouldn't tell it. This could be offensive."

210

"Don't!" I pleaded. "I'm tired of all the jokes."

"You've started," my mother insisted, never shifting her eyes from Moshe. "Go ahead. You're a joker anyway, aren't you?

"Okay," he said finally. "The difference between a pizza and a Jew is that a pizza doesn't scream when it's put into an oven."

For a moment, I giggled. Then I lifted my coffee cup, watching all of them over the rim.

Several seconds passed until Bella said, scrutinizing me, then Moshe, "Very nice."

"You tell us about your parents' war experience and we were, of course, concerned," my father said. "Then you tell that—"

"Abomination," Bella added.

"Did you hear about the pregnant Polish woman? She didn't know who the mother was," Moshe said.

"Let's forget about it, please," I begged.

He stood up, starting to raise his voice. "Who do you think told me that joke in the first place?"

"It's almost ten-thirty," I urged.

"My father. He thought it was a good one. People told jokes in the concentration camps. It wasn't sacred."

Bella stared at him. "You still haven't told us why the door to my daughter's bedroom was blocked when I came upstairs."

"As a matter of fact," he said. "I wanted to discuss that very subject with you both."

"Don't!" I cried, grabbing his arm. "We were just—"

He ignored me. "It seems as if you're both unwilling to accept the fact that Hannah's a growing woman." He looked at them sympathetically. "I can imagine that it's difficult letting go. It always is. But that's very neurotic, if you ask me."

"What do you know?" my mother demanded.

"She's just eighteen," my father argued. "And she has a lot of independence anyway."

"You're going to discuss this with him?" Bella asked. "I can't believe my ears."

"In Middle Eastern countries, females far younger will often have several children," Moshe lectured. "And they're perfectly healthy. The problem with Americans is this period of extended adolescence."

Bella's voice rose. "You come here, you little college *pisher,* to our house"—louder and louder—"and then you're going to tell us what to do?"

"The times have changed, don't you know that? As have the mores. This is the era of the sexual revolution—"

"Are you sleeping with my daughter?" my father demanded.

"No!" I cried. "We're not. I swear to God."

"Honesty is the necessary ingredient to bridge generational gaps—" He made a bridge of his hands. "For an authentic communication."

"Get him out of here," Bella growled.

"So we can all grow," Moshe continued. "I really like you both and feel as if we could—"

"Shut up, Moshe!" I screamed, dragging him away from the table. "He doesn't mean it. He's really not this way. You even said so yourself, Mom, he's a nice guy and he has a good vocabulary." I was dangling dangerously from the tightrope of the heart. No net. No North Star. The horizon line a membrane. "Remember?"

25

Slowly I hoisted myself down the plumb line of Moshe's body, kissing each rib like white keys of a piano, that he would sing, his navel, nuzzling my nose, lips, face in the dark curls of his stomach.

"Do you like that?" I asked unsurely.

"Oh, yes," he sighed. "Don't stop."

Something drove me on. I had dreamed of it, him, coming under the roof of my mouth. Safety was there. Nothing could hurt us. I wanted it. His legs trembled. My parents couldn't stop me, even Bella-tio, who I had told I was going to the Museum of Natural History, as I had gone to the Museum of Modern Art, and, the weekends before that, the New-York Historical Society, the Frick, and the Planetarium.

But I was scared too, in unfamiliar woods, no bread crumbs in my pocket to guide the way back. A hibernating bear lurked in the midst. It was awakening below me, stretching its furry torso. Was it fear, the transparent hairs on my body standing at attention? A trillion goose bumps, everything erect. I thought of graffiti on the subway which made it sound obscene. I wasn't even sure it was done by normal people, that it was legitimate and not some kind of perversion. Leathered buttocks, bicycle chains. He nudged me. I didn't resist. Instinct led me. Hand over hand.

I studied it for a moment, eyeing the hole, which was the size of a pinhead, and how many angels could dance there? A Swiss dot. Suppose something leaked out: urine, semen, whatever. I stared into it but couldn't see anything. What did I expect, a little man who would stick his tongue out at me? Birds, butterflies soared past in Moshe's room. *It* was monolithic.

"That's so nice," he said, drawing me to him.

"I don't know what I'm doing," I called.

"Don't worry. It's fine."

I took him in my mouth ever so slowly, gently, like an operation, dental work. I was afraid of hurting him, accidentally biting down and swallowing the whole kit and kaboodle. Then what would I do?

He filled my mouth, precariously close to the opening of my throat. I gasped for air, trying to breathe through my nose. Suppose I suffocated? It was ten times as big as a chicken bone. I pulled away.

"Press down," he whispered. "It feels wonderful."

I nodded, mouth full, wrapping my tongue around him like a silk sash, sashaying to the rhythm of his breathing. My breasts rubbed against his thighs.

He held me tightly. I closed my eyes as if making a wish. How his legs quivered, then, bucking to climb into me. I swooped down as he raised himself, erupting molten in my mouth.

While he lay there with his eyes closed, his arm over my stomach, I tickled his penis, which now looked like it was covered with a lace doily.

"Don't," he muttered, turning to his side.

"How are you?" I asked.

"Resting," he said. "Just five minutes, okay?"

Why was he so tired? I was the one whose mouth had been plundered, gums sore, lips chapped. Could I get pregnant, seeds trekking down my digestive system, to the uterus?

"Did you like it, at least?" I asked. "I never did anything like that before, and I was pretty unsure at first—"

"I told you, it was swell."

"Is that all you have to say about it?" I demanded. "Like it was a piece of pie?"

"You want an Academy Award?" he asked, sitting up.

"I can see you're not going to let me get any rest."

"But you didn't do anything—" I paused, embarrassed. "With me."

"It doesn't always have to be simultaneous. The best kind of lovemaking, in my opinion, is serial. So you don't get distracted." He wiped himself with a tissue.

"One at a time?"

He nodded. "Six, then nine. Sixty-nine is rarely successful."

"Do you love me?" I asked.

"Why can't you wait until I tell you, of my own free will, instead of asking all the time?"

"I've never loved anyone as much as I love you," I said, looking into his eyes. "Not even my parents."

"I'm just your first. There'll be many more after me."

"No, there won't." I pushed him away. "How can you even—"

"That's why you're getting so emotionally involved," he said. "You haven't had very much experience."

"You don't take my feelings seriously. Besides, I've had a couple other boyfriends," I protested.

"You never slept with them."

"But we did everything else," I said. "It's not fair for you to condemn me for my lack of experience. I can't help that."

Moshe shook his head doubtfully. "Look, I feel as if you're becoming too dependent. It worries me."

"What do you mean?"

"You're too young to settle down—I have undershirts older than you—and think I'm the end-all, be-all. You should have more experience. Besides, it will carve out your character and make you a fuller person."

"I love you," I said simply. "I really do."

"You're a girl from Queens," he said. "A nice girl. An upper freshman at Queens College. You don't know anything about love."

"You don't love me," I said, beginning to cry. "You don't! I see that now."

"Stop crying, will you?" he said. "Babies cry. Women

can discuss things. You've transferred all your dependency from your family to me. That's too heavy a burden."

"I thought—" I chewed on my lip, sobbing. "I thought you cared about me."

"You should see other people, open yourself to life's experiences. I'm telling you this for your own good. You'll thank me one of these days."

"Why are you torturing me?"

"You're going to be a very miserable person if, at thirty, I'm the only man you've ever known. Believe me."

"Why aren't you satisfied with me?" I wailed. "I try. I really do. I wouldn't do that—thing, you know—for anybody else."

"Hannah," he said, putting his arms around me. "You're misinterpreting what I'm trying to say. It's not that I want us to stop seeing each other—" He kissed my nose.

I threw him off me. "Stop playing with me!"

"Why? I love to touch and squeeze and kiss you."

"Then why were you saying that?"

He leaped out of bed, taking my hand. "Let's get something to eat."

"But what about"—I held back—"me?"

"We can talk at V & T."

We took a corner table, passing a signed photograph of Frank Sinatra. The waiter laid down two red paper mats with a map of Italy and two brown plastic glasses of water.

"Some wine?" he asked. "Cocktails?"

Cock what? The waiter's hair was dark and greasy. He spoke with an accent.

"One for me, please." I looked at Moshe.

"Make that two. The house red," he said.

The waiter left two oversized red menus on the table. Moshe grabbed one, studying it. I stared ahead.

"Remember, this is Dutch," he said.

*I gave you my body and I bet I could charge at least $20
each time, which is cheap, and that would come out to—* I
didn't say anything.

"Look, we could go Jewish."

"What's that?" I asked.

"We don't go out."

"I don't want to see anybody else," I blurted. "I don't
even know anybody else, and I don't see why you want
me to—"

"Their special pizza has anchovies, mushrooms, sausages," he interrupted, looking at the menu.

"Did you hear what I said?" I demanded, pressing his
arm.

"We should order first. It really takes a long time."
He turned to me, taking my hand. "You do eat sausages, don't you?"

"I don't care."

"I think we should try the special pizza. How much do
you eat? Should we get a medium or large one?" He
didn't wait for my answer. "We might as well get the
large one. That way, if anything's left over, I can have it
for breakfast tomorrow." He poked me under the table.
"But you should, Hannah. Just as a homework assign-
ment. To check it out and see what it's like with other
men."

"You mean, you want me to sleep with them?" I
asked.

"That's not necessary," he said quickly. "But who
knows? It might be part of the experience. Oh, there's
the waiter. Waiter!" he called. "We're ready to order."

When he came to our table, Moshe told him, "One
large special pizza with extra cheese and sausages."

The waiter left two glasses of wine. "Large special
pizza," he muttered as he walked away. "Extra cheese
and sausages."

"He'll probably get it completely wrong," Moshe
said.

"You really wouldn't mind if I slept with someone

else?" I asked, amazed. "Their body naked next to mine?"

"Not if you were honest and we could bring it into the arena of our relationship. As a matter of fact, if it was a woman, I'd love to watch."

"Moshe! I know you don't mean that."

"I believe in living out fantasies. Sometimes I can even imagine necrophilia!" He tapped my glass with his. "Skol."

"Well, you're not sleeping with anyone else," I demanded, "are you?"

"I might be."

"I don't believe you'd do that!"

"I didn't say I was."

"Are you? Answer me." I shook his arm. "You better tell me, Moshe. This minute."

"Okay," he admitted. "I have."

"Since you've known me?" I asked incredulously.

He nodded. "But only a couple times."

"Who?"

"That's not important."

"I just don't believe it." I pulled away from him. He ducked as if he expected a blow, knocking the glass of water with his elbow. It tumbled over, spilling, then rolled to the floor.

"See what you did!" Moshe grabbed his napkin, trying to soak up the puddle of water on the table.

"You care more about that little bit of water—which I didn't spill, you did—than you do about me," I accused. "How could you? You've been using me all this time."

He sat down. "We better get the waiter to wipe this." He looked around, then turned to me. "Maybe you've been using me. It goes both ways."

"Are you kidding? I didn't even really want to, at first."

"You seemed pretty ready to me."

"That's a lie. You know it is."

"Why'd you wear a Tampax on our first date?"

"You're not going to get out of this one. Who'd you sleep with?" I demanded. "Ellen?"

He dropped his head, nodding.

"No."

"I called her after Homecoming," he confessed. "But only for my books, I swear. And she was wearing a transparent blouse and started—"

I stood up, clutching my bag. "How could you!"

"Don't go!" He rushed to me, knocking over his chair. Several people turned to look at us. He picked it up, lowering his voice. "Please, Hannah. She's not a threat to you. It was just sex."

"Leave me alone, you creep!" I tried to disentangle myself from his arms. "I'm going home."

"Don't make a scene. I eat here all the time, and everyone—"

"I don't care." I pushed him off. "I don't give a good goddamn!" I ran out.

"What about our pizza?" he called, running after me. "We'll be right back," he called to the waiter.

"Hey, mister! Friend!" the waiter shouted. "Special pizza."

"Keep it warm," Moshe said, racing past the cash register. I was already halfway down the block.

I ran as fast as I could, around the corner to 112th Street. Moshe was close behind me. I gasped for breath but continued, reaching Broadway.

He leaped ahead of me. "Slow down a minute," he said, winded. "You want me to have a coronary?"

"Get away from me. I never want to see you again," I screamed. "Do you hear me?"

"Come on, Flushing." He tried to embrace me.

"No way." My arms flailed threateningly.

"Let's go back to my room. I want to tell you something."

"Not on your life. Why don't you go make love to Ellen?" I said sarcastically. "And *shtupp* her?"

"But it was just sex. Can't you understand that?" he

asked. "Sex and love aren't the same thing. I don't have feelings for her like I have for you."

"Then why'd you go to bed with her?" I glared at him.

"Males are different. Every so often, you need to exercise, you know, keep in shape," he equivocated. "But you're the one I'm involved with emotionally."

"I don't buy it."

He belched loudly.

I made a face. "You're disgusting, too."

"What do you have against good honest *grepps*? That always happens when I run. Besides, it gives me a chance to re-experience the last thing I ate. Like a dying man, I saw it all before me: my eggs over easy, toast, home fries, orange—"

"I don't want to hear about it," I said.

"All in one second. It looked like a modern painting."

"I feel miserable."

"You? A child of joy, of normal parents? I'm the one who was born out of the ashes of the Holocaust, a child of sorrow and despair." He put his arm around me. "I don't know what I'd do if I lost you."

"Why didn't you think of that when you were with Ellen?" I crossed my arms, refusing to budge.

"I told you, it was just sex."

"And what's it with me? Non-sex?"

"It's more complicated between us. I care about you. And you know that sometimes emotions, particularly because I feel protective of you, can preclude eroticism. But to tell you the truth, I kept thinking how much better it was with you." He grabbed the bus-stop sign, shaking it. "I mean it."

"Bullshit!" I cried. "If that's what you thought, why'd you do it a couple times?" I kicked the other side of the pole.

"I didn't," he said, staring down sheepishly.

"You mean, you went to bed with someone else too?" I asked, eyes distending with disbelief. "Besides Ellen?"

"I can't totally change my habits overnight. Before I met you, I went to bed with lots of girls. I even took out an ad in the *East Village Other:* 'Young, handsome collegian seeks to learn the ways of love.' I'm still getting calls. But most of them were weird—hookers, married couples where the guy wants to watch, men who tried to fake female voices. Anyway, that's what I'm used to. I have an insatiable sexual appetite." He held my shoulders. "And you're all the way in Queens."

"That you can do that," I said, turning away from him, "with other people, like it's nothing."

"It's one of the differences between men and women," he said. "Men get off on pornography, underwear, whatever. Women are turned on by one thing."

"What?"

"Love. And sometimes a person wants a change of pace. Like let's say you're really into chocolate ice cream. But one time, just for a change, you try strawberry or rum raisin. It's not a tragedy. That doesn't mean you're giving up chocolate for good."

"You're awful!" I cried. "How could I have—"

"But they don't mean a thing to me," he insisted.

"That's what you probably tell them about me," I said, starting to walk to the subway station. "I'm going home."

"Call your parents! I really want to be with you tonight. There's so much I want to share with you. I feel so close to you. It's important that we—" He embraced me. "Make up some story for them. I don't know! You broke your leg or something and were rushed to St. Luke's—"

"No, Moshe."

"I want to put you into my bed and tuck you—"

I pushed him away. "Leave me alone! That's all you want to do—to everybody!"

"I didn't say that!" he cried. "You misunderstood what I said."

"I want to be alone," I said sorrowfully.

"You're angry at me. Aren't you?" he asked.

"It's hopeless." I shook my head slowly.

"Depression is anger turned inwards," he said. "I didn't mean to hurt you. I swear to God."

"I'm not angry," I argued, continuing to walk. "I just want to go home."

He put his arm out. "Punch me. Go on, punch me. You'll feel better if you express your anger. Then we can go back to my place—"

"I'm not angry!" I said, raising my voice. "You never listen to anything I say."

"You see. You're seething under the skin—"

"I am not, damn it!"

"And when anger is repressed, it can be an extremely destructive force. That's what gives people migraines."

I turned to him. "You want me to go out with other people so you won't feel guilty. Isn't that it?" I demanded.

"I just thought it might be good for you, open your eyes. But if you don't want to—"

"Maybe I do."

"Come back with me, please," he begged. "I want to come in all your orifices. Your ears, nostrils, armpits, ass—"

"I said no!"

26

Up the block to 141st Street. I walked past windows glowing with the blue light of the evening news. Earlier, it had been the soapy moans of violins as small children gathered stockades of snowballs in their mittened hands. One girl lay in the snow, flapping her arms above her head, singing, "I'm an angel. Look at me!" As I went by, she darted after me. "You see?" she insisted, pointing to the outline where she had lain. "Those are my wings." She indicated them with her red boot. Now glasses clinked as flatware was set, ovens slammed.

I walked two blocks until I came to Jewel Avenue, which I followed for half a mile, the selfsame trail I walked every day. The red tract houses knew me, their golden numerals flashing. It took twenty minutes.

I entered Queens College through the Melbourne Avenue gate, staring at the gray stone rectangle which was Remsen and past it to Fitzgerald, the gym, with its towering smokestack. The sun had just set, and orange formed around the lip of the horizon. You could see Manhattan, silver in the distance, a mirage of buildings like so many broken teeth of a giant's comb. I passed the Science building, a dark concrete structure without windows, and walked toward the Paul Klapper Library, which some called the crapper and others claptrap.

As I wandered into the Language Lab, I thought, this is what it's like to die: zombies seated at desks with partitions around three sides of them, bathed in fluorescent light that turned their skin a jaundiced grapefruit. I spotted Greta.

"*Apra il suo libro,*" Greta repeated. "Open your book. *Io apro il mio libro.* I open my book."

I tapped her on the shoulder. "Let's talk."

She looked up at me. "Sure. The small caf? Harvey's in there, I think."

It was next door and considerably smaller than the stadium-sized big caf, its white-washed walls decorated with abstract murals from Queens' art department. We took a table near the entrance.

"So is it still *it?*" Greta asked as soon as we sat down.

"What would you do if"—my voice grew grave—"if Harvey was unfaithful?"

She looked into my eyes, turquoise powder gleaming in the creases of her lids. "Frankly, I can't imagine it. Oh, there he is!" She pointed across the room. "Last week, ZBT decided to sit in the small caf from now on."

I observed his puffed face, puckering up for a dime-thin burger which he splattered with green relish, ketchup, and hot mustard. He sat next to another boy who wore the same navy blazer and white fraternal badge. "He has late classes this term?"

She nodded. "Sexy, isn't he?" Before I could answer, she told me, "But only I know how good he is. That's what he's always telling me. 'You're the only woman on earth who knows how good I am. That's why I love you.'"

"Are you really in love with him?" I asked.

"Sure," she answered. "I wouldn't be pinned to him otherwise."

She was pleased, I thought, watching her eyes meet Harvey's in a robust embrace. She waved with her fore-finger. He didn't take out ads in the EVO, compose feces theses, arrange songs to himself on tape. He waved back. But did he ever discuss the philosophic implication of getting out of bed in the morning?

"Do you really think he actually made it with someone else?"

"I know it for a fact," I said. "He told me."

"Why'd he do that?"

"I told you, we're totally honest with each other."

"Oh." She glanced across the room momentarily. "Maybe Harvey's doing it too, but"—she shook her head—"I just can't imagine it."

"Well, Moshe did it with Ellen, his ex, and a lot of others too." I stared miserably ahead.

"Why don't you go out with someone?"

"I don't want anyone else," I stated quietly.

"That's stupid," Greta insisted, pointing her finger. "There's a lot of guys around. I could get Harvey to fix you up with someone from ZBT."

"Did you hear me?"

"Joshua just broke up with Peggy. . . ."

"He said he has an insatiable appetite—" I began.

Greta interrupted. "So does Harvey! Sometimes he even wants to do it during the day." She lowered her voice to a whisper. "We once did it in the basement of Remsen."

"Introduction to Psych, Remsen 101?"

She nodded.

"Moshe said that love and sex aren't the same thing."

"Of course. It isn't."

"You don't really think that," I retorted. "You didn't even do it with Harvey until you got pinned."

"My dear," she informed me. "Love and getting pinned aren't the same thing."

I turned to her. "Tell me the truth. Do you, when you do it with Harvey—have an orgasm every time?"

"Yeah, sure."

"What do you feel?"

"It's hard to describe."

"Please try," I urged her.

She studied me for a moment. "It's kind of like a trembling that gets bigger and bigger." Her fingers cupped in a circle expanded like a balloon.

I grabbed her arm. "Then what?"

She dropped her hands on the table with a thud. "That's it."

"But does it ever feel like you reach a peak and you're kind of stuck on top of it?"

"That's what coming is," she told me. "The peak. Reaching Fuji." She giggled at her own joke.

"Yeah," I insisted. "How are you supposed to come down?"

She shrugged. "It just happens."

"Do you think it means anything to Moshe with the other people? Like he's in love with them or something?"

"How am I supposed to know? I'm not a guy. You want me to ask Harvey? He could tell you, from the male point of—"

"No!" I cried. "And if you tell him anything—"

"Men are so weird," Greta said, shaking her head. "They think with their dicks."

"Not Moshe. He's—" I paused gravely. "*Sensitive.*"

27

I lay on my bed, staring at the ceiling, its cracks a map of the world I hadn't seen. Above my window, a splotch of plaster was Japan; in front of my desk, near my framed Arista certificate, Italy. A skinny drip. It was the same bed where I'd had German measles, mumps, chicken pox, and recently, while Bella was in Cleveland for a convention, Moshe.

"Do you masturbate?" he had asked.

"No, not too often," I answered shamefacedly. "Do you?"

"Of course. Everybody who's horny masturbates."

"Well, I'm not that horny," I lied.

"Do you do this to yourself?" he asked, bending over to kiss my stomach. "Bet you can't. Although I once met this guy who could give himself a blow job."

I picked up the receiver. Stevie's voice commanded, "Whoever it is, hang up!" I wandered into the bathroom, applying Chapstick, blush-on, my mother's Rose Milk hand lotion. As I waited, I peered into the mirror, as if there might be some answer there, in my own face.

Finally, I dialed Moshe's number. It had been twelve days since our fight. My breath lurched higher into my throat with each digit. Five rings. I hung up, dialing slower. This time, I slammed the receiver. He was undressing a black woman, her hair an aurora borealis, jade in her ears. He unbuttoned her blouse. I tried again. He stuck his hand into her brassiere, fondling her dark breasts, pinching the nipples lightly. I dialed his number every few minutes. He grew harder, rubbing his penis against her lips. "Let's do it forever," he whispered. "Every time I get close, I'll stop. . . ."

Before I knew it, I was stroking myself, but it was his fingers that tiptoed stealthily, teasing each breast momentarily, stealing to rub the crotch of my panties, dipping under the waistband like kids into a movie. Oh, so sneaky! I moved back and forth, my fingers crawling into the valley of the sluice. Why was it called self-abuse? It didn't seem like I was abusing myself. Oh! His mouth and tongue, my ankles tightly crossed, grinding my thighs against each other, a pebble between them, longing to be pulled back to the sea.

I washed my hands as I always did afterwards, good girl, so no one could smell it, especially me. Why couldn't I do that with Moshe? I tried him once more.

Stevie called from the kitchen. "You want some matzoh and peanut butter?"

"I'm not hungry."

"There's some Tab."

I shook my head, sitting down at the table.

"Are you okay?" she asked, looking at me.

"Where'd they go?"

"Visiting. Somewhere in Forest Hills."

"He's probably out screwing right now!" I raged, grazing my hand against the table's edge.

"So he fucks around. All men do," she said.

I ignored her. "And it wasn't even only with Ellen. He slept with some other women too."

"I don't know who'd want to sleep with him," she said, making a face.

I stared at her. "What's that supposed to mean?"

"He's funny-looking."

"He is not. Thanks a lot. He happens to be brilliant and sexually masterful too."

"You must be blind," she retorted. "He's a creep and a phony too, the way he sucked up to Bella. I thought I'd puke."

I stood up angrily. "I thought I could talk to you."

She caught my arm. "Don't get uptight. What do I know, I've never been with anyone more than a few times."

"I love him," I wailed, sitting down again. "I really do." I took a matzoh from the box, cracked it into three pieces, and smeared peanut butter thickly on the first.

"Come on, Han. Just because you went to bed with him a couple times doesn't mean—"

"It's not that," I interrupted. "We had something very special together. There was love in the presence of passion and vice versa." I bit into the matzoh. It crumbled all over my shirt.

"And where's a violinist when we need one?"

"You don't know Moshe," I insisted. "He's the most fascinating person I ever met."

"He's your first, that's why you think that," she told me as she dipped her matzoh into the peanut butter jar. It cracked, so she had to fish out the crumbs with her fingers. "I mean, it's not like you've known a lot of people." She licked her fingers. "Let's go downstairs."

We sat in the womb of the finished basement. It was dark except for a star-shaped candle's glow. Stevie ran her finger through the flame. Out of the speakers, Mick Jagger screamed, 'You can't always get what you want. . . .' She sat cross-legged on the floor.

"Sometimes I wonder if there's something wrong with me," Stevie said moodily. "Do you ever feel that way?"

"How?" I asked.

"You know, my not having had a real boyfriend and all. Most of my friends—"

"What do you mean? You have tons of them! You're always going out," I said. "More than me, anyway."

"But it's not like someone who calls you up and asks you to the movies. I mean, not that I really want that. I just sometimes think about it." She ran her finger through the flame again. "Even for one month."

"I thought you weren't into that."

"Just to see if I could be with someone . . ." Her voice trailed off. "I don't know if it would work out."

"What should I do about Moshe?" I asked, lying down on her bed.

"He's an asshole," she said.

"He is not," I answered. "You're just judging from your first impression."

"It never seems to work out anyway." She raised her shoulders, then dropped them with a shrug. "Fuck."

"What?"

"Nothing."

"What were you going to say?"

She turned, looking directly at me. "I want to ask you something."

"Sure."

"You're going to deny it, but I want to know." She paused, staring down at herself. "Do you think there's a reason why?"

"What do you mean?"

"You know. My not having had a boyfriend . . ."

"I never thought you really wanted one," I observed.

"It's my figure," she stated. "That's why."

"What are you talking about?"

"I'm fat."

"You are not!"

"Sometimes I really freak getting undressed. Like the guy's looking at me and he couldn't tell in my clothes, but it really turns him off."

"Come on, Steve." I touched her lightly on the arm.

"Just like Bella. A goddamn blimp. I ate half that box of matzohs."

"So?"

As I watched her, I thought of how we used to jump off the house steps. I was in fifth grade; she was in third. It was our favorite game. We jumped two steps, three, four, building our nerve until we got to the top, seven. Then, like Peter Pans, we would fly to the ground. Sometimes we fell. Bella would rush outside, screaming.

But we always bounced back, un-Humpty-Dumpty-like, and began again.

"Do you remember the Flying Wolves?"

She turned to me, "Our jumping contests?"

"Wasn't it great? We used to talk about running away to the circus."

"That's right." She smiled.

We listened to the record. "But you get what you need. Yeah, you can't always get what you want. . . ."

"Do you think I'll have a real boyfriend one of these days?" Stevie asked suddenly. "One who takes you out to a restaurant? It wouldn't have to be expensive."

"It's not so terrific," I said glumly.

She paused. "I did meet someone."

"You did!" I exclaimed. "Who?"

"Kingfish."

"I couldn't get along with anyone named Kingfish in a million years."

"He has a motorcycle—and you know what?" she added. "We were bilingual."

"What does he speak?" I asked.

"First, he used his tongue on me, then I used my tongue on him." She grinned broadly. "We met at a Dead concert."

"Did you do it there?"

"No, of course not. We went to his place. He lives on Avenue C."

When the phone rang, I leaped for it. "Moshe!" I cried. "Hello? . . . Oh." I passed the receiver to Stevie.

"Linda? Hey, what's happening? Yeah? Great!" she exclaimed. "Really? When?"

I sat for a while, watching her as she stood on one leg, scratching the back of her knee with the other. Her overalls hid her whole body like a tarpaulin. Then she slipped to the floor, leaning against the wall.

"He was there? By himself? How'd he look?" she asked excitedly.

After a few more minutes, I stood up to leave. "I want to call Moshe." She nodded absently.

• • •

I dialed information, then Columbia. "Wayne McMillan," I told the operator. "He's an undergraduate, Engineering."

"What's his dorm?"

"Something like Abe Lincoln. A president."

"John Jay?"

"That's it!"

"Just a minute."

As I waited, I twisted the telephone cord around my wrist like a noose.

"Hello?"

"Wayne?" I began shyly.

"Yes?"

"It's Hannah Wolf. . . ."

"How are you!"

"Fine. And yourself?"

"Not too bad," he answered. "I really didn't think I'd hear from you."

"Well, it's me. At least, I think so."

"So what's happening?"

"S.O.S.," I said. "Same old shit."

"Did you make that up?" he asked.

"I guess so. Anyway, I thought since I had to be in the City tomorrow, and if you're going to be around—"

"I'll just be doing laundry. But I have to study for this calculus test on Monday."

"Don't worry," I said. "I won't stay long. Besides, I've got this dentist appointment—"

"You want to come over to my dorm?" he suggested.

"Your room?"

"Sure. I mean, it's kind of messy. I share it with this guy, Burrell, from Chicago—"

"Will he be there?"

"I have no idea."

"You see, I just wanted to talk. . . ."

"Great. We can talk here. Do you remember where John Jay is?"

"Yeah."

"Why don't you stop by around six."

"Well," I said doubtfully. "Okay."

"There's a guard sitting at a desk. I'll meet you downstairs."

"But Wayne, wait!"

I wasn't sure I heard a click. "It's important that you realize," I continued. "Hello? Are you still there, Wayne?" No answer. "I just don't want you to get the wrong idea...."

28

I halted before setting forth on Columbia soil. I adjusted my dark glasses, the scarf which masked my hair. Tiptoeing past Ferris Booth, I peeked inside, then continued, fully exposed, running across the great lawn. On my left, I passed Low Library, Alma Mater, and the sundial. Would Moshe and I actually meet in five years? Suppose I was married? Or lived in Tanzania and traveled all the way back and he wasn't there? JOHN JAY was carved in stone over the entrance, black wrought-iron lamps on either side.

The uniformed guard sat at a desk, a large Christmas tree behind him, reading the *Daily News*. I cased the place. Several students milled about by the oversized bulletin board and mailboxes. I ducked past them and found a fountain, sipped several mouthfuls, scrutinizing them, then returned to the guard's desk.

"Are you looking for somebody?" he asked.

"Not exactly." I checked down the hallway in the other direction. "Hmmm," I muttered conclusively.

He turned the page of his newspaper, which featured—I studied it upside down—chicken specials at D'Agostino.

I strutted outside, retying my scarf, staring up at the windows. Which one was his? Could he see me? I restrained a jig bursting out of my feet. How much after six o'clock? Fifteen minutes. Would he come? No, ten. From the corner of my eye, I saw a large red shape bouncing. It was a laundry bag. "Hannah!" Wayne called.

An enormous smile ballooned on my face. "Hi!" I waved, blinking disbelievingly at this boy with Marilyn Monroe hair, a Miss America smile, this ski-jacket-clad Yankee who belonged in the worlds of O'Hara, Fitzgerald, *Peyton Place* with Ryan O'Neal, not Philip Roth's and mine, was jogging toward me—and I knew him.

"Well, hello there!"

"Have you been waiting long?"

"Nah."

He grabbed me by the waist. "How's things?"

I leaned away from him, holding my jaw with my left hand. "I got a Novocaine. So my mouth's stiff." Lying through my teeth. "Ow," I groaned.

"The dentist?"

I nodded. "That's why I had to come to the City, so I figured, since I was here anyway, I could stop by."

He looked thoughtful. "I guess you can't eat anything."

Was that a *double-entendre?*

"You want to see my room?" he asked.

"Couldn't we take a walk or something, so—uh, you could show me around?"

"I've got to drop this laundry off."

"Oh, right."

The guard didn't look up as we passed to the elevator. "Don't they check?" I asked.

"They're just unionized seat warmers."

"But suppose a murderer came or somebody like that?"

Wayne shrugged, pressing eight. "It's not too neat," he warned.

"Is your roommate around?" I asked casually as we walked past painted blue doors.

"Burrell? Nah, he's with his girl friend at Barnard. He'll probably stay there tonight. That's what he does on most weekends."

I thought of Saturday nights in Moshe's foldaway bed, going out to Duke's for eggs afterwards, then a Times

Square double feature. We passed a lounge with a TV set.

"He loves to party. Wait till you meet him," he said, slipping his key into the lock. "You'll really get a kick out of him."

"I'm not going to be able to stay too long," I said. "Besides, what about your test on Monday?"

"Don't remind me."

With his shoulder, he pushed open the door. I followed behind, into a tiny room with a bed on either side, a wooden desk next to each of them, one medicine cabinet over the sink, a bookcase filled with cans of cocoa, soup, tuna, and instant coffee. Wayne turned on the light, a Japanese lantern which bathed posters of the Marx Brothers and a groveling Sophia Loren from *Two Women* a bright pink.

"Be careful," he said, taking my hand. "Everyone falls over the wires."

I looked down. Fifty wires crossed near the desk with several extension cords like ganglia between them.

"There's only one outlet," he explained. "Which means you can't shave with the lights on, or listen to music and have the hot plate going at the same time, or you blow a fuse." He dropped the laundry bag on his bed. As he dumped its contents, he asked, "How are you on socks?"

I took off my dark glasses and scarf. "Okay, I guess."

As he folded T-shirts and shorts, which I scrupulously did not look at, I tried to match the socks. Although they were dark brown, black, or navy blue, of different lengths and knits, they all looked the same. I pulled out a black sock from under the pile. Our fingers met for a moment. He smiled as I snatched my hand from his.

"How many cavities?" he asked, a mock-pained expression.

"Oh, he just took X-rays this time."

"How come you got Novocaine?"

"I give up," I said, shaking my head. "Listen, I didn't

go to the dentist. I just wanted you to not think I came in especially to see you." I avoided his eyes.

"Did you?" he asked.

"Sort of. But I've got this boyfriend, you know, who I've been going out with for a couple months—"

"The bald one at Homecoming?"

"He's not really bald. It's just thinning a bit."

He picked up a pile of clothes and laid them in a drawer. I carried the socks in my arms.

"Here," I said. "So anyway, I found out something about him which upset me deeply."

"He was making it with someone else?"

"I wasn't going to say what it was." I added, frowning, "The creep."

"How come you called me?"

"Well, I felt sympatico with you and"—I paused nervously—"I figured that maybe I could talk to you about it." I turned to him, summoning my nerve. "Do men really separate love and sex?"

"I don't know."

"Like they're two totally different things. Like meat and milk dishes—oh, you don't know about them. Anyway, you know what I mean?"

He stared perplexedly at me. "Kind of."

"What do you think?" I demanded.

"That you ask some pretty heavy questions."

I crossed my arms. "I wanted to know." I paused, dropping my voice so it only echoed in my shirt collar. "I need to."

"I guess it's different for every guy," he answered finally. "I don't think you can make generalizations."

"How about you?"

"Me?"

"Wayne McMillan."

"This is not what I usually discuss with girls I don't know too well. . . ." He paused, thinking about it. "I guess I prefer to screw someone I like."

"That's kind of the way I feel," I admitted.

He pulled me to him. "Do you smoke?"

"Cigarettes?"

"Dope."

"You mean grass?"

He nodded. "Would you like to smoke some?"

"Why?" I demanded suspiciously.

"It's relaxing," he said, taking my hand. We sat on the bed. "You'll like it."

"I tried it once with my sister and smoked a lot. Absolutely nothing happened."

"This is good stuff," he explained. "I got it from a guy in the chemistry department. He has acid too."

Wayne fetched a Nescafé can from the top shelf of the bookcase. Lifting the lid, he removed a Baggie of brown marijuana, a tweezer, and Bambu paper. The seeds rattled at the bottom of the can. "Would you hand me that cover?" he asked, pointing to the chest.

I passed him the Cream's *Wheels of Fire.*

"You can turn on the stereo if you want," he said. "Just hit the power switch."

I did. Jonathan Schwartz was talking about the Byrds' concert at Madison Square Garden. Their song, "Turn, Turn, Turn" played in the background.

He crumbled the weed between his fingers over the album's surface. Then, tilting it slightly, he swept the grass with a matchbook cover so that the seeds rolled to the bottom. He began rolling a joint with two fingers, his tongue licking the paper to seal it.

"I'm not sure I'm actually that much into it," I began cautiously.

"That's cool." He lit up, inhaled through his nose and mouth, then passed it to me.

I puffed lightly, then exhaled the smoke.

"You can't get high that way," he said. "You've got to keep the smoke in your lungs. Like this." He demonstrated by taking another hefty drag, pointing with his finger to show how it filled his lungs, where he held it for several seconds as he passed the joint to me.

"Okay," I said, taking another light puff.

"First, force the air out of your lungs," he suggested.

"Isn't it hard for you to run track if you smoke pot?" I asked, choking on the smoke.

"You're not supposed to talk," he said. "Here."

"I'm sorry." I exhaled hard so my lungs collapsed. Then, slowly, I inhaled the smoke, squeezing my nostrils, tightening my legs. "But don't you think it's dangerous?"

"How?"

"You know, a crutch—and a person can become dependent on it even if it's not physiologically addictive. What about psychological addiction? . . . Nothing's happened so far," I said, squinting at the paper lantern, that it might suggest some cosmic truth to me about the universe.

"You probably haven't had enough yet," he said. "I'll roll another one." He grabbed the Bambu package. "Empty! Damn it!"

"Oh, well." I shrugged my shoulders with some relief.

He began to search in drawers of one desk, then the other, in the bookcase. "You don't have any cigarettes on you, by any chance?"

I shook my head. "I've got some tissues in my bag," I suggested.

He turned to me. "You wouldn't have a tampon with you?" he asked, somewhat embarrassed.

I flushed as I thought of my first date with Moshe. "Why?"

"The paper it's wrapped in is perfect for rolling."

I made a face.

"I guess girls react that way. To me, it's like a Kleenex or something." He continued hunting around the room.

"Look, forget about it," I said. "I've had enough."

"Wouldn't you like to really get high?" he asked.

"I'm not sure."

"Hannah!" he cried, pulling an empty beer can out of the garbage. "You're about to witness Old Boh turn into a bong."

Making a fist, he punched a depression in the top of the can. Then, with a pocket knife, he began to bore several holes. "Now watch this," he said, dropping large clumps of marijuana over the holes. He lit them with a match and passed the can to me. "Breathe through the pop-top," he instructed me.

I put my mouth over the key-shaped hole and inhaled as hard as I could. He continued to light it. The smoke rushed into my throat. *Whoa!* I coughed, passing it to him.

"Try to keep it in," he said. "Even if you feel like coughing."

I gagged slightly, eyeballs popping.

He covered the top with his fingers, lifting them as he puffed on the can. "Mmm," he sighed.

"I still can't feel anything at all," I said ruefully.

"Have some more," he said, passing the can back to me.

"I could smoke the whole bag and nothing would happen. My grasp on reality is too strong," I mused. "Which isn't so bad, in my opinion." I laughed.

He lit the mound of dope again as I inhaled strenuously. "That was a good one," he commended. "Are you feeling anything yet?"

"You should know something about me. I mean, in my case, reality has an impermeable membrane around it." I released the smoke like a white satin ribbon. "Like virginity, I suppose. The way there is a hymen. I mean, it's not final. And one can be penetrated." Suddenly, I looked up. "How did I get to that stuff about virginity?"

"You were talking about—"

"Right, the impermeable membrane of reality. That's a good line. The impermeable membrane of reality. Someone ought to write a book about that...." I leaned dreamily back. "But do you know what I mean? I mean, a person can be penetrated and still nothing happens."

He put his arm around my shoulder. "What I like about you is that you're intelligent. You wouldn't be-

240

lieve some of the fuzz brains I meet."

"You really think so!" I exclaimed, delighted. "That I'm intelligent? I think I'm mildly stoned." I giggled.

"You know, that would be a great name for a rock band. The Impermeable Membrane of Reality. Or Membranes of Reality—"

"Come on!" I laughed. "Seriously, I have a hard time having things penetrate me. Somehow nothing ever gets through, even though I try hard. You know what I mean?" I leaned toward him. "Do *things* enter you?"

"Not like they *enter* you, but I'm not sure what you're talking about," he said.

"You know, experiences, people that you've known, memories, so they somehow carve themselves on your consciousness and you're transformed. I don't think I'm expressing myself very well." I dropped my hands, two squirrels skittering in my lap. "Do you consider yourself introspective?"

"What do you mean by that?"

"Like when you're alone, you're not lonely because you have something inside of you."

"I guess so." He shook his head, studying me. "Why don't you relax," he suggested.

"Maybe I should have some more." I grabbed the can.

The smoke rushed down my throat, filling my lungs, rising into the aorta of my heart, tweaking me between the legs before it rushed out of my mouth. "Mmm," I sighed ecstatically. "I think I'm getting something."

"I told you it was nice stuff. Real mild. I can't stand hyper grass."

I nodded. "I see what you mean. You know, everything has a slight fuzzy edge around it and seems a little bit brighter." I peered at the room. "Yes, I think I've gotten slightly stoned, which means that the membrane may be permeable and can be broken—and penetrated. . . ." My voice trailed off as I sank, head first, into the doughy implications of that statement. "God," I said as Wayne kissed my neck.

"Where are you?" he asked.

"I don't know." I was staring at the shadow of our bodies cast on the bed like a flash-forward in a foreign film. "And you know, it doesn't even matter." I chuckled softly to myself. "It doesn't."

His lips swept over my neck, down my collarbone to the upper strata of my breasts.

"Wayne." I looked at him as sternly as I could. "I told you, I have a boyfriend."

"I won't tell him."

"You don't understand. We have an honest relationship. I'd have to tell him—"

"Shhh." He slipped his hand under my shirt, traveling across my back to my bra, which he snapped open.

Was it the grass or a demonic side of me: pure, raging, libidinous id? But maybe this was reality and I should try to experience it in a spontaneous way, instead of always fighting. Be penetrated in another way.

And I desperately needed real life experience, to be transformed by the erotic, the passionate, the bizarre, and not to be a sheltered girl from Queens leading a ho-humdrum bourgeois existence for the rest of my days and nights. Experience was knowledge and power. George Sand had many lovers. So did Doris Lessing in *The Golden Notebook*. And Brett. Moshe might even be pleased. After all, in a certain way I was doing it for him so I'd become more worldly, a worthier mate. But I still felt unsure as Wayne pulled my shirt over my shoulders.

"I really don't know if we should be doing this," I began doubtfully. "At the very least, we should discuss the ramifications of introducing sex to our Platonic relationship. . . ."

"It'll be all right," he whispered, slipping my bra off.

I gazed into his eyes. Did I want to swim there, diving under the surf, letting it crash over me? Or could I rise with it so that finally I crested and everything was white? I was afraid. He unzipped my jeans.

I held my hand against his chest to push him away. He guided it down to his crotch.

242

"Wayne—"

He started to kiss me, his tongue burrowing inside my mouth, engaging mine. Before I could pull away, my tongue launched to meet his, say how-de-do, tongue talk, get acquainted. *Oh, perfidious tongue!*

In a matter of seconds, he leaped out of his slacks, boxer shorts, Columbia T-shirt, leaving only his socks and track shoes on. Was he planning to jog first? *Where?*

Since it was now inevitable, too late to decline, I stepped out of my jeans and red bikini underwear and gathered them, along with my shirt and bra, and laid them on the other bed. Moshe would have been proud of my neatness.

Now is the time for all good men, I steeled myself; Peter Piper picked a peck of pickled peppers. . . . *It* stood straight out, at a right angle from his body. I turned away, scurrying under the sheets.

He added several more flakes of pot to the can and took a long drag, then passed it to me. I took one puff, then another, which swirled through my head: piped music, painted horses, and all, I swear.

"What about birth control?" I whispered as he slipped into bed next to me, starting to caress my breasts, squeezing the nipples which perked up attentively, flitting between his fingers. *Nefarious nipples.*

"Don't worry, I won't come inside of you."

"You better not."

"I promise."

As his hand traveled over my body, stopping at historical buildings, tourist traps, taking pictures, buying postcards, window shopping, stroking my stomach, thighs, poking around, I studied his face. It reminded me of the doctors in romantic comic books. Fair hair and skin, light eyes, straight nose, stony jaw. Not only did I prefer Ben Casey to Dr. Kildare but I even had one of his shirts which buttoned down the side. I missed Moshe.

He kissed my breasts, then squeezed them together, taking both of them in his mouth, nibbling. I was letting him make love to me but I didn't love Wayne, I told my-self. There was no poetry here. Sensitivity. Like Moshe, whose history had carved a depth in him that was like the black holes of outer space. No darkness to contrast with the light of his hair, his eyes so blue. It was a sum-mer of sunshine without storms, thunder, lightning de-stroying trees, flooding, catastrophes. He was blithe. And I had longed after, hankered for, would have dropped my *samedi* pants for, just this. He. Wayne Mc-Millan. To be with one of them and escape my own be-sotted skin.

"Where are you?" he asked again.

"Next to you," I said, putting my arms around his waist. I could feel him against me but I wanted Ur lan-guage, intellectual rapport, psychic bonding, eye con-tact, devastating closeness, and, most of all, love. Oh, Moshe.

His fingers stroked me. I put my arms around his neck, closing my legs. He forced them open with his knee, climbing partially on top of me. I struggled un-derneath, but he only split my legs farther. Momentari-ly, I relented.

He touched me softly, his fingers diaphanous, teasing me. A tumultuous squeak of delight escaped. I tried to clamp my legs shut. He didn't let me, holding one leg with his hand, the other restrained by his leg. He kissed my neck, biting lightly, harder, surprising me again, pecking at my earlobe. I grasped his shoulders as his fingers began to play with me, getting closer, kneading, retreating, tantalizing me. Closer! I bit into his shoul-der, covering my teeth with my lips. He swooped down, fingers slow at first, then building. I bucked against them wildly. My body shivered, becoming almost fever-ish, my pulse, heart, especially my vagina palpitating, rubbing against his fingers as hard, as precisely as I could. I whimpered softly, wanting to say *things.*

What was this, an orgasm? I asked myself, but didn't have the time, concentration, to answer. Oh, no! This wasn't supposed to—it hadn't ever happened with

Moshe. Only when I burned in my own bed, alone, my fingers doing it over and over again. With fair Wayne.

"You know, you're very handsome," I gasped, trying to regulate my breathing, catch my breath, my arms trying to push him away as my legs wrapped around his. Suddenly, the feeling started again. I feared I was going to pee on his fingers. Stop, I wanted to scream. But I didn't want him to—stop. I tried to clasp my muscles, make them hold back. But they flapped open, an ocean breeze whistling through them, and I couldn't. Finally, I let go. Something whooshed through me, my legs quivering uncontrollably.

That moment, he rolled on top of me. I bent my knees, encircling him with my legs. He entered immediately, hard, crash, *shlang*, bang. I held on to his waist as he filled me, further, saturated me, and still more. I pressed against his pelvis, moving like a pendulum, trying to match his movement, collide with him full force. Clock-wise, counter-clock, cock-wise!

"Mmmm," he sighed.

"Mmmm mmmm," I purred, my eyes closed, colors darting out of the darkness behind my lids. "I can't believe this."

"Did you come before?" he asked.

I nodded guiltily. "I think so. Yes, I'd say I did," I admitted slowly. "I did, I think. It felt so weird. That never happened to me before. Not, at least, when I was with anybody else. Did you learn that in Buffalo?" I inquired.

"Shhh."

Halfway, all the way, in, out, on the edge, filling me, my *innards,* almost into my stomach, back and forth, leaning forward, thrusting, thirsting, I was!—again! My head spun as if watching a tennis match inside of my own body, concentrating on him, then me, back to him. I grasped his waist to hold him inside. But I had to ask him something first.

I called his name softly.

He stopped. "What's the matter?"

"No, don't stop. Please! I just want to know one

thing. Do you think this is meaningful sex or casual, like *a night stand?*"

"What?" he asked breathlessly. "You want to know that right now?"

I nodded. "You made me come. That's something." I gazed up at him. At that moment, straightening up, *homo erectus* above me, he looked exactly like a surfer, the sun lighting his hair a golden white.

"Don't come inside of me, okay?"

"I told you I won't," he whispered huskily. "Your eyes!" he cried, grabbing my ass. "They're so incredibly dark"—he started thrusting faster, faster, faster, *faster!*— "and in—intense!"

Pulling violently out of me, flaming cock in hand, he spurted semen, boiled milk, all over my stomach.

I blocked the passage to my vagina with my hand.

He sighed, burying his head into the pillow. His penis curled into itself, soft as an embryo. I held it as I had so often held myself, falling asleep.

29

I scratched my stomach. Something flaked. Looking down, I discovered spots of caked semen like rubber cement. Sunlight rippled through the window. I leaned over Wayne to reach his watch, inside of his track shoes. It was eight-thirty. A.M.! We had slept through the night. I bolted out of bed.

"Where are you going?" Wayne murmured sleepily.

"The bathroom?" I asked frantically opening the closet door, then shutting it. "Where's the bathroom? I have to get out of here."

He sat up, one eye open. "Down the hall. But you better put something on. You want my shirt?"

I grabbed it from the desk chair. "How could I have done this?" I paced by the door. "I just wanted to close my eyes for a minute and then, it's now. Oh, God!"

"We got pretty ripped last night," he said, smiling wryly. "Even with your impermeable membrane."

"I didn't even call them!" I ranted, ignoring him. "My parents are going to die, if they haven't called the police yet. Or Moshe. Where's your phone?"

I dialed the number slowly, reciting to myself: 'I'm almost nineteen—in February—an Aquarian, the humanitarians and risk-takers in the astrological circle. Besides, if I went away to college, I could do whatever I pleased. I'm a maturing woman with thoughts, feelings, and desires. I will not be treated in a denigrating—' It was ringing. 'And not only did I do it but I came. I bet you don't even know what I mean. . . .'

"Where were you last night?" Bella demanded. "Now

she doesn't even come home anymore. Did we bring you up like this?"

"No!" I exclaimed self-righteously. "I didn't do what you think I did!"

"I know what you've been up to!"

"I was with this girl from Queens who lives in the City. Ellen! She goes to Barnard." I stopped to amend my story. "You see, she transferred and's having problems adjusting, so . . ." Wayne was shaking his head incredulously as my tongue tied itself like a cravat in my mendacious mouth. "Anyway, I had to do something important."

"Young lady, the only important thing is that you didn't come home. How do you think we felt? I almost called that—that"—in her rage, she sputtered his name—"that Moshe."

"You didn't." My voice quaked. "Did you?"

I listened to the sound of water running in the sink. "Why are you acting as if you don't know if I called him? I know where you were last night. And I suppose you don't need our permission for anything anymore."

"Did you call him?" I implored.

"No," she admitted. "I should have, though. And given him a piece of mind."

"Mom, I swear I wasn't with Moshe," I began. "On the Five Books of Moses, the American Overeaters Bible—"

"We'll talk when you get home," she said firmly.

"But I can't! Not right away. I've got to take care of something." I clutched the telephone cord. "You understand, don't you? One woman to another."

"Hannah, I'll take care of you and so will your father if you don't come home immediately."

"I'm sorry," I mumbled.

She slammed the phone.

Typed names were taped to wooden shelves in the bathroom. Wayne McMillan, I read aloud, opening and shutting his electric shaver kit, sprinkling his Ammens

Medicated talc like fairy dust on my recently exposed pubic area, suddenly so open to the public, hiking my leg on the toilet seat for a better view.

Like some hothouse flower, it was vividly mauve, violet, fuchsia—fucked by two different men!—with lugubrious petals that hung tongue-like. And I'd had an orgasm *here*. I spread the lips open. But exactly where was *that*? In all the biology diagrams and Tampax instructions, I had never seen an arrow that pointed to orgasm.

Wayne had made me come, and not Moshe, who I had deep feelings for and we shared a religious background. And it wasn't as if it were better or lasted longer. "How could we do that?" I had asked Moshe. "I'll stop every time I get close. . . ." Yet I was always left stranded. I stepped into the shower, clearing the hairs around the drain with my big toe.

When I returned, Wayne was covering the bed with a green army blanket. I began to dress. "Are you feeling better?" he asked.

"Awful."

"But I thought you liked it last night."

"I did," I acknowledged guiltily. "Too much. But I haven't known you for very long and you don't really know me, and there's Moshe, you know, who I'm in love with even though he's a creep sometimes, and besides, my parents . . ." My voice dropped into my bra. "It's all very confusing."

"I'm sorry to hear that." He slipped on his underwear from the night before, then his jeans.

"Don't you ever get upset about anything?" I asked crossly.

"Sure, I get bummed out sometimes. I mean, really bummed. But last night was an up for me." He sat down next to me on the edge of the bed.

"I had a nice time too," I admitted, bending over to lace my desert boot. "I really did, especially considering I never did anything like it." I looked at him. "I guess this could definitely be considered *a night stand*, right?"

"You're funny," he said, putting his arm around my waist. "It's one-night stand, Hannah. How about one more for the road?"

I shook my head. "I've got to talk to Moshe."

"You're going to tell him?" he asked, amazed.

"He has to know."

"I wouldn't," he said doubtfully.

I stood up, pacing as I spoke. "He's a very unusual person who understands lust and sensuality. Besides, we have a relationship based on honesty." I paused, saying softly to myself, "But I don't think I'll tell him about the orgasm. He might misunderstand that."

"Could we get together one of these days? Nothing heavy," he said. "See a movie or something?"

I shook my head. "I can't."

"How come?"

"I told you. I'm involved."

"You didn't seem that involved last night."

"I know." I turned to him. "I'm sorry."

He looked down at himself, flicking a piece of lint off his jeans. "So what'd I do wrong?" he asked.

"Wayne—"

"I thought we had a really good time together. You were the one who called me—"

"But I tried to explain that—"

"Let me finish, please." He reached for *Wheels of Fire* on the floor. "And you wanted to talk about love and sex as if you were—"

"I know, but you see it was the first time I ever, uh—" I paused for a way to say it. "That I ever did anything like this."

He laid the album on his desk. "I understand what it's like to be a girl and feel used."

"How'd I use you?" I demanded.

"You haven't yet. But when you tell him, you will." He replaced the Nescafé can on his bookcase.

"You don't understand," I said, shaking my head. "We have the kind of relationship where we can talk about anything. If there are lies—"

"Nobody talks about that unless they get caught with their pants down. And then they can just pretend they came upstairs for a glass of water."

I hiked my pocketbook over my shoulder. "It was nice. You're nice," I added. "But I have to go."

"Well, let me know if it doesn't work out with the bald guy—"

"I told you, he's not bald."

He shrugged. "Whatever."

I met his eyes. "I think you're a great guy, and I would have given my eyes and teeth for a date with you."

"Come on." He grinned, thumbs hooking the belt rings of his jeans.

"And not only that but I think you're gorgeous. Really. The first time I saw you at the bookstore, I almost died! I was so excited. I really was! And then I came but you weren't there."

"I wanted to come but I had to—"

"I ran to the College Inn, to the bookstore, back and forth, searching for you. Finally, I decided I'd wait inside the bookstore, which is what I did." As I raised my shoulders, then dropped them with a fatalistic shrug, my pocketbook slipped to my wrist. "That's when I met Moshe."

"I lose," he said.

"I wouldn't say that. Remember, you don't know me," I warned him.

"But I like you," he said.

"Why?"

He shook his head. "If you don't know, I can't tell you."

For a moment, we stood there, eyes locked in a mirrored room where there was only us.

"I've got to talk to Moshe!"

30

"Whoever you are, get out of this building or I'll call the cops!" Moshe's voice, distorted by the intercom system, boomed. "Do you hear me, you junkie! Where the fuck's my TV set?"

"Moshe," I said faintly. "It's me."

"Who?" he demanded.

"Hannah."

"What the hell are you doing here? Do you know what time it is?"

"I'm sorry to wake you up," I apologized. "But I have to talk to you. I've come to an important realization that could—"

"What?" His voice screeched. "I can't hear you."

"Couldn't I—uh, we—talk for just a few minutes?"

"It's not even ten o'clock. I'm still asleep."

"Moshe," I implored.

"On a Sunday morning," he growled.

"Please."

"Okay, already." The bell continued blaring as I began the four-flight climb.

Armed with my recent trial-by-fire worldliness—and I had learned more in one night than in my whole semester and a half at Queens College—the desire to forgive Moshe, as I confessed my own transgression, for us to be close, in love again as we had been before I overreacted like the green girl I was, I mounted the stairs.

I now understood Moshe's desire for others. I could hardly wait to tell him. How I had discovered that sex could be nice, you could even have an orgasm, ten of them, ten thousand. I was flowering, white sprouts puckering, pressing their lips to be kissed in my hair, under my arms, between my legs, the lobes of my brain and heart. But I still preferred meaningful sex. Really and truly, Moshe.

Last night, I had realized that I never wanted us to be apart again. No matter what. I had to tell him. I couldn't be without his jokes and imagination, the way he was, his eyes, his hair—yes, that too. Besides, I never wanted to become jaded like a divorcee.

As I reached the fourth floor, winded, I saw him standing in the doorway of his apartment. His hair was freshly combed and he wore a red and navy striped terrycloth robe over his blue pajamas.

A wave of love splashed over me as I gazed down at his feet, which were white, pointing out like a duck's in brown Hush Puppy slippers.

"Long time no see." I cupped my hand in a timid but coy wave.

"It's not even ten. Do you know that?"

I followed him into the apartment. "It's just, I thought, we haven't spoken to each other in a while. . . ." I paused, sending him a woeful look. "Since we had that argument at the Italian—"

"You're the one who had the argument," he interrupted nastily. "I couldn't believe how you ran out of there. After I ordered the pizza already."

"I know."

"A guy's got to be able to feel free. You know, some breathing space is necessary in a relationship." He sat down on his unfolded bed, primly covering his knees with the bathrobe.

"Look, I've realized I was wrong. That's why I had to see you." I sat down next to him, taking his hand in mine. "I'm sorry. And I want you to know that. I've given it a lot of thought."

"You acted like I'd committed some murder."

"But that's the way it seemed to me, then. You see, I always thought that love and sex were the same thing."

I turned to him. "What do you think is the true meaning of—"

"Can I go back to sleep?"

"—sex."

"The gratification of a need," he said, looking bored. "That's all it was to me. I told you that."

"But do you think it has other implications too?"

"What kind of implications?"

"I don't know. Large ones."

"It's the kinesthetic experience of pleasure which doesn't have to be genital. And it definitely doesn't have to be romantic or emotional."

"Well, that's what I realized too," I announced proudly.

"Great."

"No, really. In a profound way."

"Wow," he said unexcitedly.

"In other words, you don't think it's such a big deal, sex. Like when you made love to Ellen?"

"Is this what you woke me up to tell me on a Sunday morning?" he demanded.

"You don't understand. It was a real stumbling block for me. Like religion; I didn't know whether I was an agnostic or I could go all the way and believe—"

"What are you talking about?" he asked impatiently.

I tried to catch his eyes with mine. "You know how you've always said that we should be honest with each other? Well"—I paused—"I had an experience."

"Really?" he declared, retying the sash of his robe.

"Yup."

"What kind of experience?"

"A sexual one."

His eyes grew enormous. "You didn't."

"Uh-huh."

"With a man?"

"Yes, I went to bed with a man. We had sex," I reported truthfully. "I want to tell you, since you told me, and a good relationship is based on honesty. And it was very nice, but I realized—"

"Wait a minute," he interrupted, his eyebrows forming a dark cloud across his forehead. "Who did you go to bed with?"

"That doesn't matter," I said. "Just someone I met. It was casual, but the important thing is that I realized I too could have sex and it wasn't such a big deal. So I could empathize with you and understand—"

"Hannah," Moshe said. "You're not making any sense. Did you go to bed with someone?"

"Yes."

"Who?"

"Wayne." I volunteered his name.

"When?" he asked.

"Last night," I admitted.

"Oh. I see." He stared at me.

"It was a really positive experience for me, and for our relationship, I think."

"You had intercourse?"

I nodded. "I feel as if I've grown as a person and as a woman. Anyway, that's why I came. I wanted you to know that I'm not mad at you anymore because I now can identify with your feelings. You see, I thought that sex was this incredibly monumental thing."

"How did you meet—er, Wayne?"

"At Columbia," I answered.

"You're kidding, aren't you?" His left eyebrow floated up to the middle of his forehead, suspended like a black worm. "You mean, he goes to Columbia?" he asked incredulously.

I nodded, looking down. "But it wasn't anything serious at all."

"What year?"

"Moshe, that's not important."

"Maybe it is to me," he said.

"Okay," I conceded. "He's a sophomore, I think."

"Oh."

"Do you want me to leave so you can go back to sleep?" I asked, growing uneasy.

"What school is he in?"

"Engineering. And that's the last question about him that I'll answer." I stood up to leave.

He peered strangely at me. "Is he Jewish?"

"I don't want to talk about it anymore." His expression frightened me.

"He isn't Jewish, right? With a name like Wayne," he said. "Was he circumcised?"

"How am I supposed to know?"

"Did you go to bed with him or didn't you? It has this piece of skin over it like an umbrella case."

"I swear I didn't notice." I began to walk toward the door. "You went to bed with other people, including Ellen, so I figured—" I looked at him. "I better go."

He grabbed my hand, which was on the doorknob. "Was he better than me?"

"Moshe, I refuse to answer these questions."

"Was he bigger or smaller?" His face flushed, eyes darting. "You ought to know that."

I felt frightened. "Moshe—"

"Answer me." He squeezed my arm.

I tried to pull away, but his hold on my arm grew tighter. "That hurts," I whined.

"I want to know."

"Okay, already. I think you're about the same. But Moshe, it's you I really love. I'm never going to see him again. I told him that."

"Was he on top? Is that the way you did it?"

"I don't remember."

"Hannah, tell me!" He squeezed my arm until it turned white.

"Uh!" I cried, "Stop it! You're hurting me!"

He released me, then walked over to the window. I stroked the red splotch which smarted on the inside of my arm. For several minutes, he stood silently, staring out at the courtyard.

Finally, I said unhappily, "It isn't fair if you're going to be mad at me. You did it."

He didn't seem to hear me.

"You're not really angry, are you? You can't be. It's

the same thing you did. And I know I got mad, but I was naive. You're much more experienced, so you understand that it doesn't really matter that much, right?" My voice trembled in the silence of his room. "That it can be casual and not mean anything. You're the one who said I should go out with somebody else."

I waited for him to say something. When he didn't answer, I approached him slowly.

"Moshe." I touched his arm gently. "I really didn't think you'd react like—"

He threw my hand off, slamming his fist down on the window frame. A crack formed. "You cunt!" he screamed.

My body was shaking. "You don't understand," I whispered.

"I thought I could trust you." He kicked the baseboard, crying out in pain. "Shit, my foot! Damn it! I really did."

"But you're the one who said it's just the gratification of a need," I insisted, starting to cry. "I heard you. That's exactly what you said."

He covered his face in his hands. "How can anyone as stupid and shallow as you—how could I have let you into my life?"

"I didn't mean to hurt you. I swear. But I thought you wanted me to experience more and not just be a girl from Flushing—"

"Get out of here already!" He unlocked the door, opening it. When I didn't stir, he shouted, "Did you hear me?"

"I'm sorry," I said, trying to reach out to him again. "It was just an experience. Like you had. And I wanted to be honest—"

"Get out." he shrieked, pushing me. "I never want to see you again."

In the doorway, I wept. "Don't be like that. Please, Moshe. You're just angry. I know you don't mean the things you said." I stood sobbing. "You can't. You took that ad out in the—"

He slammed the door.

31

Those subways, that bus, that street, that damn semi-attached house: I returned home to Queens. And they waited inside, as I knew they would, through the proscenium archway that led into the living room, the totalitarian state that was my family who loved and cared about me.

I was afraid of Bella. Afraid for Stashek. I yearned for a cell where I could seal myself off, life-tight, between two speakers, listening to ". . . and one very special person, a feeling deep in your soul, says you were half, now you're whole. . . ."

"Look who's come home!" my father exclaimed, *The Week in Review* balanced on his stomach. I bent over to kiss him. He bolted forward, his hands on the arms of the recliner, so it sprung to an upright position. Standing up, he removed his glasses first, then hugged me. "You know we were sick with worry about you?"

"I didn't mean to—"

"Oh, do you still live here?" Bella rushed out of the kitchen. I moved away from my father. She wiped her hands on her checkered apron.

"You really should have called," he scolded. "Told us you weren't coming home—"

"I know, but it got late and I didn't want to wake you up, so I stayed with this girl, Ellen."

"And we're supposed to believe that?" she demanded. "Do you take us for fools?"

"I swear to God, Mom. It's the absolute truth."

She lurched forward, suddenly. "I can't stand a liar!" She slapped me with a whip of her hand.

I winced, grabbing my cheek.

"Bell!" My father raised his voice, turning to her. "That wasn't necessary."

"She thinks she can get away with anything. Now she doesn't even call if she doesn't come home." She searched in her apron pocket for cigarettes.

His tone was severe as he spoke to me. "It wasn't right what you did. We didn't know where you were, if you were safe. Suppose something really happened to you? That's the city you're in. Where people are like animals. How do I know that one hasn't taken it in his mind to harm you?"

"Dad, I'm careful. I really am."

"You're my responsibility as long as you live here—"

"You spoil her, Stashek," she interrupted. "You know that? It's your fault."

"You won't even listen to me," I cried. "No one around here ever does."

"Because we know what you're going to tell us." Bella shouted. "Lies. That's all you know."

"A person is innocent until proven guilty," I insisted.

"Okay, Hanny," my father arbitrated. "Why don't you tell us what happened."

"Forget it." I walked away from them, toward the stairs.

"And where do you think you're going?" she railed.

"Is Stevie here?" I asked, stopping halfway so that I had to lean over the rail to talk to them.

"Who knows where that one is?" She shook her head hopelessly. "Look at how our daughters behave. Like they've never learned anything at home. Like they're from the street and no one cares when they come in. . . ."

I climbed two steps, then stopped to listen.

"That's not true," my father argued. "They're good girls. They get good grades in school. Nowadays, children behave differently. They're more free. It's like

Hair, that play we saw. They live in a different world. Values have changed, mores—"

"You with your cockamamy ideas!" she answered furiously. "I don't know what to do with her anymore."

I perched at the top of the stairs.

"You shouldn't have hit her. If you can't talk with her, it's too late for hitting. That'll just make her rebel more."

"Something has to knock some sense into that head of hers, or she's going to get into big trouble."

"She has a boyfriend," my father said, dropping his voice. "If things were different, we wouldn't have come home either."

"I don't like it," she grumbled. "Not one bit."

I slammed my door loudly.

"Don't you bang doors in this house!" she screamed. "Do you hear me?"

I pulled at the chain she had given me, wanting to rip off the gold heart suspended over my black ribbed sweater. Instead, I unfastened it, opening the locket. Bella had cut out her and my father's faces from a photograph, pasting them inside. I carried the locket into the bathroom. Flush! It would be so easy. I dangled the locket over the bowl. "A genuine antic," Bella had raved excitedly. "I found it at the temple bazaar. Only five dollars."

Lying down on my blue carpet between the two speakers, I closed my eyes.

32

"The fact that he goes to Columbia was the real death blow," Moshe began. "Couldn't you have found someone at Queens?"

"I didn't think it would matter." I took the phone to my bed.

"You know, we might end up in the same class when I go back. How do you think that would make me feel?"

"I don't see why—"

"He knows you've been unfaithful to me. I was the chump. It would be so humiliating."

"But you're the one I love," I insisted. "He knows that too. He wanted to see me again, but I said I didn't want to. That I was involved with you."

"What a laugh. You two must have had a pretty good time together," he added nastily.

"It wasn't that great," I lied.

"What did you do?" he asked.

"I'm not going to answer another question. Every time I do, you use it against me."

"Hannah," he said vehemently, "I have to know everything. It's the only way my imagination won't fill in details, which I assure you are much worse than what actually happened. I need to know. Otherwise, there isn't a prayer for us ever to—"

"Moshe," I cried. "I never meant for any of this—"

"How did it happen?"

"I don't know if I should tell you."

"Well, then, let's forget it. I'll hang up."

"No," I implored. "Please don't. Okay, I'll tell you. But then you can't—"

"How did you meet him?"

"Remember the guy at Homecoming? I took a walk with him?" Then I added pointedly, "While you were talking to Ellen."

"The blond one? Him!" He gasped. "I knew you were turned on to him. You couldn't keep your hands off him. That's why I was angry."

"It's not as if you didn't spend half of Homecoming with Ellen and then go to bed with her!"

"What did you say his last name was?"

"McMillan."

"Okay, that's good to know. Just in case we run into each other. So I can identify him. He looks like half the jocks at school. Your average bland sexless Wasp."

I didn't say anything.

"How did you two get together?"

"I called him," I admitted.

"When?"

"After we had our fight. You see, I was trying to call you and you weren't there. Friday evening. And I was sure that you were with Ellen or somebody so I called Wayne, just to talk—"

"For your information, I was having *Shabbus* dinner at my parents' house."

I gulped. "I didn't know that."

"So you called him. Then what happened?"

"He invited me to meet him at his dorm."

"Which one?"

"John Jay."

"Oh, no," he groaned. "Do you realize that my friend Pete Lester lives in that dorm? I can't go in there anymore. He probably knows Wayne, who's probably told him, even—"

"He wouldn't do that," I assured him.

"How do you know? Do you have any idea how guys talk about girls they've had sex with? He's probably told the whole dorm. And he knows who I am, right? How could you do this to me?" he said desperately. "Do you see what you've done? You've ruined everything."

"I'm sorry. It never occurred to me—"

"It's my school. I'm the one who showed you around, took you to the football game. Is that the way you repay me? I'll never feel the same about Columbia again." He paused. "So you went to John Jay. What time was that?"

"You're cross-examining me."

"I have to know."

"Okay, I got there around six. We were supposed to meet, but he was late. He came about fifteen minutes later, carrying his laundry."

"Laundry?"

"You see, I didn't want to go up to his room. I suggested that we walk around. I had actually called him to talk, since he was a man and I figured he might understand—"

"And he had to take his laundry upstairs, right?" Moshe asked.

"How did you know?"

"He was probably just carrying that bag so he'd have an excuse to take you to his room."

"But it was full of laundry. We went upstairs to his room, and I matched socks while he folded the rest."

"Then?"

"Then we just sat around talking. I was telling him about you, our relationship and all. Then he asked me if I smoked pot and wanted to get high."

"You didn't mention that part before," he said.

"I was going to. So we smoked some grass, and at first nothing happened. I was even talking about how nothing ever gets through to me, you know, how I have this impermeable membrane of reality. And then, all of a sudden, I began to feel it. I heard things differently, I saw colors—"

"How much did you smoke?"

"I don't know exactly. He ran out of rolling paper so we smoked through an empty beer can. Isn't that weird?" I tried to engage his interest, make him laugh.

"A pothead!" Moshe rebuked. "Do you have any idea how harmful marijuana is? It can cause brain damage and psychosis."

"Everyone smokes," I said.

"Well, everyone's being self-destructive. I wouldn't touch that stuff. And you see what happened when you did?"

"I don't regret smoking the pot," I insisted defiantly. "It helped me break through. I needed to experience it."

"Do you need to murder someone too, so your spectrum of experiences will broaden further?"

"Smoking pot's not like murdering anyone."

"I see why you did it. You were getting back at me, expressing your hostility," he analyzed. "You know, you have a lot of anger in you. You're actually seething. I've always suspected what was under your sweet innocent facade was—was—murderous rage!"

"That wasn't why. Really. I just thought—"

"You got high. Then what? How did the lovemaking start?"

"It just happened," I said. "I tried to stop him. I said I had a boyfriend, but he just—wouldn't stop."

"You wanted it, that's why," Moshe accused. "Just like that time with me."

"That was different."

"Did he take off your clothes or did you?"

"Half and half."

"And—"

"Then we just did it. That's all."

"Did he touch you first?"

I twitched. He had found the exact spot, no searching and pecking like a person who couldn't type, and forced my legs open, not stopping, until I couldn't hold back.

"And then he came inside of you?"

"I wouldn't let him do that!" I protested. "He came outside of me. On my stomach."

"You mean, he didn't use a rubber?"

"It was perfectly safe."

"You don't know anything!" he yelled. "Don't you realize you can get pregnant that way?"

"But he pulled out of me. Then I covered myself with my hands," I reported. "I would've felt something leak in."

"Jesus!" he cried. "You had your period two weekends ago, didn't you? When we went to the Green Tree. Remember, I gave you a quarter for the machine?"

"I'm not sure."

"So besides taking the chance of having picked up some disease or crabs, you might have gotten pregnant too. Do you know there's a very good chance of that? How do you feel now?"

"That's impossible!" I blurted, beginning to cry. "It couldn't happen. After just one time. You're just trying to scare me."

"What if you have to get an abortion in Mexico on some kitchen table?" He hurled the words at me. "And a butcher with a knife—"

A click on the phone made me start.

"I'm just concerned about you—"

"Shhh!" I hissed. "Someone's on the line."

"You didn't talk enough all night?" Bella inquired.

"Five more minutes!" I tried to control the quiver in my voice. "Please."

"You've been on for twenty-five."

"I know, but we're having a pivotal conversation."

"Give us a break," Moshe snapped.

"Five minutes." The phone clicked.

"You slept over there?"

"Yes," I admitted guiltily. "I fell asleep, and the next thing I knew it was morning. But what about when you went to bed with Ellen or whoever, didn't you—?"

"You break my balls about staying over, and then you just do it with him. Terrific."

"But it was an accident, Moshe. Like in 'Wake Up Little Susie.' And you've done it. What do you have to say to that?"

"Look, I wasn't a virgin like you were with me. That was never an issue between us. Besides, I need to test my adequacy. Yours is intact."

"What do you mean by that?" I demanded.

"You don't come from a family like mine. I've met your parents. They're normal. They don't have nightmares like mine. But I do think you should go to a V.D. clinic. Just to make sure you're all right."

"I've got to get off," I said finally. "Otherwise she'll pick up again."

"So have a nice life. You'll meet a lot of interesting people. You can go to bed with all of them—"

"Can't we talk when we see each other?" I interrupted.

"I don't know," he said quietly.

"What?"

"If I can ever see you again."

"Are you serious?"

"It might really freak me out. That's my most vulnerable area. David agrees. I called him up after you left, and he said it would be better—"

"But I told you," I insisted, tears clogging up my nose, dropping into the collar of my sweater. "It didn't matter at all. It was just sex."

"This could turn into a real crisis. I've got to be careful, after Claire and Ellen."

"That's them and I'm me."

"It doesn't matter as far as my psyche's concerned. And one thing's for sure, I can't go to bed with you."

I took a deep breath. "Ever?"

"I wouldn't be able to relate to you. Each time, I'd be thinking of his cock inside of you. It's almost homosexual. If he had a disease— You didn't think of that, did you?"

"Moshe," I pleaded, shaking the receiver. "Couldn't we—I don't know. Just somehow forget it?"

"Forget? Like it was nothing? And did you suck his uncircumcised cock too?" His voice lashed out at me. "Huh?"

"Stop it!" I cried. "Please."

"If you want to know, that's why I can't see you," he told me. "Those kinds of thoughts would constantly be on my mind. Which is unhealthy." He paused. "Just for the record, did you?"

"No!" I sobbed.

"I don't know whether to believe you."

"Does it matter?"

"I suppose not."

"I've been too honest with you already," I wept. "If I hadn't told you, you'd never know."

"I would have found out," he said. "Just like I did with"—he hesitated momentarily—"the others. I have a highly developed sixth sense about these things."

"Aren't we going to see each other again?" I implored.

"Maybe when some time has passed. I don't know how I'll feel. I really don't."

At first, I crushed my face into the pillow, but I couldn't burrow deep enough to smother the tears. So hot. So bitter. Then I began to punch the pillow as hard as I could, crying, "Damn you, Moshe! Goddamn you! You shit! You prick! I hate—"

33

A knock startled me to my feet. "Just a minute!" Desperately, I fluffed up the pillow. "Don't come in!" I screamed as Bella opened the door.

"What do you want?" I demanded, trying to wipe the tears with my sleeve, looking furtively away.

"I don't understand," she said. "You stay out all night, then you finally come home and you're on the phone with him for an hour. You didn't talk enough?"

I stared out the window. "I told you, I wasn't with Moshe."

"Please, Hannah." She sat down on my bed. "I'm tired of being your jailer and you telling me your stories. Why can't you admit that you were there? That would be better than you lying to me."

"I wasn't."

"Could you turn around while we're talking, please."

"I don't want to," I said, my shoulders shaking as sobs wrenched out of my body. "Leave me alone," I pleaded.

She stood up and walked over to me. "What's the matter?"

"Nothing."

"Something's happened. Is it Moshe?" she asked, trying to brush strands of hair from my face. "It is, isn't it?"

I shook my head, pushing her hand off.

"Your hair is in your eyes. How can you see?"

"Maybe I like it like that!" I cried, tears streaking. "Will you leave me alone?"

"Where's your locket?" she asked, touching my neck.

"I flushed it down the toilet."

"No, you didn't," she said. "You wouldn't do that."

"How do you know?"

"Because even if you're mad at me that I hit you—and I shouldn't have, Daddy's right—you know how much I love you."

I bit my lip. "I almost did."

"I'm sorry I smacked you," she said gently. "I was so upset, I didn't know what to do."

I covered my face in my hands. "I want to be alone. I don't want to talk to anybody."

"We're a family and we have to care about each other. Even if we hurt each other sometimes." Her voice dropped to a conspiratorial hush. "It is Moshe, isn't it?"

"No, it's not."

"What happened last night?"

"I told you, I wasn't with him."

She looked shrewdly at me. "Did you go out with someone else?"

Surprised, I answered truthfully. "Yes." I added, "Sort of."

"You were with him last night?"

I nodded penitently.

"Oh." She nodded thoughtfully. For a few seconds, she studied me. "That's a different story." Finally, she patted me on the shoulder. "You're not married. What's the big *shmeel?*"

"You don't understand."

"What's not to understand? Moshe was jealous."

"But it's not that." Guilt oozed through me. "I mean, it was more than that."

"What then?"

"I can't talk about it," I said, watching a red Mazda pull out of the driveway next door.

"You know, I had a couple boyfriends before your father, and even when we began to go out."

"Did he ever get jealous?"

"Sure. That's why he married me." She laughed slyly.

"To take me off the open market."

"But it was different then," I said firmly.

"I doubt it."

"Did you ever—um, kiss—or anything?" I asked, my face flushed. "With them?"

"A woman needs some experience. I just wanted you to be a little older, to know more how to take care of yourself." She shrugged. "But you couldn't wait."

"You had sex with other—uh, men? Really?" I asked incredulously. "Than Dad?"

She smiled. "Don't forget, I was an *artiste*."

"I can't believe it," I said, sitting down on my bed.

"Did I ever tell you about Leppy Feinstein, the actor?"

My mother. Sex. I didn't stir.

"That he looked exactly like Montgomery Cliff? Very handsome, a fine actor, and could he dance! On Sunday afternoons, we would go to the theater together. To all the shows. Then we'd eat at the Ukrainian restaurant on Second Avenue. What was it called?" Her forehead wrinkled as she tried to recall the name. "I think it was something like with a V or a W—"

"Vaselka?" I asked.

"That's it! Vaselka!"

"It's near the Fillmore. I went there with Stevie once."

"Leppy was something else!" Her eyes twinkled, eyebrows wiggling wickedly. "That was his nickname for Leopold. He could tell a story, you know, where you'd want to pee-pee in your pants from laughing so much. What a man!"

"Why didn't you marry him?"

She slipped a Newport out of her robe pocket and lit it. "You have to know something very important. There are some men it is fine to go out with, eat, dance. They're wonderful to have fun with. Such charmers. They could charm the English queen out of her crown. But when you marry, that's something else. A woman has to think about what kind of father he would make, would he be responsible, down-to-earth, keep a job or what. Leppy made me laugh so hard I cried. And he wanted to marry me." She paused, inhaling deeply on her cigarette. "But when I met your father, I recognized something else. I knew immediately that he would make a good husband and father. No, he wasn't brilliant, talented like Leppy—"

"Are you kidding?" I interrupted. "Dad's a genius."

She shook her head in amusement. "A genius, huh? He's a good and kind man. Solid. That's what matters."

"But his poetry is brilliant," I insisted. "And his ideas for *The Baking Times* are clever. And his essays too."

She smiled patiently, taking another puff of her cigarette. "One of these days, you're going to have to settle down too and have a family. So this is the time to live. I'm not saying, you know, be too free with yourself, because what men really want, even if they tell you to be free, is stuff that costs and is unused. And they can hurt you. But it's not a tragedy, and it's good, I suppose, that you've known Moshe, though he's an awful boy in my opinion."

"I love him," I said, starting to cry again.

"Do you think he loves you?" she asked softly.

"He's crazy about me!" I answered vehemently. "It's just that he's mad at me. But—" I covered my eyes. "He says he doesn't know if he wants to see me again, that—that—I don't know," I said finally.

"Would someone who loves another person make them feel like this?"

"I don't care what you say!" I screamed. "I love him. I really do!" Dropping next to her on the bed, my head on her shoulder, I clutched her waist. "Oh, Mom!" I cried.

"Hanny, my Hanny." She stroked my hair. "My big girl. . . ."

"I want to die," I muttered into her lap.

"What, my radish-face? No, don't say that. That's not good. Wait, I have a story for you. But it's a dirty one,

I'm warning you. I heard it in Cleveland at the convention."

I didn't answer, hiding my face in the shelter of her robe.

"Okay, ready or not. This woman, let's call her Ethel, Ethel Shapiro, she gets a phone call from the director of the funeral home where her husband has been taken, let him rest in peace. So he tells her, 'Mrs. Shapiro, we're having a problem here.' 'What's the matter?' she says. 'I didn't pay enough money for a rosewood casket?' 'No, no. It's Harvey,' he says, hesitating. 'What about him?' she asks. 'Well, I don't know how to tell you this but— he has an erection.' 'That horny I'm not,' she answers him. 'No, Mrs. Shapiro, you don't understand. We can't close the casket. Every time we try—' 'Oh,' she says. 'That's a problem.' 'We're at our wits' end. We don't know what to do.' 'It's simple,' Mrs. Shapiro finally says. 'Just chop it off and stick it in his *tuchis*!' " She tapped me on the shoulder. "Don't you think that's funny? I laughed until my guts almost spilt."

"I want to die," I repeated, my arms tightening around her waist.

34

I entered his apartment shyly. He helped me out of the sleeves of my Dr. Zhivago coat, staring admiringly at my purple embroidered Indian shirt, borrowed from Stevie, and my black velour miniskirt. His eyes traveled the length of my black patent leather boots, then met mine. "I forgot how lovely you are," he said, kissing my neck. My violet-shadowed eyelids fluttered, as my glossed lips brushed against his. We held each other.

Then without warning, he threw me on the bed, forcing himself on top of me. "Oh, Hannah!" he whispered huskily. "It's been hell, all these weeks without you. I've missed you so. I'm only a man and can resist you no longer." His hand ran over one breast, the other, across my stomach. "Oh!" he exclaimed, lifting my skirt. "You wore the garter!"

I waited outside Moshe's door. Finally, he unlocked it. "Don't look at me," he growled. "I look awful." He wore his bathrobe, blue pajamas, socks, and slippers. His nostrils were swollen, a vivid rose, which he tried to cover with the tissue in his hand.

I moved to touch his shoulder, but he pulled away from me.

"No, you don't!" He blew his nose loudly. "I just knew this would happen. I told you it wasn't time yet."

"I had to see you," I said quietly.

"This could be a major setback for me."

I crossed the room, looking around. There were crumpled tissues on the bed, the floor next to it, and the garbage teemed. I laid my coat over the chair. "It looks like the attack of the Kleenex monster," I joked.

"Very funny," he sneered, wiping his nose. "I feel lousier than a dried-up turd."

"Would you like some tea?" I asked.

"No, I wouldn't like some tea," he answered nastily. "Forget the solicitous bullshit."

"Oh."

I stood in front of the Horowitz-Margareten calendar. A black border was drawn around today, Saturday, the 22nd of Kislev, 5728, with FIN scrawled in large letters.

I chewed on my lip as I turned to him.

"I've been crying since yesterday," he declared. "Mourning our relationship, what we had together." He paced back and forth. "I've realized that I have to protect myself. I just can't afford to be masochistic."

"But I never meant to hurt you," I said softly.

He blew his nose loudly. "You were my best friend."

"You were mine too. Isn't there a way for us to somehow—I don't know, you know—"

"I wish there was. I really do." He wiped each nostril separately, making a small tent out of the tissue. "But I can't. I keep thinking about how innocent you were when I met you. I loved that about you."

"No, you didn't." I shook my head vehemently. "You kept criticizing me."

"That's the way I express affection," he insisted. "You should have known that." He retied his robe. "It would have been different if you'd slept with someone before you met me and weren't a virgin."

"But that's why I did it. You said I was inexperienced, and how I'd regret it when I was thirty—"

"I really cared about you." He blew his nose again as he walked to the window. "I thought you were different from the others. That we could be together forever. I had such hopes."

I followed him. "So why won't you—"

"No," he answered flatly. "I'm going to be alone again as I've always been. I'll spend this New Year's at Orange Julius again, watching Guy Lombardo and that fucking ball."

274

I reached for his hand.

"Don't touch me!" he cried. "You're defiled, by an uncircumcised goy, no less."

"Ellen's a shiksa," I argued, my bottom lip quaking from the effort of holding back tears so I didn't crack a water main and couldn't return.

"Who knows what kind of bacteria he had in his fore—"

"Moshe," I interrupted. "Couldn't we just—"

He sneezed. "This damn cold! It's your fault. I wouldn't have gotten sick if I wasn't seeing you today. But you insisted. Are you satisfied?" he demanded.

My eyes bounced off titles of books on the shelves. *Journey to the End of the Night. Coming of Age in Samoa. The World of Goya.*

"So talk," he commanded. "What do you want from me?"

"I wanted," I began, "that we— You hate me, don't you?"

"No." He stared coldly ahead. "It's my fault for having trusted my emotions to you. I must have been out of my mind."

"But—" My eyes and nose filled. "I love you. I really do. I wouldn't have come here if—"

"Sentimental crap!" he cried. "A person can say any old garbage. It's what they do that counts. And it isn't the sex either. You betrayed my trust."

"I never thought that—"

"How can I ever share anything intimate with you again?" Moshe asked, then answered himself. "Well, I can't."

"Do you mean that?"

"No, I'm trying out new comedy material."

"Okay," I said, eyes fixed on *Let Us Now Praise Famous Men.* "I'm going home."

He turned to me, surprised. "But you just got here."

I picked up my coat off the chair.

"It's a long ride and you don't have to yet. I mean," he said. "What's the rush?"

Wilhelm Reich: Selected Writings. "I better go."

"Why?" he demanded. "This is the last time we'll probably ever see each other. Do you realize that? This is it." He lowered his voice. "Why do you have to go?"

I burst into tears. "I thought, maybe, if we talked, we'd be able to—" I slipped one arm into the sleeve of my coat. "But you won't let me."

"Why don't you wait a few minutes," he said, trying to take off my coat. "Don't desert me," he whispered.

"I thought I repelled you."

"I didn't mean it, I swear." He laid my coat over the chair again. "It's not you. I can't get along with anyone."

I sat down on the edge of the bed, wiping my eyes with the back of my hand.

"I'm a monosexual," he said flatly.

"What's that?"

"Oh, I've been having a lot of sex lately." He stared out the window. "With myself. One of these days, I might even start a movement. There'll be bars where people can dance by themselves, pick themselves up. Only one cover charge, though. All closet monosexuals, married, homo, or whatever, can come and have an intimate time with the one person in the world who really understands. For the self-made man and woman." He sat down next to me, running his fingers through his hair. "I feel so alone. I really do."

"I better go," I repeated.

"You don't have to," he insisted. "Don't you understand? I'm the alienation kid. Screw-it-yourself enterprises. I can't help it, Hannah. But—" He paused. "I loved you." He reached for me. "You're my friend."

I held back. "I thought you said—"

"I didn't!" he cried. "Or I didn't mean it if I did. Let's make love," he pleaded. "I'll be so good. Don't go, please."

"First you say all these horrible things, and—'

"I know! I'm sorry. I really am. I won't do it again. Just don't leave, please."

I sat stiffly, watching him. "You're confusing me."

"How about if we just made out and pretended we never heard of sex? I'm sorry for being so crazy." He stroked my hair. "I don't want to hurt you."

I looked into his eyes. "Do you mean it, or are you going to—"

"I won't. We'll make believe none of it ever happened."

"I don't—"

"Hannah, please...."

At that moment, I imagined I could see his heart. A robust porterhouse encased in a glass box. If you touched it, your fingers stuck to the ice, burning.

"You have to believe me."

"I wore the garter," I said tenderly.

"You did!" he exclaimed. "Where?"

"Under my clothes."

"You're wonderful! You really are." He blew his nose loudly. "Got to clear the passages first."

"Are you sure?" I asked.

"Just give me a chance," he implored.

"Will you give me one?"

He took my hand. We moved to the bed. "One more time." He blew his nose, then kissed me. I closed my eyes tightly.

How familiar it felt, his penis growing hard in my hand, his hands moving over my breasts and thighs, his fingers pulling the elastic of my panties, stroking me. Our clothes fell on the floor. I grasped his back. The garter wrapped itself around my ankle.

As he opened the night-table drawer, pulling out the blue plastic case and a rubber, I felt his body shudder.

"What's the matter?" I whispered.

"I can't!" he cried, drawing away from me.

"Moshe—" I tried to make a bridge between us with my arms.

"No, you don't!" he shouted, crawling to the other side of the bed.

"What?" I covered myself with my arms, moving away from him.

"We were so close. Why did you have to fuck everything up?" He turned to face the wall.

Slowly, I sat up. The garter lay on the red, white, and blue sheet.

"You're all the same!" he accused. "Women are incapable of love. You never loved me."

"That's not true!"

"Then why did you—"

"You know," I cried. "I told you. Because I thought you wanted me to. And I was mad. You did it with Ellen and everybody else and took an ad out in—"

"I didn't," he said quietly.

"What do you mean?"

He turned to face me. "I wanted to see what you'd do. And you did exactly what I knew you would." He spat the words out. "You slept with someone else."

"But you—"

"In order for you to be able to exercise free will, to do what you really wanted to and not feel constrained by me."

"You didn't sleep with Ellen?" I demanded.

"She wouldn't give me the time of day."

"What about the others?"

"Zero."

"And the ad?"

"I made all of it up. I wanted to know if you really loved me." He stared up at the ceiling. "I thought you did. You were so sweet and innocent. I'll never forget your face when we first made love and I pulled the Tampax out of you—"

I stood up, beginning to dress as fast as I could.

"You were mine," he whispered. "Slowly, I tutored you so you'd be ready, so you could open up like a flower. And you did. It was like watching a time-lapse photograph."

"I'm going," I said, throwing my coat over my arm.

"There's no love in this world. Everyone's out for

themselves. I should've known." He covered his face in his hands. "But I don't want to believe it."

"Moshe, I'm going," I repeated.

He didn't look up.

I spotted the garter on the bed. As I reached for it, he said, "I'd rather you left that."

"It's mine." I crushed the garter in my hand.

"I want to have something—"

"You gave it to me," I insisted, pocketing it.

He stood up to open the door. For a moment, we were next to each other. "Well, this is it," he declared.

"I don't know what to say," I mumbled. "Except that I'm sorry that things had to—"

He cut me off. "Look, I'm just the first guy. Don't worry. There'll be dozens more, at least. And you'll have this scene with each one of them."

"Don't say that!"

"That's the way it is."

"No!" I cried. "I'm never going to be that way."

As the tape thinned to a sliver, Moshe declared, "I'm going to say goodbye now, Hannah. But one of these days, I'll come knock, knock, knockin' on your door. And you know what I'll say?

"Are you ready? Wait a second. Okay. The Contours doing it. 'You broke my heart 'cause I couldn't dance. You didn't even want me around. And now I'm back to let you know, I can really shake 'em down. Do you love me—I can really move. Do you love me—I'm in the groove. Do you love me—now—that—I—can—dance, DANCE! Watch me now and work, work—' See you in four years at the sundial!" he screamed over the music. " 'Work, work, work it out baby. Work, work, I'm gonna drive you crazy. Tell me, baby, you like it like this. Just a little bit of soul. . . .' "

Acknowledgments continued from the copyright page.

Jobete Music Company, Inc., Hollywood, California: Selections from "Do You Love Me?,"words and music by Berry Gordy, Jr. Copyright © 1962 Jobete Music Company, Inc. International copyright secured. From "You've Really Got a Hold on Me," words and music by William Robinson, Jr. Copyright © 1962 Jobete Music Company, Inc. International copyright secured. All rights reserved. Used by permission.

New Directions Publishing Corporation: A selection from *Nausea*, by Jean-Paul Sartre. Copyright © 1964 by New Directions Publishing Corporation. All rights reserved.

Random House, Inc.: Selections from *Ulysses*, by James Joyce. Copyright 1914, 1918 by Margaret Caroline Anderson. Copyright renewed 1942, 1946 by Nora Joseph Joyce. Copyright 1934 by Modern Library, Inc. Copyright renewed 1961 by Lucia and George Joyce.

United Artists Music: A selection from the song "Goldfinger," by Anthony Newley, Leslie Bricusse, and John Barry. Copyright © 1964 by United Artists Music Ltd. All rights administered by Unart Music Corporation. All rights reserved.

Viking Penguin Inc.: Selections from *A Portrait of the Artist as a Young Man*, by James Joyce. Copyright 1916 by B. W. Huebsch, 1944 by Nora Joyce. Copyright © 1964 by the Estate of James Joyce.

The Welk Music Group: A selection from the song "Goin' Out of My Head," by Teddy Randazzo and Bobby Weinstein. Copyright © 1964 by Vogue Music (c/o The Welk Music Group, Santa Monica, CA 90401). International copyright secured. All rights reserved. Used by permission.